In The Name

Of

Ben Dunn

For my Daughters, Ruby and Marnie

PART ONE

CHARLOTTE

They don't check for a knife. Why would they? I'm small, a woman, no menace at all and they are men, or will be soon. Two skinny boys, tall and lanky, all ribs and muscle, late teens at most and too young to have fat. The Third is older, thirty at least, a gut and pallor speaking of how he spends life. They smoke, roll-up after roll-up, talking about drugs, violence and women.

I am sitting on their black leather sofa. I am flanked by two blue armchairs that do not match and each is occupied by one of the teenagers. The single window is covered by heavy green curtains. The view will be a spectacular sight over estates in London, a panorama of lights from up on high in the darkness of a winter night.

The boys have tattoos on their necks, the outline of a heart with two balls inside. It is the mark of a gang they run or joined. Sally is in a bedroom with the Dealer. She won't come out, not for a long time, at least not alone. She had wanted her hit and came for nothing more. She knows what will happen, she knows the three men will visit.

The two teenagers watch me, trying at the dead-eyed stare of street gangsters from LA.

Sally told me her name, she wasn't lying, I know who she is, I did my research. She is nice in an innocent way, easily convinced and trusting. She is pretty if gangly and awkward with long blonde hair and a crooked nose. She is unconventional beauty turned dull and sour on injected peace.

It is ten o'clock on a Friday night and this is all she lives for.

The Dealer comes into the room and the two teenagers continue to stare as the Dealer smiles and nods his head. I am next, he is ready. The two teenagers stand.

"Are you ready?" the Dealer asks. "Sally is in a happier place. We'll keep her safe here. We can do that for you too."

The two teenagers cannot help but smile.

My plan had been to come and see, check out who and what they are, to see where they live. I had an idea of the dirt and squalor even if the Dealer has kept the grotty green carpet clear of take-away debris. The air smells like the windows have not been open since I was at school.

But this is the moment, I need to leave or fight. Taking a hit, monging out, and being molested by heavy handed adolescents is not on my bucket list. Sally has been and done before, as she will again. Defending her would mean nothing. She doesn't want defending.

"I've lost my desire. As long as Sally is OK, I'll be on my way," I say.

I'm small, quite stocky, thirty-eight, five feet five and muscled. I wear my blonde hair short, styled with wax. Men leave me alone because they think I'm gay. They're wrong, but I like the hassle free nights. I'm not scary or intimidating but I know how to fight. I'm not the pissed-up lady in mini-skirt in December who's downed her shots and taken offence with a sexy lady getting all the attention. I don't grab hair and swing women around; I strike, I wrestle, I can hold my own with lesser skilled men. These three, without their weapons, pose no threat. But they have weapons, they carry knives. I know this, which is why I carry my own.

I lift my small brown leather bag from the floor, placing the long looped strap over my left shoulder. The zip I left open. My knife, a six-inch double-edged blade with short stubby plastic handle, is the only thing inside. I do not want to risk plunging my hand into confusion, rummaging around and trying to defend myself with a handful of tissues.

"Who are you?" the Dealer asks.

He walks across the room always between me and the door that leads to the corridor, bedrooms and exit. He looks out of shape, but his shoulders show he had once been active. They are broad for a slob, a little exercise and he would be back. Muscle memory is strange like that.

"A friend of Sally's," I say.

"She's got no friends," the first teenager says, exhaling smoke. "Junkies don't hold onto people. Unless they're Junkies too. Which you clearly ain't."

"You think she's police?" The second teenager asks.

The pair of lanky kids appear to be trained like guard dogs. The word 'Police' brings them to attention. I expect them to bark.

The Dealer smiles, any room he is in, with any person from anywhere in the world, he will believe he is the smartest.

"She isn't police," he says. "This would be entrapment. Not at this time. Not with Sally."

3

He turns to look and gives me a smirk that tells everyone he already knows the answer to his next question.

"Who are you?"

"I'm nobody," I say. "Thought it'd be fun coming here. It isn't. I'll go."

"Go where exactly?" Teenager two asks as he lights the end of his roll-up.

"Home."

"And that would be where?" Teenager one asks. "Because you ain't from here."

The Dealer takes a step forward, calming his friends by patting down air at his sides. He loves his audience.

"A young woman looking for a little rough," the Dealer says. "A little danger. Well, I think you've found it. I suggest the injection. Things are so much smoother."

Teenager Two stares at me, with the attempt at dead-eyes like he has lived a life. He comes across as the messed up little shit he is.

"What did you think? You'd come up here, smoke some weed with the local gangsters, have a laugh and then tell your story to your friends on Monday?" he asks.

The Dealer laughs too. "You guys do what you want. I'm off to the bedroom, see how Sally is going. Leave some for me."

The Dealer winks and leaves, closing the door behind him. The Teenager on the right sits back down in his armchair, the one on the left steps toward me.

I had convinced myself I would come, look and leave. I am not naive, but I am kidding myself. I have come here for this, to test myself, to cause chaos, to see if I would lose. Three week's surveillance to place myself in a situation I could have created in an hour by simply knocking on the door.

Teenager one pulls the roll-up from his mouth. Thick white smoke slips between his lips. He offers me the joint.

"Take a pull, it'll make things easier," he says.

There is going to be confrontation. Do I judge these two to be below my level? Easy prey? Quick kills? Or do I give them credit and assume they are good? The first makes sense and is not difficult. But I need to incapacitate one quickly and then the next. The Dealer will hear, come in all big man, rag-dolling Sally, and she has enough problems.

4

I wonder how it feels to kill a man.

I move to my left with a quick step, and then forward as I spin clockwise. I place my hand in my bag, removing the knife. I have trained for this, I know the moves, but I have never sliced flesh. I know where to cut and how deep.

Teenager one hasn't moved.

I'm fast but no ninja. The kid is stoned and arrogant, his reactions are turned down all the way to dead. I reach up with my left hand and grab his chin from below. I lift up and his neck is exposed. With my right hand I slash across his throat, from his left side to his right. Blood streams down in the rhythm of his heart, and I let him drop back. He feels at his neck as he sits back down. I step to my left again. Teenager two has inhaled the roll-up and is choking as he stands. He reaches to the back of his tracksuit bottoms, going for his knife.

I am behind him before his fingers can lift the oversize baseball jersey. He won't even know the rules. I am between him and the armchair. I grab his chin; the move was a winner first time so why change? He tries to pull away with a jerk of his head but he exposes his own arteries as a consequence. I slash across again, like an old-time Jewish butcher cutting open a pig to make it kosher. I step away and ease the teenager into his armchair. The first is dead. The second's feet shake, he stares in shock, he gargles and he dies.

I step back. I have blood on me, not too much considering the litres that have flowed. The room is sprayed red like an A-level artist believing he is Jackson Pollock and a shitty council flat is his canvas. I have been quick and silent. The Dealer is in the bedroom. The right or left side of the corridor? It doesn't matter, I can leave and phone this in. This would cause him trouble. He has a stash to put him away for a while, but the murders would never be his. Too clean.

Sally is in there too.

The kids were easy but I am here for the Dealer.

He is smarter than I thought but not as much as he believes. I wait five minutes, standing still, dripping blood, watching pools of red in blue material expand and soak. Two open-eyed teenagers are quiet company.

The Dealer opens the door. It opens into the room. I am two metres away. Sally is in front of him. He sees the blood and pushes

Sally forward as he turns and runs. I leap the coffee table and sprint for the door. Sally is in another world; she can't understand what she sees. She smiles or is it a grimaced? I can't tell which. She lies down for comfort and sleep, she lies in blood.

The Dealer is going for the front door. It is locked from inside, attached to the frame by a crude slide-bolt fitted by someone who cared little for finesse. He opens the bolt, turns a circular knob and pulls the door inward. He pulls fast but the door jerks to a halt when it snaps on the chain. He pushes the door closed and scrabbles at the hook that keeps the chain in place. He pulls it free but he takes too long. I arrive and without breaking step, I launch the sole of my right foot at the side of his left knee. He has his weight firmly placed, and his knee has nowhere to go but sideways.

I hear the snap as his ligaments go. He buckles, but doesn't drop. He tries for the door again. He scratches at the circular knob and I kick with the sole of my right foot, trapping his hand between it and the solid metal lock. I hear a bone crack and his wince of pain. He doesn't scream, he tries to keep sound to a minimum. He wants out. I drive my right elbow down at the back of his head. He is bending forward rasping for air, a sense of what is coming makes him reach up and grab my waist, throwing his right arm around me. He pulls me close, I open my mouth and bite down on the base of his neck where it meets his shoulder. He grunts, lets me go and pulls away. His skin is split.

"What do want?" he asks.

I don't answer, I pull my left fist back, and he raises his hands to block what he thinks is coming. I swing my right foot and throw my weight behind a kick that lands squarely on his cheek. I hope for a fracture, an exploded eye socket. I have missed his nose. There is no pouring of blood but he loses control of his movement. He sags to the floor and tries to stand. He falls again, like Balboa getting up from a beating at the hands of a nemesis. Only he is having no fairy tale ending, no shouting out to the woman he loves. He is going to die. I have decided to kill.

I drag him back to the front room by his hair, he stumbles and falls all the way. Sally is lying and grinning on the floor, blood seeping into her clothes and covering her hair and face. It is difficult to tell who is closer to this world, her or the Dealer. The Dealer is

6

having balance problems and mumbling incoherently, she is having the ride of her life. I wonder how long the full trip takes.

I sit the Dealer down on the coffee table, he lurches forward, not to escape, but to make sense of balance. He vomits, not at the macabre scene, the kick to the head has caused concussion. He is feeling all the pain.

I grab the top of his head by his hair and lift up. He looks at me but his eyes are in and out of focus, pupils dilating and shrinking. His chin is speckled in vomit.

"Look at me," I say.

He does, or at least appears to try.

"Who are you?" he asks.

His voice cracked and wavered over different tones.

"What's the problem here? We can sort something out."

"Look at me," I say. "Who am I?"

"I don't know."

"Look at me."

He stares, his eyes holding focus. "I've never seen you before."

"Do you remember Michael Simmons?" I ask.

He knows, I see the recognition in his face, a brief tense then relax. He knows the name; he will never forget. He looks down at the floor and I ready myself. I have said the name and he knows what is coming.

He springs forward and I catch his upward thrust with my right elbow. I connect with the bridge of his nose and his momentum stops. He reaches out with his hands, his eyes closed in pain. He scratches at me, hitting my shoulders, wanting to grasp. I slash at his left hand, cutting deep, a flap of skin and blood an immediate effect. He winces again, but he never screams as if his vocal chords have numbed to paralysis. I stab his right shoulder, nothing deep, a warning, and he lurches back. He tries to stay up straight, flapping his arms around like an old man returning to the ice rink after fifty years away. His balance is shot.

"You remember the name?" I ask.

"I had nothing to do with it. I'm not the man you want. I was nothing in that."

"You boasted otherwise."

7

He moves now, all hands and arms and gestures, a man making a speech with empty words.

"I'm a bullshitter," he says. "I was shooting my mouth. I was not involved. He was a whole other level. I'm small time."

"You know who did it."

He looks into my eyes, looking for the salesman's connection. The struggle at shared empathy.

"I. . .I can find out," he says. " I can help. They'll speak to me. I can help you."

I watch him, he is sure he can convince, he thinks a line like that will turn his fortunes.

"Give me a name," I say.

"And then you'll kill me."

"Not if it's a name that means something."

He slows now, speaking with the pace of the conversation.

"I wasn't there," he says. "I don't know."

My turn to look into eyes.

"That's a lie. I was there. I saw. I saw you."

He looks at me. His eyes widen.

"You?" he asks. "Charlotte?"

I nod.

"I wasn't involved," he says.

"You were there."

"I was told to be."

"By who?"

"You know that."

I smile. I know. It doesn't take any leap of imagination.

"Humour me," I say. "Who told you?"

He looks around the room. He is scared the man might be there. He drops his voice.

"Scully," he says. "Scully told me."

"A man moving up in the world."

The Dealer stands, he is unsure on his feet. He is faking a little, looking for sympathy. I am not buying.

"I can help you," he says.

"You could but it would mean I would have to trust you. Believe what you tell me. Scully scares you. I don't. You wouldn't help."

8

He understands what I am saying, his tears are close, he makes a move to me but his strength and desire has gone. I drive my left hand into his stomach and he bends forward wanting to fall. I grab his hair and pull him up. He flips back quickly and I slash across his throat. I go deep and blood spurts. He falls back over the coffee table, arms outstretched, like a young girl trying to form a bridge. He trembles and shakes. I watch him, just as I had watched Michael, my husband, die. He slows and stops. I look at him for a long time, not moving, not understanding.

I have killed three men.

I feel nothing.

I hear a scream, I turn, Sally is watching. Her magical mystery tour is at an end.

RAUCOUS

The Idyll doesn't last because it doesn't exist, not for me.

I am walking to collect three thousand pounds. Drizzle hangs in the air, my stubbled face dripping with cold rain. Six in the morning, the early bird calls are difficult to start but easy to finish. People like Darryl can't operate in the morning, not even on a litre of espresso. This is a monthly routine for another man but this is my second time. The plan is for it to be my last. Darryl Jones is a regular payee, but he's missed his day and I am the go-to when men need persuasion to hand over illicit cash for unpleasant deeds.

Darryl lives on the third floor of a tower-block built in the sixties by architects who loved communist counterparts. A new modern London built believing Functionalism is an art-form. Builders followed the plans but the theory was as flawed as the materials. It is a heap, ten-storeys high, with small two-bedroom flats in ruin and occupied by people who have grown up to be every stereotypical person in an inner-city slum.

Burned out cars and teenage shitbags, stairwells used as toilets.

I'm not scared, I live and grew up here, an inner city London boy, who has come to be exactly what is expected. I am an ex-con with a record for murder, a hardman with nothing to show for my thirty-eight years except prison violence and the look of a man who

9

works for crooks. And that's what I am, all the way down to my shaven head, inked arms and shit existence.

I walk concrete steps, which are chipped and worn, exposing rusted iron wire. Dogs bark, curtains move and everyone knows I am here.

Darryl's door is green and closed. I don't need to do the smash, walk in, smack him around and take what my boss wants. I tried that once, and just as it always does, the routine only causes problems down the road.

I want to hit him; I know I would take great pleasure from inflicting pain. He is a man who uses others, who makes money from women in the most ancient of ways. But he is protected and untouchable until he doesn't pay. He hasn't now, but he is a shrewd man, he takes no risks. He is a little weasely joke, not one capable of winning a fight with me. I hope something has happened, something to make him penniless, something that gives me free pass to have my kind of talk. I am operating under rules, yet here I have free rein.

I turn off the stairs, the long landing is empty except three women in their thirties. They are in slippers and pyjamas, leaning against the blue, chipped metal safety-rail. It is a wide concrete walkway with different coloured doors coming in pairs with each flat a mirror layout of its partner. When they see me their faces of defiance drop. They cut short their conversation of gossip and men and hurry to their holes.

I am not famous but I am known.

Two months ago I had dragged Darryl from his third-floor flat. He was wearing tracksuit bottoms and a white shirt, his neck and wrists heavy in silver chains. He was bleeding from his broken nose and busted mouth. His reluctance to follow me had caused his discomfort. I took him to the middle of the green square that stood protected on three sides by the three tower blocks. I shouted out his name, I stated what he had done, I told them I was his punishment. He struggled, tried to run, but I kicked his thighs and he couldn't walk. He lay back on the overgrown grass, his hands out, his palms raised. I grabbed his right hand and snapped his fingers. He screamed as I stomped his head, and as I broke his arms with stamps of my booted feet. He had tried to make the wrong girl one of his own, a family had complained, a family who had favours owed. My

10

boss called and told me to make sure everyone saw what happened to people who went on ahead when the OK was never given. Kids watched, the young teens who all believed they would make it to where I was, as if being a numb meathead who people feared was the goal in their lifelong obsession with respect. They watched and nodded, their gangs loving the violence and seeing a real man. They had no idea who I was, no one ever did.

Darryl's door is ajar and I take this to mean a trap. The way he is, the man he wants to be and the business he runs means the door should be locked. I have not arrived in secret; my approach was not by stealth. He knows I am here and he knows why. He knows I am coming.

I think: guns are hard to come by and they make too much noise. The police don't like to visit the area but a gunshot will bring the big boys in vans, vests and semi-automatics. Daryl can't have uniforms running through his storage. He needs to do this quietly. Maybe they have decided to go independent, maybe they think they have enough power to break free and start up alone without percentages to pay, without protection. They are wrong, but put enough arrogance in one room and the collective intelligence drops until the impossible is so easily achieved.

I figure they will wield bats or knives, there will be Darryl plus two. Numerically, three on me, but reality told me two. Darryl does not fight. If he has local boys, they'll be skinny and school-age kids, would-be tough guys who have stabbed before but only in ambush. The cowardly act of jumping a target as a group and stabbing away so there was no way of telling who did the deed and no way of being hurt in return. What once were cowards, are now the men.

I remove the fifteen-inch iron bar from my sleeve. Heavy in my hand. I have read about blackjacks in old detective fiction, but they sound like snooker balls in socks. I had been hit with one once, knocked down and beaten. I never took a fancy to them. I push the door open with my empty left-hand.

I wait as the door slowly bounces against the hallway wall. The light is on, a bare bulb shining on the grubby corridor. It is needed as no natural light enters. The cream carpet has a brown streak down its middle where people walk dirt. This is not a house where you wipe anything let alone your feet. I hear nothing, no

11

breathing, no music, no movement just a silent flat with crappy carpet and yellow plaster walls. The dank smell of a thousand smoked cigarettes mixes with the aroma of alcohol sweat. I tap the doorframe with my metal rod as if the sound would attract would be assailants like zombies to a kill. Nothing stirs.

I doubt Darryl has run because he has nowhere to go, and letting a profitable business slide is not in his nature. What is he going to do? Run to the city and get a job as a financial suit? He'd be great given the chance, he has no morals and sees everyone as a possible victim. He can work numbers too. But his CV is lacking in certain essential elements in the education section. His personal interests, if he were to break with tradition and be honest, would amount to destroying the lives of the vulnerable to turn a profit no matter what. He would be the managing director of an off-shore, Caribbean hedge fund if only he had gone to university.

I step into the hallway, it is three metres long with a door on the left and one opposite. They are painted white but dulled to a dirt grey. There is another door at the end of the corridor and all three are closed.

I have to think, how intelligent or dumb do they think I am? If they think I am dumb, they'll have a man behind the door on the left and the door on the right. They will expect me to walk past to the front room at the end. I'd be trapped as I got there, two men bursting out behind me as one came from my front. What if they tried imaginative? Would they expect me to smash down each door as I got to it and be tired and vulnerable on the third? Darryl is a smart coward, he'll be in the front room at the end of the corridor, listening and waiting, devising a plan of words for whoever came through first. A congratulation for his henchmen or an apologetic sermon on being misunderstood if I come through.

I walk, the doors I pass open into the room. I will have enough warning if there are kids intending on jumping out with bared teeth and knives.

I reach the end of the corridor and still no sound. The door is closed. I turn the gold-coloured plastic handle and push. The door moves but is blocked. I push again and some of the weight moves. I push again and the door bursts open. The carpet is worn and shiny. I take in the room, think, and make my mistake: I step through.

I've been set up. I didn't need to come, I was picked out and told to call. Here I am, faced with a scene. The locals saw me arrive, they saw me walk in. I am here, I am a known man and this is so obviously me.

I've broken my nose four times, my sense of smell is poor. A stink I can pick up, but subtleties are lost. The room stinks of stale air, smoke and men. There will be more for a person more educated in such things, a metallic smell, a sour odour or something similar to describe a connection between what you inhale when you walk into a room full of blood. I only see, and my eyes while not perfect, can see up-close. An abattoir with three slaughtered humans waiting to be sliced into prime fillets.

Three men. Three bodies. Three slit throats.

CHARLOTTE

I left Sally, but I should have called in Medics, I should have done something other than let her shoot up again. She saw the stash, had the opportunity. She had to take.

I needed that time, not to clean the apartment, I can't remove my DNA and CSI were going to find a whole generation of filth, contamination on top of contamination. My details are not on record, not in anything police can read. The bath will contain my hair, pieces of me. I took the risk as a blood covered woman walking the streets of London in the early hours is likely to be picked up quick. I can't take the chance.

I showered as quickly as I could in their bathroom. The recently deceased residents, from the evidence at hand, used the place to douse themselves in piss and scrub themselves clean with a matted ball of pubic hair. I stood under the showerhead fully clothed, blood washed from me, staining the crap encrusted bath. I was wet through, but didn't look like a Halloween Zombie. I was scared someone had called the police, I was scared about leaving with all eyes staring and marking me out as a blood-covered killer. I can't talk my way out of triple murder, not even if the police found out who I really am. A year or two from a sentence, maybe an easier ride inside, but free and at peace was not going to happen. Nothing stirred and nothing sounded as I waited to drip dry as much as I could before stepping out.

I left damp prints through the front room and corridor. I had to walk through my slaughter scene to escape. I had helped Sally to a corner of the room where she refused to move. I covered her in sheets from a bedroom. The sheets would stick to her if she lay down too long. The three were there as I had left them. The Dealer I cared nothing for at all, the two boys I doubted. Was rehabilitation possible? Had I taken the right lives? I wasn't feeling anything, no regret but that would come when I returned home.

The night air froze me. The tower block quiet, a party was happening within the estate, a distinct beat throbbed in the distance. I had a flimsy top of sequins. A coat would have singled me out as not knowing the rules on a lady's night. Booze was the way to keep warm on a night out in winter and flesh was the calling card. I hoped fashion would change.

I walked and saw lone people walking home, swaying and drunk. I saw two small groups of youths, male and female mixed. They showed interest in me, but only so I didn't see their own actions in the dark. I should have been scared but I felt only power. I had started. The build-up had been two years. I had trained. I would never be ready, as that would mean I could achieve my aim with ease. I wouldn't, I knew that. The Dealer was a way to start, a calling card, even if they wouldn't know who it was from. That would come later, I was sure. I could see where I was going, the final act but I needed to plan better, not make rash judgements after long surveillance. These people were uneducated but not thick. They knew, they understood. One or two got there through brute force, but those that stayed, those that grew when reaching the top, did so through intelligence as well as fear. I had experienced the fear, I had seen others crumble, and some try and run. No one succeeded. They all died and so would I but I wasn't going to live scared.

I could be a thousand miles away, free of this slum, free of this culture. I chose to stay, to fight. And I will.

The buildings closed up, became more cramped, gardens shrank, and uniformity of old redbrick houses grew. There was less space, as if the whole street was cuddling up to keep warm through winter. I had the feeling the summer would bring terraced housing to be detached. The whole place was organic, a system that operated within itself to support all those inside, and if needed to help everything that lived here to keep on reproducing generation after generation. I was part of that, a beach in Bali with a rum and coke, and burnt shoulders was fun for a week but a lifetime there was a waste.

I opened up my apartment, one I had been renting for less than two months, a ground floor flat in a once large single, three story dwelling. There was no basement flat but my windows, despite the upgrade in area from the Tower blocks, were barred. It had been a thirty-minute walk into this, my middle-class area. I shut my door behind me and locked, and rechecked. I stood with my back against the solid front door, I breathed in and felt it come. I ran to the bathroom, dropped to my knees, held the toilet seat as I bowed my head. I vomited, I retched and I saw the boys' faces, not angelic, I saw the emptiness in their eyes, the delight they would take in pain, the horrible things they had done and would do. I saw their throats opened. I saw the blood.

When I had nothing more to remove from inside, I washed myself again, hot water against my frozen skin and removed my clothes as I heated up under the spray. I bundled my clothes into a black bin bag. I dried and dressed, I was awake and buzzing. The sleep I needed was not going to come. I needed to do something, I needed to be moving. I decided to dump my clothes, lose them, but I knew what I was doing, I knew where I would go. I was going back, going back to see.

RAUCOUS

The three men are not long dead. I'm no forensic expert, I have no knowledge nor study but the blood drips and trickles down walls. Nothing has congealed, this is recent. I am at the scene and hundreds of local scared folk could put me right here.

I hear nothing.

Two of the men were young, each sat on an armchair as if to fulfil the requirements of a macabre scene. The one on the left in his gangster hoodie and oversized jeans, sat back, open-eyed with his right hand clutching his slashed throat. Blood had spurted. His chest and lap are covered in red. A blood splatter expert could read

15

the scene, walls and floor space with paragraphs of actions written in dark red splash. His friend lies in a photocopy position of the first. The men's hearts had been pumping strong. Darryl lies over a long coffee table. He looks like a small girl trying to arch her back and take the shape of a bridge with his arms flung out and his body bowed. Someone of great skill slit his throat and threw him down. He bled out quickly and in volume. The kid in the armchair on the right wears white trainers with a high-tide mark in blood.

I hear nothing.

I am here physically. I can't deny I was at the scene. My prints are on the door, my traces all over. I've been here before, DNA lingers, but the blood is everywhere. No one in this room at the time of the slaughter would be untouched by blood. My walk up had been quiet, no real movement or noise, no locals talked. They must have seen something; a red someone walked from this flat.

I scan the room and see no knife. They took the blade and left money and drugs. This is not a turf war, a simple hit, but a smart move. Dump the weapon a long way from here because no weapon, and no witness means no conviction. I am clean, a half-drunk solicitor could argue me out of this. No blood on me means I am not the man.

I hear nothing.

The man I work for is a smart operator, he has to be. If he wanted me dead, he would do it quickly and with force. He is no James Bond villain, he wouldn't give me the chance to talk. If he wanted me gone, he would come fast and hard, with two or three men like me and that would be it. A set-up like this is a waste to him, no complex tricks, a man, a gun and dead. But something is wrong, this shouldn't be.

I don't need to run, not yet, not from here and not from what I have been for the last eight months. I can stay, do what I have to do, work my way to achieving what I set out to achieve. This isn't a sign, this isn't a lucky escape, this is coincidence. Three dead men, taken out with ease, taken out with skill, and I am the first to find them. Without traces of them on me, I am free.

The corridor is dirty but free of blood, a little damp in places, but the way this heap has been maintained I am surprised the whole thing isn't caked in mould

No one walked out clean, no one walked out unseen.

I hear nothing.

I step back and feel arms reach around my waist. I turn, I grab across my stomach at a small forearm with my left hand. I spin and pull my right fist back, loaded and ready to strike. I see a gangly blonde with highlights of red, her face and hair matted in blood. She stares at me. She is shaking, in shock, trembling unable to react. I stare at her, I should push but she is no threat. She moves forward, she places her arms around my waist and hugs. Her head is on my chest. My arms, without thought reach around her shoulders. Comfort, a reaction no one would call natural. She pushes forward, driving her weight through her legs at my centre of gravity. We fall and I land on my back and she on my chest. We slide against each other and the floor, I turn, and she releases her hold. I look at her, she is Sissy Spacek in Carrie, a bucket of pig's blood poured over her head. And there is me, her victim, a man covered in the still warm blood of three murdered men.

No solicitor is talking me out of this.

My connections, my protection would vanish on sight.

I stand, the woman lies curled in a ball. I pull my phone from my pocket. Colleagues laugh at what it is, nothing flash, nothing new. I need texts and phone calls, I don't need to stare at a screen because it holds all the information in the world. I don't need to check a page where everyone I know posted pictures and comments about how their day was going. I don't need to show compassion with a horrific event from a far off land by changing a picture to a flag I do not know. I do things. Real things.

I call the number. It rings four times. The other end picks up.

"This is Raucous," I say. "Tell Mr. Scully we have a problem."

CHARLOTTE

I expect chaos but I find silence.

I drive my small silver Seat, smooth running but ten years old. I park up a street away and walk, ready to drift by when I see commotion. I'm a passer-by with a rubber neck. I have my bag, the one I always leave home. It is a leather satchel, the size of A4 paper, as wide and as thick as a magazine. It bulges in the middle and hides little. Ten seconds of staring and a simple thought is enough to see what is inside. My husband's gun, old fashioned, a cylinder with six bullets, not the clip to load magazine. It is silver, a vanity gun. It fires, it will kill but it is built for show not efficiency. I leave it in the bedroom. Now I take it with me. My fear is growing. I believe it is confidence.

I carry my knife in my Jacket pocket. I am wrapped up warm, black Parka, thick jumper, black trousers and gloves. I'm wearing black boots, not light, but warm. It isn't smart taking a weapon back to a murder scene but I haven't been smart in two years. My obsession is eating my sense, I want to speak, to discuss, but I only have me to listen and debate the point, not someone intelligent enough to point out the flaws in my thinking.

I want to be caught, I'm sure, or maybe I want the end. No patience, I have no patience. I need the fix, a rush of adrenaline so I know I am still alive. I am acting dumb, not being cautious when I have to be cautious. You get nowhere without that. Stupidity acting on impulse, starting without a plan will get you killed, and that is what I am doing.

I had waited but what was I doing? Me the angry woman. But am I angry? Has the rage not gone? I have nothing else to do, I want to die, I've said that before. Not want but accept, I accept I will die, accept I don't have the courage to do it myself. Maybe I am a teenager who wants to die, but not entirely, not really. I want the attention because who am I now? Who speaks to me? Who needs me? The queen of old is gone, sitting in black, mourning a past that died with my husband. I am finished as anything. But I killed and I found it easy. The anger at seeing Michael that way, my husband, seeing everything they did. That changed me. I am not who I used to be.

You never go back. That makes sense. The smart guy in the wheelchair, the guy with the electronic voice, the brain, the genius, the Simpsons character, a black hole theorist. He states that time travels only forward. You can't go back, but you can jump forward. Time travel into the future a theoretic possibility, but never ever back. DeLoreans to 1985 were good films but not science. Flux capacitors and funky haired madmen with nuclear waste. The ideas of a creative mind. Fast forwarding your life was science.

I want the future, the point of showdown and I want it now. Not a boy's western in a graveyard, three men staring down as seconds click. An ugly one who isn't ugly, good but not good, bad but not entirely. Michael loved it, I sat through it. Men never grow up, not fully.

I am my own time machine, taking steps too big to a point far away, missing the middle and costing myself dear by paying no attention to the here and now. I have started, an official point to look back on and say, Yes, this is when it began.

I think of the police, how they swarm, the vans and detectives and door-to-door enquiries of pure silence. Yellow tape and dogs. I fear the dogs. They smell, they know, they find the scent and here it is mine, and here I am going back.

RAUCOUS

I want out of the apartment. Nothing to do with fear or panic or shame. I'm not angry at the problems three deaths on my round will cause. I want fresh air, need the cold to think. Scully's secretary assures me I am safe. He has phoned me on the business line. The boss himself will be there soon. Hold the fort, he says. Hold the fort? Who says that anymore? There is nothing to hold.

Inside is a smarter place to stay, I am covered in blood, and while not the scarlet red of shocking films, I look a mess, like a man from an abattoir on a cigarette break. Outside I would act as a gruesome scarecrow. The police aren't coming, Scully has seen to that. He wouldn't come if there was a risk of having trouble from official circles, and Camp Freddy the secretary, is not inclined to lie. Scully is coming so I need to read the situation. Three murders, a lot of blood, and no idea why they are important enough to kill. This is a pretty big message from someone but I have no idea who needs to send one and what the message says. Someone has decided to shout out in action and I don't need any part of it. I'm not volunteering to find out more. I smile, maybe I have competition.

If I step outside I will be a flesh lighthouse in front of a green door. I am a white and red beacon warning addicts to stay well clear of Darryl's lest they crash and drown, or simply get thrown off the walkway.

I am not the clean-up guy, if they would even need one. I figure Scully is coming to look assess and decide. It is only Darryl, no one is going to toast his achievements nor mourn his demise.

Darryl had no one, I know that much. He is younger than me, but not by many years. He came up through the system just like I did. Maybe he started out different. I heard he was dumped on a doorstep, but I also heard he was a baby left in a bin. The origin matters little. Mine could have been the same. No one cares, it's the upbringing that has meaning. Place to place, moved on because he was difficult, then difficult because he wanted to move on. No ties, no bonds, and no one to be at his funeral.

The two youths I don't know. I have probably seen them, maybe even spoken to them at some point. Paths cross here all the time. But I don't know who will miss them, don't know their family, don't know if they have connections. I doubt it because being the scare for Darryl sure didn't indicate they had any foundation round here. But they would be missed. Teenagers have friends, and even when they don't, tragedy brings out the amateur dramatics in people you vaguely know. Another opportunity for attention to the kid who needs it. They were probably living at home, bossing the parents, doing what they liked, but not able to get out. They still needed that nest.

The call is for Scully to make. The murders known to all, or three bodies vanish. A pair of teenagers become missing persons if hidden well. In the ground, in concrete or dissolved in acid. No one will find them because no one will look.

Their disappearance could trigger a teenage tit-for-tat, a consideration Scully will have to make. The vanishing of two teenagers being mistaken for a hit from a rival gang. How those children could escalate. Random violence, because, why not? Any excuse is as good as another.

It looks like a one-man job, a competent man at the very least. The three were not finely tuned killers, but they were three and taking down three, no matter who they are, is a difficult task. Whoever did it was fast, didn't blink, didn't hesitate, decisive, killed and left. Not easy to do. I couldn't have done it, not in that way. They'd have stabbed me to death before I had choked out the first guy. I can't use knives, not like that.

But whoever did it was not without conscience. Sally saw and heard everything. She is no reliable witness, but who was to know that? She saw, she heard. She knows. Maybe a person with local knowledge. Sally is connected by blood, a family with history here. A black sheep, but death always brings forgiveness. Vengeance is a lot easier than admitting you never cared.

Scully will talk to her, hope for some information but she is off in the land of pure pleasure, a different dimension where you can never stay. You are always thrown out to feel the agonies of hell burn your flesh and rot your mind until you pay for re-entry by handing cash to gatekeepers like Darryl. The invite injected straight into your bloodstream. Leaving Sally alive was a mistake, no one leaves a witness behind, no matter how far gone. A professional-style hit with amateur heartfelt mistakes. The thing makes no sense and Scully will come to the same conclusions, quicker than me too. That's why he is the man around here and I am nothing.

Was it for Darryl or the flat? The flat is important, tactically perfect. The rock of Gibraltar to a drug dealing empire. Physically the centre of a massive market. Police don't need to come here, why would they? A small den, a flat with nothing in particular. There are plenty of them about if they need their arrest stats boosted. There are easier places to raid, more stashes to seize, more early evening local news to show drugs with a street value of millions when the reality is less.

Here there is a negative truce, an estate that governs itself, polices its inhabitants and has its own set of social justice. Scully is the de facto President and everyone, whether they acknowledge it or not, owes him their peace.

The outbreaks of violence are Scully's, carried out by men like me, a punishment or warning. The kids don't try to hold or take this turf. It is his. An area like the armed neutrality of World-War Two Switzerland, if Switzerland were a corrupt, deprived violent land with nothing to offer and everything to hide.

The bodies will go, the flat will be cleaned, not perfect, blood will linger but covered in paint, carpets re-laid on black stains. No one will come to check, no one will ever know. No body, no murder, no cares.

But three people have seen inside. Sally laid out on another hit, me and the killer.

And why Darryl? Why like this? No sense in it all, but not my problem, this isn't for me. As soon as Scully arrives, with whatever crew he chooses to bring, I'll be told to go.

Scully can make his decision, spout some shit in his Brummie twang, and leave. He'll make sure he rubs palms, kisses babies and donates to the local charity. But he will make sure everyone here is clear, if they say a word they die.

He is good at what he does: he has to be. An outsider here, running the roost over those born and raised, a ginger man from Birmingham, calling the shots on a prime piece of London. I am nothing but an enforcer, a slab of meat with local knowledge, and the local's knowledge of me, a figurehead, a manipulated figure. Scully's own set up, 'Look, I have Raucous, one of you, trust me because your man does.' A cheap politician's trick and one that works.

Camp Freddie calls again. I have two phones. I answer the one that is vibrating. He tells me to get outside, to warn people off, make a show. I tell him of the blood problem and Sally. He tells me to put on some of Darryl's clean clothes and to make sure Sally comes out of whatever dreamworld she is in and not to let her go.

I follow instruction.

Darryl's clothes are too small, so I keep my trousers after wiping them down. They are black so nothing shows till up close and looking. I put on a green jumper I find in the bedroom. There is no order to it, piles here and there. It stretches tight across my body. My ever increasing gut protrudes, as does my chest. It had once been solid, now it sags like a big-breasted old woman in an ill-fitting bra.

I look at my second phone. It is new and unused, a void. No saved numbers, no calls or messages received or sent. Nothing. I need to call a number set it up to wifi and track my every move. I am holding it in my right hand. I have no recall on why it was there. The most expensive thing I own but never use. A gift from Scully, a sign he cared. But I am not fooled.

My death, if deemed a positive to anything, to any overriding aim of whatever Scully thought he was going to achieve, was nothing. And my death would be that. I should throw the phone away. I should never have taken the thing. There is nothing to achieve through this. A moment of madness on my part, a moment when I thought I could do something right. But that's not who I am.

I am a man they call Raucous. A man who has already chosen his life.

CHARLOTTE

The square opens out as I trace my steps back to the flat. The three tower blocks, the large grass space and the early morning light bouncing on unbroken frost. There are no foot prints because no one moves. I am here alone and a plume of white escapes my mouth on every exhale. I'm wearing warm clothes so the chill doesn't bite.

The flat remains empty, unsearched. I have killed, gone free and no one knows. The three men lie dead and undiscovered. I look up at the walkway, the door, the green paint, still closed and no one discovered. The addicts will start coming. They will knock. The door is unlocked and they will enter to search because an addict won't give up. They will find, take what they want and leave. They won't call the police, why would they? Nothing more important than the hit.

Am I disappointed, or relieved? There is some anger too. I don't know how to feel. What was I thinking? Why did I assume because I want fast action the whole world would revolve around what I need? What am I doing here? Stupidity. Proving that is my reason to be here. What do I expect to find? Too soon, not patient. I expect it to be all over in a day.

I turn, deciding to head back to my car. I would have gone, vanished and never returned. This is what I tell myself but my eyes stay on that green door and as I turn my body away, the front-door opens. A large man in green jumper and shaven head steps out. He holds something, a phone I guess, in his right hand. He is small in the distance, but I have been on that walkway. I know his bald head is much closer to the ceiling than mine. Six feet four is my guess, and carrying weight, a lot of it muscle, like a body builder who has long since given up the hard hours down the gym.

He holds the phone like it is a delicate animal on the edge of death, a new-born chick or a child's hamster. I freeze, standing up in the open space, not hiding, not thinking that I should, staring at the man, a small dark figure on the edge of a walkway above a large green square.

He doesn't look my way, he just stares at his hand and I watch him. Time slows and I watch every movement, transfixed. Two seconds drag like minutes and I would have stayed that way. A seagull makes its awful screech and I come back to reality. I start to move. I walk to the tower block on the right and I turn the corner. I lean my back against rough grey concrete and pant, my heart racing. I am out of sight.

I stay here, my hands deep in my pockets, my right grasping the handle of my knife. I watch my breath bloom, my ears so cold they burn but my nose numb. I lift the hood on my parka and crush the fur lining against my face. I wait for police, for something to happen. Chaos and shouting, anything to tell me they know what I have done. I don't understand, I wait in my place, my back against the wall, watching the estate evolve. It starts to stir, dog walkers and smokers. It is no jogger's paradise.

RAUCOUS

I walk back in, people now know I am here. The estate is quiet but beginning to stir. Dog walkers and people hacking on their first cigarette of the day. Husbands and wives out in the cold so their houses don't stink, or their kids don't passive smoke. I only need a few to see me, so I stand large and look people in the eye. Some stare back, surprised I am here, one even stops in the middle of the square and looks open mouthed at me. I guess I still hold some type of fear.

Word is out, I have done my bit, now I need to sit tight. Scully won't need me, and I don't need to be here. This is a nothing event for me.

Sally has made her way through the shakes. She is on her way to the person she should be. She won't be there long. Her body will cry for another hit, or her mind. A moment of panic, an inability to cope with who or what is in front of her will force her back to oblivion.

Sally is twenty-four, she's been dead-end for ten years. I don't know what happened to her but I can guess. She is a pretty girl,

24

innocent too and trusting, which are rarities here. Her father is an old man now, but he had been someone. An enforcer, a lot of time inside. Unlicensed fights and a popular guy. Everyone knows the family. Sally isn't part of that but she had been growing up. Her father has washed his hands like Pontius Pilot from Peckham. No one is dumb enough to touch, no one but Darryl. But this isn't her father gaining revenge. He is old school, beat a man to death and make sure everyone knows who did it. Sally is safe through family.

I need to make Scully understand.

"You want something to drink?" I ask.

Sally nods. She is slumped on the edge of the bed.

"Coffee?"

She nods again.

Probably the only drug Darryl doesn't have.

CHARLOTTE

Why would he come? That is the first thought I have.

I watch him step out of his expensive sports car, he glides, his pale skin, freckled, his hair more white than red now. He is wearing a shiny blue suit, slim fit, with waistcoat, his jacket is joined by two buttons. He is tall, six-feet-two and in shape for fifty, there is a little paunch, a thin man but not sickly. His glasses have thick black rims. A businessman in look.

Scully straightens his tie as he straightens his back stepping from the car. I have no idea what it is. It isn't flashy, no low-riding Lamborghini or bright red Ferrari. But the car is expensive, powerful looking, and silent. No motor roar, but a smooth silent glide. Top end Electric. It looks calm and smooth and darkly blue. It doesn't stick out. The only statement it makes is, don't look at me, I'm not what you think.

He looks around and sees no one because no one looks at him. I step out from my hiding spot and I am three hundred metres away, none of my features obvious. I stare at his eyes, dark blue, almost glistening is how I remember. They are bigger now, magnified slightly by his lenses. He is an attractive man but he never smiles.

I know I should move. It would be my advice to anyone like me. Move, get away and get hid, this is not the time for silly games. I touch the satchel that hangs from my shoulder.

He knows me, but I look different now although maybe not enough. He has no memory of me, I am not important. I'm dead and were I not, he would kill me. I am someone with whom he has shared company in formal evenings. It won't be in his mind because I was nothing then and am less than nothing now.

Scully walks once he is joined by his driver. He is a young man in look, but I know he is thirty-five. He walks on tip-toe, effeminate almost, but a sign of the athlete he is. I know him, or at least of him. His name is Merrick. I can't see his face as it is turned the wrong way. I can only see his right side but I know the scar that runs clean down the side of his nose. He was slashed at thirteen, took his revenge at fifteen, borstal then prison, bare knuckle fights and a late entry to the Mixed Martial Art scene. A middleweight and in his prime. They walk in unison.

Scully looks around as he walks, maybe he senses me, I can't help but stare. I want him to see me, I make no effort to hide. He keeps pace but he stops talking and squints slightly. We play eyeball. Does recognition flicker? There is something there. I touch my satchel. I am not a random lady in layers of black, I shouldn't be here and he knows. The out-of-place is his speciality. Scully's mouth moves and Merrick turns his attention to me.

It isn't a conscious decision; I don't know what I am doing until it is done. My hands grab the fur edge of the hood on my Parka, I pull the hood back, away from my face, exposing my head to the cold. I shake from side to side but I don't have long enough hair for the action. I used to have flowing locks, long blonde, with waves, I took them two years ago. My short hair flicks up, light hits my face and my features are clear to see. I haven't slept, I look like hell, but I look like me, the person I have become.

The two men stare as they walk but Merrick unable to ignore, unable to accept being challenged, changes course and comes to me. Scully reaches out with his left hand and gently grasps Merrick's right forearm. They have more pressing things to do. I put my right hand inside the satchel.

RAUCOUS

"This is a hell of a mess," Scully says.

Merrick nods his head like the good dog he is.

We have left the front room and the bodies, and made our way to the bedroom to the right of the corridor as you enter the flat. It is cleaner, but not clean. Darryl's room, I imagine, dirty sheets, full ashtrays, and clothes all over the floor.

I don't like Merrick, I've met many like him inside, always has to be the man, no off switch. Scully rules him because he pays, because Scully never says he is the bigger man. Scully needs a minder and Merrick is better than most. A relationship that could never break. Merrick will never be top man, he lacks the patience and intelligence. The intelligence told him he is working the only job he can. There is no career development. This is what he is and soon enough his speed will slow and he will be beatable. Yet right now he is dangerous, one-on-one he is trouble. I can lift more weight, hit harder in a single shot but he is fast, trained in all the martial arts that those cage fighters learn. His speed and strength are his assets, he isn't weak, none of those guys are. He can kick, punch, wrestle and he has that nasty streak. He'll bite, gouge and scratch. He doesn't believe in rules. He's lost professional fights, been choked out, tapped a couple of times, but never knocked out. He lost on skill to men who have lived the life since they were kids. He is tough and I have every intention of avoiding him.

"Was this you, Raucous?" Merrick asks.

I'm tired and I cannot be bothered with this.

"You ever seen me use a knife other than to butter toast?" I say.

"Raucous would have made a lot of noise and a lot of furniture would be broken. Someone else did this," Scully says.

"Not for drugs," I say.

Merrick and Scully look at me.

"The other bedroom. Rammed full of the stuff. Doesn't look like anyone took anything. And there's plenty of cash, which should cover the debt he owes."

"They were killed just to be killed," Scully says. "What kind of message is that?"

"A stupid one," Merrick says.

Scully defocuses his eyes. He isn't looking at anything. I've seen it before. It is his processing face. I've seen him do it dozens of times, the longest over a minute and when he came back, he told me to kill a man, and I did. He comes back, he turns to Sally and smiles, nothing friendly, a forced grin in an attempt at building empathy. Sally is shaking, she sits on the edge of the bed, her head turning left to the door every two seconds.

"You're Sally, right?" Scully says, his voice low and calm.

Sally tries to smile back. Her teeth are still there, and while yellow, they aren't black.

"What did you see?"

Sally shakes her head in short sharp darts back and forth.

"It's OK, Sally," I say. "We know who you are. You know who I am. You're safe. Just tell us what you saw, what you heard. That's all we want."

Sally shivers, her teeth chatter, she hugs herself and smiles at what she was.

"I didn't see the killing. Saw them dead. I think. Didn't see the killing. Didn't see her."

"Didn't see her?" Scully asks.

Sally nodded again. "Yeah, her," she said. "The woman. My friend. I didn't see her. Where's her body?"

Scully glances my way, I shake my head. There is no female body.

"What's the name of your friend?" Scully asks.

Sally opens her mouth, no sounds come, she pauses and thinks.

"I don't know," she says.

"You forgot your friend's name?" Merrick asks

His voice louder than anyone's in the room. Sally flinches at the sound. Scully shoots Merrick a glance. It is quick but it tells Merrick his silence is required.

"Sally, who is your friend?" Scully asks.

"The. . . the. . .little woman. We met up town. In the Italian bar."

"Last night?" Scully asks.

He moves forward a step and places his right palm gently on Sally's shoulder.

"Yeah, last night. Before we came here."

28

"Who was here?"

"Darryl and the two young guys. The usual people. No one else."

"Your friend?"

"She was here, she was with me."

Merrick walks over to the curtains and pulls them open, he has a view of the walkway, past the green and onto another tower block. The light shakes Sally and she turns from the window. Scully gives Merrick the same look but it is wasted as all he can see is his back.

"What hairstyle does your friend have, Sally?" Merrick asks.

Sally looks to Scully then me, we nod, it is OK to answer.

"She had blonde hair," Sally says.

"How long?" Merrick asks

Sally looks to Scully for help again. Scully pats her shoulder.

"It's OK," he says. "Are you going somewhere with this Merrick?"

Merrick turns, "Yeah, I am."

Merrick walks over to Sally and grabs her right arm, pulling her to her feet. He marches her to the window.

"Look down there," he says. He points to the distance. "Is that her?"

Sally squints. "I. . .I . .I can't see," she says.

Merrick pulls her up to the glass. "Is that her?" he asks.

Sally turns to Scully, twisting her neck as Merrick holds her tight.

Scully walks to the window and stares at the lone black figure in the middle of the grass.

"You think that's her?" Merrick asks.

"I think it is," Scully says. "And I think she's here to see what the hell happened after she left."

"Proper witness?" I ask.

"More than likely," Scully says. "Probably saw someone coming up as she was going down."

"Who is she, Sally?" Scully asks.

"Just a friend. She was nice. She likes me."

Merrick snorts. A fake laugh of contempt.

"Yeah, maybe," he says. "But she's different to you. You would never have come back to see if she were OK. Not unless there was some hit in it."

Scully is deep in thought again. "Too many people saw. There is no sense in this."

"Do you want me to go and grab her?" Merrick asks.

"No," Scully says. "That's for Raucous to do."

CHARLOTTE

They've been inside for five minutes. I wonder if Sally is still there, that poor woman. But she made choices, that's how it is. I made mine, I killed three people and only one of them on my list. Collateral damage, or simple practice? I don't care, they can come and haunt me all they like but they are not people to be mourned. They have no place in the world, no kindness owed, and it brought Scully here, out in the open. Merrick is with him, and that massive slab of meat in the green jumper. He needs to start thinking about what he wears, he is no teak hard muscle boy now. He needs to embrace baggy and quick.

Merrick I don't like, he is too good, better than me all round. One-on-one in a straight up fight, I am gone in seconds. The knife might cut him, but he has no fear of blades. He knows how to handle that. This is England, knives not guns. He won't expect the gun. Could I do it? I think I could, less involved than slashing with a knife. I remember pulling a trigger at the firing range but not with this gun, not with this type of gun. Would it fire? I don't know. I know it has because Michael used to have a small club where he went to shoot cut outs as he ran around a course. A competition of some sort. Men never grow up.

I am waiting out in the open. They've seen me, sneered like they do at everyone. What am I but a short stumpy woman in a massive coat? What threat am I to the two fine specimens of masculinity? They didn't recognise me; Merrick was coming over because my stare was rude. Scully didn't care, cogs were turning in that mind of his, but the print-out read blank.

I could go queen sacrifice, that would work if death is what I want. Merrick would get me soon enough but I'd swap my life for that of Scully and let the rest of the pieces play the end-game. Any other way and I would have to survive Merrick, and I don't think it possible. I could get Scully but it would mean I die too. Or could I shoot them both? Double tap was the phrase Michael used, a double tap, chest and head, or two to the chest, rapid, bang bang, and on to the next. Four shots, recoil going, target one and move to the next. I would have to be quick. Merrick first? But what if I miss? That's it, no chance to kill Scully. If I miss Merrick, Scully pulls a gun just like Merrick will. A small gap, a brief hit of time to take down two armed men. Scully first and hope Merrick is slow on the attack?

I smile. He is never slow.

RAUCOUS

I come out through the side entrance. She won't see me. I know the layout, and know the buildings. The fire escape busted open years before that no one wants to fix because it would be busted again. If she is where she was, standing in the middle of that dull green square of council cut grass, the tower block will be between me and her. I hope she got bored and moved on. I am not rushing, I don't want to take a small woman out. There is more chance of irreversible violence if I bring her back to the flat too quickly. Sally is in no danger, I have seen to that, I made it clear she was a piece of this place. Her death is not going to be forgotten smoothly. But if I bring in this woman the chance of nastiness will increase. They need information and if they think she holds it, she is going to get hurt.

I lumber around the back of the tower block. The council hasn't been so efficient here. Like someone who painted the front of their house and kept the garden neat, only for inside and outback to be a dumping ground of waste. Black bin bags ripped open and potato peel spilling out, rusted bikes and discarded washing machines all hidden from the normal view. There is a break of four metres to the next tower block. It is way off to her right but still in her peripheral vision. I want her to see me, to make the connection and run. I need to make a show. Scully and Merrick are watching and any sign I am making a mess of this will have repercussions on me.

I walk slow and large, I look to my right and see her. I am not in her mind, she stares up at the balcony, at the dark window, oblivious to the fact at least two faces are staring back.

She should have moved when she saw me leave. What is she waiting for? I walked out of the front door and moved along the walkway. There is no other way to go. She should have turned heel as soon as she knew I was coming. She maybe had an eye on the front door. Maybe she thought she was safe at that distance. Maybe she was just too far gone to care.

I need her to run. I would chase, but I have no foot speed, I never have. Big lumbering and slow. She could outrun me, I would make sure of it.

I pass behind the second tower block and she doesn't move.

I walk around, coming from behind as I knew I had to. They are watching me, expecting that move. Are they the only ones with interest in me? I don't know, people are always watching. I look from a distance like a man tip-toeing to prey. I am making as much noise as I can because I want her to hear and turn heel. I walk closer trying to do the opposite of what I should be, stealth is needed but I am crunching earth with every step. She has to hear me but her hood is up, her head enclosed. The front, I imagine is a cocoon of fur, a synthetic tube she stares through like a goose down telescope. She can't hear, self-imposed deafness while waiting for a hit. There are twenty metres between me and her, and I hope she bolts before I halve the distance.

She doesn't, but I keep on crunching.

I am close, I could, in two steps, reach out and grab her. I know what I need to do, reach out and grab her bag. She would be free to run. She could wriggle free, and go. I hope she is quick. She needs to run fast and straight away from here. I'll do my impression of sprinting hard.

She will win.

I reach out my right hand and grab her shoulder. I grasp the strap on her bag, she turns but I don't want to see her face. I pull her to me, her face forward. She needs to struggle and shake but she does nothing. I shake her, my left hand grabbing her other shoulder. She is dead to the world, standing but not resisting. She is gone, a ragdoll, the strawman in The Wizard of Oz.

"Run," I say. "You have to run."

She does nothing, a dumb mute.

I shake her and from a distance it looks like a struggle. She starts to wake and she shrugs but pushes without force. I look up to the walkway hoping I am fooling them all.

I hear a scream, guttural and scared. It isn't her. I look up at the walkway, and see. Merrick at the edge, leaning over, looking at long arms and legs, flailing, a helicopter of limbs as she accelerates to the floor. I flinch at the thud, and the woman I hold does too in a duet of shock. Blood oozes, quickly forming a red halo and Sally doesn't shake. She is dead on impact, her head bent and dented at all the wrong angles and her legs spread like a messed contortionist. Merrick looks at Sally, he looks up at me and he waves me forward. The woman I hold finally understands.

She dips at the waist with force and twists, my natural reaction is to squeeze and lean my size. But I realize this is a chance to let her free. It matters little, she knows angles and levers, and places to push force. She is no zombie now. She is free of my hold, fast and smooth and stepping away. She hits speed instantly but two, three paces and she taps her shoulder. Her bag is gone and she pulls up like a racehorse refusing the jump. She turns, her face still cocooned in a tube hood. She checks her shoulder again, but she can see I hold her bag.

"Give me the bag," she says.

Her accent is forced posh but she isn't good enough to hide the local vowels. She is from here, from birth too. It takes a long time to pick up the sounds, and you never can lose them.

"Just run," I say.

She doesn't understand and she steps toward me.

"Give me the bag, Raucous," she says.

She is real local, she knows me, knows my name, must know what I do, or what they think I do.

"No one knows who you are," I say. "Not right now. You have a chance to get away. Run."

She looks at the balcony and so do I. Merrick has gone, racing down here. I know and so should she.

"Give me the bag, Raucous," she says.

I shake my head, Scully is watching and there is no way I can explain a handover.

"Run," I say.

We turn to the noise, a bang as the front door to the block of flats bursts open, spinning against the wall which holds it. Merrick sprints out.

I stare at the covered face.

"You have to run."

CHARLOTTE

Merrick.

Shit.

He is sprinting, his slim-fit, blue polyester suit rubbing together on the inner thigh building static. His knees high, pumping, driving forward. He is no natural sprinter, using a technique taught when training for other sports. His hands like fins, alternate up and down. He has perfect form, but no speed.

I look at Raucous, that big dumb bastard, the man in the green jumper was Raucous.

Shit.

He stares, telling me to run. He has let me go, made no real attempt at holding me back. He has my bag. He has the gun.

Shit.

Merrick charges, not breaking his style. I turn and run, no stretching, no warm up, my muscles cold and tight, my hood zipped up in a wreath of warmth makes breathing hard. I push, know I have to sprint because Merrick won't quit, he'll run till he drops.

I'm not going to make this.

I look down as I run, my heavy shoes keeping my feet nice and warm, and weighing me down. I'm not running in wellies, but these won't be the next advance in road racing. I'm sluggish, I tense, I can hear Merrick gliding over grass. I look around, not knowing where to go, catching sight of the tower blocks, realising I am heading away from my route out. My car ever distant as I run away from Merrick.

I'm not going to make this. Why did I come back? Why did I wait?

Sally is dead, chucked from the balcony, without fear of repercussion. It is my fault, I killed her, me. I should have stayed away. Was it worth it? Darryl, two boys and now Sally. I'm next, I can't escape.

I have my knife, in my pocket but I can't get it now. I need to keep form, keep moving. Raucous has the gun but he won't use it, he never liked them, he was a man's man. He won't like Sally's death, she was part of here. He won't be part of that.

I run, I need to hide, I can't out sprint. Can I out run? A long distance chase until Merrick can't continue? Who am I kidding? Stop living in a fantasy. I laugh, making me choke as I break my breathing pattern. I rasp and wheeze and I'm back to normal. I listen, tense myself for the attack. He'll bring me down, taking my legs I think, a traditional rugby tackle. He could dive and take my shoulders, but that would leave him exposed. I listen for his steps, ready to be brought down, ready to go for my knife. I could surprise him, slice the inside of his thigh, or armpit, slash down his forearm as we tangle on the floor. I can't stop and turn to stand my ground and invite him in, a square go I would never win. That would take the surprise away, he would slow and stalk, coming at me on his terms. I would have no chance with the knife.

I run but the attack doesn't come. I am still breathing well; I'm fit but I'm not fast.

I watch around me like a steady cam on TV, always remember to keep stride, not to slow, no rubber necking, foot down, go faster. I see the door to the third tower block. It is open, jammed by a brick, to let a breeze run through.

Inside? Is it better to fight inside? Can I surprise? Can I hide? Out in the open, what happens? Inside, confined space, a back door, an escape, a maze, more people, more doors, more room. The police will come, they have to, Sally bled out, contorted and twisted. Someone will call police or ambulance. They have to, not everyone is under Scully's spell.

Time, I need to buy time.

I dart left and head for the entrance.

RAUCOUS

I watch the woman run in her big boots, big coat, and her zipped up hood. She could be an Olympic level athlete, but dressed like that she can't outrun, her only chance is if Merrick self-combusts on arrogance set off by the static electricity in his cheap suit. He flays his arms like a man who has seen sprinters run and thinks copying their moves will make him fast. It doesn't, it makes him look like a stop-motion mannequin.

If he catches her she is dead, Merrick the bully, causing fear by killing the weak. He'll make a name for himself, and then he'll die at the hands of the next soulless hardman with issues. But what can I do? Me, a big, out of shape hulk carrying a woman's bag. I'm not in this for the pleasure, I'm in this because of who I am. There is no mid-life career change here. I'm uniquely qualified to be one thing, and I am that, I am nothing.

Merrick bounces toward me, following the shortest path to the woman. It means he has to pass me. I stare as he pumps his knees and elbows, high hands and high thighs, driving away. His slip-on shoes giving just enough grip for him not to slide on damp grass. I would love to trip him on his way, kick his legs out, break his shin and watch him writhe. But none of this is for me. The woman made her choice, a junkie with a junkie friend. Sally dead and she must know she is next.

Merrick keeps on running, second after second, closer and closer.

I look beyond him, see Sally, her right leg bent back. Her blood has stopped oozing, and she lies there dead. I told them who she was, what she meant. Merrick went and killed her. He had to have decided alone. Scully isn't dumb enough to give that order.

The noise comes in an unrecognisable burst.

"Chase her you dumb bastard," he shouts, each word emitted on a deep exhale.

I don't move, I stare at his contorted face as he blows air through pursed lips, like he needs oxygen for burning lungs. He has run thirty metres and he looks like he is at the end of a marathon.

He shouts the same phrase again; I turn my head to where the woman should be. She is sprinting, doing a good job too considering her clothes. But Merrick will catch her, if not before the tower blocks then not far after. A dumb woman for not leaving here. Merrick could take her down with ease. The woman looks in good shape, no half-dead druggie can move as smooth and as fast as she is but adrenaline is a funny thing, and it must be pumping around her body. She knows what is coming.

I watch Merrick's face as he bounds closer, his eyes too close together, the face and scar, the red cheeks, the spit coming out his mouth. A man difficult to warm to, a man impossible to trust. I don't understand why he killed Sally, there was no reason to do that. She was a good kid, had it tough, she wasn't going to speak. She had nothing to say. She didn't deserve that. I told them who she was.

Merrick swears at me, I haven't moved, Dumb and bastard are the words I hear most. Yeah, big old Raucous, big and dumb. I'd be right at home chewing on straw and living in the American deep south, playing an old worn banjo and speaking about the good ole boys. That's who I am, a city-raised man with a country bumpkin brain.

I don't care what you say, Merrick, I'm not your man.

Merrick is almost with me now, still shouting, still sprinting, two more seconds and he'll whoosh on by.

I step to my right, closer to where he'll run.

"Get out of the way," he shouts.

He swerves to his left to avoid me.

I swing my right arm, a stiff round arc, timing the movement, and judging I need to hold it straight at shoulder height. He sees it coming and tries to duck but I calculated that move. The inside of my forearm catches him clean in the throat, and I keep swinging. His feet lift, going higher than his head, his feet and legs go higher still, momentum and inertia doing the strange things Newton always said they would. He flips, over the top, like my right arm is a parallel bar and he's gripping for dear life with his Adam's apple.

I used to watch all that old American wrestling stuff, big men, with hairless bodies and little speedos pretending to hurt each other with dumb moves. Merrick, welcome to the clothes-line, this one is genuine, you aren't going to be speaking without a rasp for quite some time.

He hits the ground hard and he wheezes. I could leave him there, gasping, getting all muddy in his bullshit suit, and that is what

I should do. But doing nothing is a choice too, I just don't like him. I can see Sally, she was one of us.

I should walk up and punt his head, try and take his hair off with a toe-point pummel but I can't do all the 'kick a man while he's down.' I know most can, especially with all the MMA stuff now. Smashing someone in the face as they writhe in agony under the weight of a man on their chest, totally acceptable but not for me. I jump on the streaky little bastard anyway, and wrap my right arm from behind, around his neck, a little choke, make him pass out, get it all done and finished quick. Maybe I should leave him here sleeping until the police come because no matter how scared the locals are of Scully, someone is going to be old school enough to be angry at Sally being dead. Someone somewhere is making that call. I wasn't up there at the time, there'll be CCTV that proves that. I'm clean but the killings in the apartment, not so much. I should run really, or let them get on with whatever they need to do. The woman knows me, I don't know her. I look up and she is running, not exactly cutting through the air, but she doesn't need to, there's no one chasing her now.

And I think I've got it covered.

Merrick comes alive, from a passive nothing to active aggressive, a snap like he's been fooling me. And he has. He twists, the pressure on his neck immense as I am not letting go. He reaches, scrambles and twists and turns, his stomach against mine, his legs pincer and grip me. He can't squeeze, doesn't hurt nor affect my breathing, but he is stuck fast, a limpet scratching for position. My choke hold is now doing no choking, I am squeezing his face against my chest, like I'm a saggy old gran enthusiastically embracing a child. He moves, and squeezes, looking for an opening, and I'm already breathing hard.

His head pops from my grip, sliding down and out like it's dipped in olive oil. He moves quick and I'm grasping at air. He twists up and around and just like that he has my wrist. His legs wrap around my arm, he pushes down and extends my arm straight, twisting the joints, trying to pop my shoulder or break my elbow. I've got him on strength, but he has leverage. The little bastard is good. I'm standing and I know if I hit the ground I'm gone. Once I'm down, he'll lean back, pin me with his feet, extend and twist

38

until ligaments break and joints simply pop. I can't tap out because there is no referee.

If I hit the ground, my arm is gone. He has all the technique, experience and angles. My arm burns, the shoulder socket on fire. He is hanging down, ankles crossed at my shoulder, his hands grasping and twisting my wrist. His head dangling down as he pulls and turns my arm to angles it doesn't want to go. I crouch, the pain burning, not letting me think. I raise my arm up, the one he hangs on and smash it down. The speed is slow, the power large, and I force his head into the ground. But it isn't concrete, just damp grass, not solid enough, not nearly enough. He'll be getting a little buzz in his head, but he isn't out cold. And now he knows my plan, knows he has to take me down before I can crush him again.

A surge of his power, my reactions too late. I'm sure something tears, but I resist and lift him again. I smash him down, aiming to bust his neck. He hits hard and he loosens his grip. I take the chance and reach across with my left hand and grasp my right. I lock my fingers together so he can no longer lever. I lift him up and throw him down, knowing as long as I clasp my hands he can't hurt me. He thumps against the floor and I come down on top. He scrambles, and scratches, and is out from under me before I can push up and away from the floor with my hands.

I'm tired, breathing hard. I hope Merrick feels as bad as me.

I can't breathe, the strap whips around my neck as I'm still on all fours. It is thin, but leather, real leather, not cardboard. Merrick twists and pulls and the leather strap digs deep into my throat. Merrick has pulled the strap over my head and is leaning, pulling ever tighter. The bag, the bag the woman wouldn't leave. I should have given it to her. What the hell did I need with a bag? I can't let Merrick have it, and what feels like a purse inside, all her details, who she is, where she lives, where to go to kill her. I should have let her have the bag because now it's being used to crush my wind-pipe. I'm choking, unable to inhale. I scratch at my throat, dragging fingers into the flesh of my neck. I look to dig my finger-tips under the strap but it is pulled too tight. Merrick's balled hands, squeeze and pull, I feel his knuckles against the back of my neck. I reach behind me, but Merrick is no fool, he leans far enough away to escape contact. I grab at his right fist, scratching his hand. I follow the strap as it exits his fist. I have leverage, I pull, the force on my neck doesn't increase. I pull again, leaning forward, exerting pressure on the leather. I'm choking myself, helping Merrick's plan along. I feel the blood exploding in every capillary. My face crimson. A high risk strategy but the only one I have. I can feel my head lighten, oxygen not getting through to my brain, the artery blocked. I pull against the strap forcing myself to strangle. Merrick pulls, I push away, my right hand pulling at the strap. I hear it creak, and then feel the release as it snaps with a crack. I fall forward and inhale, deep gushing rasps. My face in pain as blood comes in and that trapped escapes. Merrick will react, he wants me dead. I know I need to move quickly. I roll to my left, and stand as quickly as my bruised body allows. My hands are up at my face, ready to protect and pounce.

I see Merrick and charge, bent at the waist, head protected. Merrick raises a knee to strike me in the face. I know it is coming and slide my head left, he catches me, a glancing blow. He has taken some of my momentum but not slowed me. I drive my right shoulder into his stomach, lift him up, and I feel his palms slap against my back. I take him up higher, and I jump. I pull his legs forward and drive him into the ground, my shoulder pushing all the way down. We hit the ground and his breath explodes from his body. I hear him try to inhale but his lungs refuse, winded and in pain. He starts to scramble, gasping, looking for the air to fuel his movements. We stand, he turns and he leaps into me, leading with an elbow, he strikes with everything he has left, and while not his best, it is enough to send my head snapping back. I reach out and grab his head, bunching his hair, pulling him down. We fall, and we are back to wrestling on the floor. He makes the same move for my arm, I lock my hands, he pulls.

"Kill each other sometime else," Scully says.

We stop and look up.

I look around, the girl is gone.

"We lost the girl?" I ask.

"We don't have time. Killing that girl was a stupid move, Merrick. But the other one, in her infinite junkie wisdom, has gone into that tower block. So she is either playing hide and seek, or more likely than not, that's where she lives. Go and get her, and then get out. This place , I am reliably informed, is about to be full of the police."

We don't move, we are still holding an embrace like we pose for a still life class interested in painting out of shape wrestlers in dirty clothes.

Scully stares at us, his blue eyes sparkling.

"Get up, and get her."

CHARLOTTE

More men, or boys, a mixture, all smoking, and the thick fog of hash drifts along the corridor. They stand as a group, three metres back from the base of the staircase. There are no flats on this level, no windows, just strip lights. A long corridor with an entrance at one end and exit twenty metres to the other. Behind the side walls are garages and cellars for storage but not cars. Who keeps their car in a garage? The old do, and that's it.

They look up and smile as I come crashing through the door. I slow down and walk and they watch me approach. There are seven of them, all in puffer jackets and tracksuit bottoms, baseball caps and bling. Teenagers, maybe two in their twenties, black, white and all shades in between, no racism here just anger. All of them in cheap shit jewellery from pawn shops or stolen from rivals. This is the base of the drug dealing pyramid. Thousands on this foundation level and each of them aspiring to reach the peak of an Egyptian demi-god to be feared men who everyone wants to kill. None of them will make it, but they each believe they will or at the very least be close enough to the man who is destined to rule.

The smallest of the seven steps forward. The joker among them, or the little hardman. I can't tell, but it'll be one of the two.

"Lady, you're running the wrong way," he says.

Maybe he's the arsehole. The mascot.

He walks forward, smiling, looking back at his gang. They want him to keep coming. They're smiling and he's making his way into their hearts with his humour. I don't have time for this.

He steps forward, he says "Lady," but whatever he thought of coming next in his improvised stand-up routine is lost to the humour gods. I step forward, wait till he turns his head to the crowd behind him. He turns back and I drive a straight right hand through his jaw.

41

He drops cold, out for more than ten. He falls badly, his left leg bends behind him as he hits the ground and I hear a snap, a ligament at a guess. The group hear it too.

"Where's the way out?" I say.

I'm on top, at an advantage, they could laugh at their little impetuous friend and wave me through without fuss.

But the pause lasts too long, too many of them looking at the little unconscious moron. They all look to the same guy, the one in the middle, the darkest of skin, the oldest.

He is calculating, judging the mood, judging what he has seen from me.

He steps forward as if told to do so in a police line-up.

He pulls a knife from his puffer jacket pocket. I see he has the same tattoo on his neck as the two teenagers I killed, a heart and ball.

"The way out is through us," he says.

Not the answer I was wanting.

I run, he's the only one to fight, at least for the next twenty seconds. His sycophants will watch how it plays out.

He braces himself, the exit behind him. The stairs to the next floor are to my right, between me and him. I turn and sprint, taking three steps at a time, and I hear his laugh but I don't hear his footsteps. They aren't chasing because we have reached an agreement and I'm free. I can only climb, I can't run outside. I will have to come back down.

I have time, how many floors? Ten? Fifteen? How many minutes for the police to arrive? I don't know. They will arrive, but will they search here? Will they hear here? I need to hide, lie low. I know no one here, not any more, I've been away too long, and too many changes. I'm not one of them, not now, maybe not ever.

I run, steps, each leading to a long walkway. On the third, I listen, I'm not being followed so I slow, take the walkway. I'm cautious, I shuffle to the edge, I look over. I see Raucous and Merrick together, walking slowly to the tower I am in, behind them, walking quickly away is Scully. They're coming for me; they have taken a break along the line somewhere. Did they make a plan? Do they know who is in this tower? Have they phoned ahead? Did the gang know to stop me? Too many variables and I know nothing.

Shit.

I turn and a woman in fluffy pink slippers and a three-quarter length housecoat lights a cigarette.

"You're in trouble, love," she says. "They're coming here. The police won't. Not for love nor money. You have somewhere to hide?"

I stare at her, wanting to answer, to tell her to go away, that I have everything covered. I have no words to shout down the obvious facts of my imminent death.

She inhales deeply knowing she has me.

I turn and run.

I hear her, "No point running, love," she says, "There's nowhere to go."

RAUCOUS

I walk next to Merrick as if nothing has happened. His suit is ruffled and stained with mud. I'm the same, but I was never going to be a male model.

Merrick breathes without rhythm and he winces each time his left arm moves. I hurt him, I don't know how bad, he won't show me, show any pain but I got him. The aches he gave me are swallowed up in my age, I ache all the time but then I'm medicated to the eyeballs. I feel little, and that has always been my superpower. There's no man I've ever met that can take a beating as well as me.

Merrick is of no concern to me now. The owner of this stupid little bag has my concentration.

The woman has to be from here, there is no other explanation that makes sense. She had the chance to escape, keep running, another six hundred metres and she would have reached streets. She could have vanished, dropped the all-consuming coat and been someone else. We would never have found her. But she ran to her safe place, her home. She knew me by name. She is from here. The accent was fooling no one.

Merrick is bristling, but not for me. I've seen it before, a man wanting to fight, needing the escape, needing the bombs of uncontrollable thoughts to be expressed physically. He is tense, bunched up, looking for confrontation, a man in a pub you do not want to bump.

The girl could and should have walked in and then right out the back of this tower block. That would have been smart, would have fooled us. We would ask questions, play hide and seek in a tower block and all the time she would be walking away into the morning light. We walk through the open door and know she never made it.

A small guy is hobbling, balance not right, left shoulder banging against the concrete wall of the long corridor, heading back to the group. I know the leader, a tall guy, named Jazz. He should have moved on, but he likes being the eldest of a teenage gang when in his twenties. He's the man here, the leader of a small, weak group. They each have tattoos on their necks, a crappy design of heart and balls. How obvious do you want to get? They filled a vacuum when the originators were killed, moved on or got to spend time inside. The small hobbled one was never going to have a happy time wherever he went. Small, gobby and overconfident in his ability to scare and fight. He was doomed to be the victim whenever he tried to step up. Accept your place, son. Vanish to a quiet life or be someone's little victim for the rest of your unhappy days.

Something has gone off, a fight and the little one lost as he always has. His left knee isn't working how it should, and he is whimpering on every step. I can't see his face, but his shoulders shake, and I know he is crying.

"Where did the woman go?" Merrick barks.

The little man twists to see us, his face streaked in tears, probably more from pain than humiliation. He is scared but wants to knock her down in words.

"That bitch," he says.

The gang behind all laugh. The little man looks to them and tries to hobble closer.

"Where is she?" Merrick says.

The leader steps forward, carrying a knife in his right hand. I notice so Merrick will have too. Pretty bad move for a leader of men.

Merrick marches forward and passes the little man and kicks his good knee as he goes. The little man squeals and drops to the

44

floor. Jazz, all six foot two of him steps forward, which is a really bad move.

"Where is the woman?" Merrick asks as he keeps walking.

Jazz smiles and walks forward too, raising his knife, showing off the splendour of its dulled four-inch blade and wooden handle.

Merrick speeds up in step.

Jazz hesitates, his confidence slipping from his face. He has read the situation bad. He had expected the little man in a suit to turn tail and run. He has just waved him in.

"Where did the woman go?" Merrick shouts.

His face has reddened, and spit flies from his mouth. He is running now.

Jazz thrusts the blade forward but he has panicked. He is too far away, and Merrick watches the knife dart toward him. Merrick is slow, not his natural self, his left arm not doing what it should. He steps inside the thrust, pushing the inside of the Jazz's forearm with the outside of his left hand. But Jazz is too quick, and he shouldn't be. The blade slices Merrick's shoulder, the cut is deep. Merrick swears, and screams, but not like a child, like the ball of anger he has become. Using his left hand, he grabs the inside of the Jazz's elbow, reaches across with his right hand and bends the man's hand up. The blade Jazz holds points toward his own neck. Merrick pushes, the momentum moves Jazz forward onto the blade, and Merrick forces the sharp knife point through Jazz's throat.

Jazz gargles, and claws at Merrick's hand. Merrick twists the knife, and any hope of survival is gone. Blood gushes out, a gargle and Jazz drops to the floor, not quite gone but never coming back. Merrick stares at the group.

"Where did the woman go?" he asks.

Each of them look to the stairs. Two point.

"Upstairs?" Merrick asks.

They all nod in unison like trained dogs on a shitty YouTube video.

CHARLOTTE

I'm on the third floor and I hear the shouts and screams, Merrick's tone screeches to me. They are in, they have met the gang and it sounds like at least one of them is down. Merrick hurting, maybe killing. Sally was a useless death, the gang downstairs less so. Maybe Raucous cuffed a couple, maybe Raucous is a killer now. I know why he went inside, know he could have come out early, but he got caught up in there too. I know all about Raucous. You can't grow up here, at my age, and not know Raucous. Hell, I even know his real name.

He'll hate the stairs, the exercise will kill him, so Merrick will be first. I need a plan, would it be better to hide? Wait it out? Knocking on doors now is futile, no one will answer, no one who would help.

A plan, what is the plan? What has it ever been? Me, the little princess with the dirty mouth, the High school beauty with a scum upbringing. The girlfriend of the man, we were going nowhere but council house and kids at the ripe old age of twenty. But he made it big, clever in the worst of ways. And now he's gone and I'm no princess anymore. I'm not going to be anything soon, just a dead has-been, someone who once was and got her just desserts. A cliché who lived the life the story dictates.

Only one way to go, and that is up. I run, step after step, hoping a plan will come. I tell myself an escape route will appear. I have to hold onto that, otherwise I would just sit and wait and hope it comes quick. I never came close to achieving the deaths I wanted, a stare is all I gave. It won't end like that.

RAUCOUS

I grab Merrick's shoulder as he tries to push past me up the stairwell. His left arm dangles, blood dripping off the end of his fingers. I doubt he could make a fist.

"What are you doing, Merrick?" I ask.

He tries to shrug me off, and I can see he is thinking of confrontation again. His eyes are glazed, he's not here, he's zoned in on one goal and that woman is going to be torn apart if he gets there now.

"Merrick," I shout.

I shake him, and he turns to look at me.

"What are you doing? You killed a woman, then Jazz there. What are you doing? This is madness," I say.

Merrick comes round, looks at me.

"It doesn't matter, none of it matters. It all ends tomorrow. One way or another. Nothing is the same after tomorrow."

He pushes on past, I have no idea what he is saying. He spoke like a concussed boxer, slurred and incoherent. A doomsday book in oral form from a man in a polyester suit with blood dripping from a shoulder wound.

I look down the corridor and the little man is sagged against the wall, whimpering and holding his knees. The corridor is empty but for us, and Merrick's steps are heavy on the concrete. I look up at where I need to go, floor after floor. The woman could be anywhere. She could live here, could have friends, could be here legally or illegally, renting, sub-letting, on a friend's sofa, living with a boyfriend, could be anywhere. But I know she'll keep running, she'll go to the top, she has made too many mistakes to do anything other than keep running like a scared child. I take a deep breath, hoping I get there before Merrick has killed her. I start to take the steps two at a time, hands on thighs as I walk.

CHARLOTTE

I don't want to unzip my parka because of a child's logic: if they can't see me then they aren't there. I hear the steps as the tower block is silent, screams tend to make people shy away and hide. They heard the yelp, the gargle, the screams, a man has died down there but it wasn't Merrick. The steps clattering up are his, no one else would be making that move. Raucous will be dragging behind, he won't run because he can't. I run, step after step but what happens at the top? Where does it go? Can I run the length of a walkway and find another escape? Are there two ways out? There must be. Which floor do I take? How sure am I? There is a way out. There has to be.

My legs burn, thigh muscles aching as lactic acid takes hold a long time before it should. I hear only my breath. I'm panting now, deep inhales when I can, lungs burning, not wanting the work, not knowing how to provide enough oxygen for what I'm doing. The energy stores in my body, the history of sugary breakfasts, are providing more than the taste I took them for.

I run, floor after floor. Do I think it is going to end? I keep going, looking for the way out.

I hit the top, and the stairs stop on a floor without flats, an attic of tanks and dirty windows, a long room across the top of the block, walls break the room every five metres, a hole lacking a door in each. That is the way through to the other side, a breeze block maze for beginners, straight through to the other side. I can see the door at the other end, old, but not worn, faded from standing doing nothing. This is my escape. I can do it. I can keep running. I have to.

I realise I have stopped, I am bent over gasping, my hands on my thighs, my Parka still wrapped up tight. I'm sweating, rivulets of salty water trickling down my body, looking for escape. I hear steps, the metronome of a man in constant and consistent motion. I hear shouts, but they don't seem to be for me, no idiot telling me to stop or hold up, we mean no harm. They have stated their aim and I have no intention of talking my way out.

I take a deep breath, stare at the door, and sprint.

RAUCOUS

Blood streaks the first two floors of Merrick's training run, the cut to his shoulder is streaming. Having your heart pumping when cut open isn't the best way to get clotting. The man is gone, spooked, something bad is about to happen, but he's too much of a man to ever back down. He's looking for a way to avoid his inevitable demise by being unruly today. He's screaming catch me, making all the mistakes. A man like Merrick spooked, that takes some doing.

He is moving fast, or at least was, he bumped his shoulder against the wall on the first two turns. He left a red streak where he stopped his momentum and bounced to take the next flight. He's slowed, I can hear that, the tap, tap, tap of his feet at a lower rate. He found his rhythm and it sounds like it'll be enough. If the woman is a junkie and hasn't dumped that Parka, then she'll pass out before she reaches the top. I hope she has a home, a friend a flat, because there's no way to escape on foot. Merrick is on a mission, he needs a death. He needs to be caught.

I quicken my pace, then slow, I'm no decathlete, if I get there in time, then I'll make a decision. The woman needs more than me as a saviour. She needs luck, she needs a way out.

CHARLOTTE

I clip a breeze block as I run, the point of my right shoulder hitting as I look back over my left to see who follows. The impact throws me to my left. I stumble, lose my footing and tumble. I slide, trying to get to my feet as I move, I graze skin from my hands, and the knees on my jeans rip. Years of dust billows up, as I fall to my side. I push myself up and get to my feet quickly. I have two more walls to go through and then the door to the way down. I walk and feel the burn in my knees. I hobble, but I have no time for that. The pain is a bruise, nothing more. I start to jog, slower than before, but I'm closer, almost there, I just need to open the door and run down. There's no one behind me, not yet.

I look at my hands before I push, my skin is slashed and grazed, small stones in the cuts. Years ago my mother would have dabbed TCP on the wound. Fallen from a bike, tripped and cracked. Every kid I know had them, most had the same on their chin. I hit the door, but it doesn't move, I look to the left and the slide bolt, which is shut but not padlocked.

I hear the scream, and I look back, I don't know the word, don't actually think there is one, just a noise, a triumph, a man thinking he has already won. I look through the long series of open doorways in breezeblock. Merrick stands, panting, shoulders slouched forward, his arms at his sides. He stares at me, his head forward, his eyes looking from just under the hood of his eyebrows. He is Jack Nicholson saying, 'Here's Johnny.'

Fuck you, Merrick.

I rattle the door, the bolt slides open, I pull, and jerk the door. It opens an inch, but stops. I rattle, pulling back and forth but an inch is all it gives. I look at the bolt, open the door, look to the other side, another bolt, slid closed. I push my fingers through the gap, try to prise and slide the latch, lift the small metal handle over the butterfly of metal loops, I scratch, push, flick but the bolt won't move. I turn and Merrick is where he was, still panting, still staring.

He sees something in my face, an expression he loves because slowly a smile breaks across his mouth. He nods, grinning with menace, stepping forward with his left foot, then his right. He walks, speeds up and starts to jog. He isn't sprinting now because he knows I'm trapped.

I try the door again. Nothing.

I turn, put my back to the wall.

He's coming like the liquid marching machine in terminator two, a John Wayne sideways walk of confident intent.

I slide my right hand into my pocket, grasping my knife.

He knows what I'm doing. He starts to sprint.

RAUCOUS

I hear Merrick's scream and if there's a word in there, I can't pick it out, just a guttural howl of achievement. He has caught her, or at least got close enough to claim a prize. I'm near the top, there can't be any more floors after this. If there are I'd consider the possibility I'm trapped in one of those impossible drawing of infinite staircases and water that flows in a continuous illogical loop.

I've taken it easy and I'm still sweating. Not much of it alcohol, mostly liquid lard from the lazy, order-out diet I have taken on in the last eight months. I'm slowly killing myself because I don't have the courage to do it quick.

I turn the last corner on the stairs and see I've made it, I see an open doorway into the attic. If it runs the length of the building, there's a lot of space up there. It is too high up for a junky's paradise, and too damn dark to be a social hub. I jog the last flight, just like I'd jog the last two hundred metres of cross country at school. I never fooled teachers into believing I had made an effort.

CHARLOTTE

He's charging, but not fluid, his left arm isn't swinging naturally. I see the stain in his jacket like a sweaty armpit on the outside of his shoulder, a dark spreading patch of blood. As he runs, flicks of red splash ahead and back, no clotting yet, which means the cut is deep. Maybe the gang downstairs loved me after all. Nothing like saving the damsel in distress from evil stalkers to balance out a life of shit. I hope they severed an artery.

Raucous is nowhere to be seen, he'll be sweating pure ethanol on the third floor like a human disinfecting machine of recycled supermarket own-brand top-strength lager. He used to be somebody but not anymore. He is now a third rate hardman living on the reputation of his younger angry self. He's become the joke he used to tell.

Merrick is coming fast, I pull the knife from my pocket, and he yells again, not a good day for knives. I spread my feet, balance myself but I won't attack, only invite him in, and use his momentum. I can't beat him on strength, can't beat him on skill. I'll admit, I can't beat him at all, not if he's thinking. I'm trapped and I can only escape if I take him to the point of death. I need luck, or for Merrick to lose his head. If he thinks straight I'm gone.

He keeps running, his arm not working, and I hear him rasp in a smoker's breath of crackles and phlegm. He's hurt, I hope Sally hurt him, I hope the gang hurt him. I hope I kill him.

I inhale as he nears, a second and we start. I expected him to slow and stop and circle as that would be the smart move. But now I see his face, close enough to recognise the eyes, I know he has gone, in a rage, a loss of control. He won't slow because he thinks I'm nothing, just a flesh bag to smash and crush. Why would he grant me respect? To him I'm a drug addled scumbag of no consequence with no training, and no fear. A woman wanting destruction and he'll take away my pain by massaging his own. He knows I have a knife but he's fast and I'm a skank. There is no fight.

You're wrong, Merrick.

He jumps at me, not feet first, nor leading with a fist. A hop, to raise his height, grab my wrist and come down with me already in his control. You wouldn't do that in any ring. You don't do that with me. He cares little for being slashed. I dip, taking inches off my height, thrust forward with my left hand, press against his chest, and slash up with the knife in my right hand. I cut through his suit, down his chest, along till his stomach. I spin away, and face him, his back is against the locked door. Face to face, two metres between us, he nods, he knows I'm not a mug. He looks down at the slash through his clothes, not as deep as I want, but I have gone through skin. What I would do to have my gun now, with a bullet for Merrick. I'd love to torture you, take you to death the slow way, but killing you is all I want. I didn't think it would be so soon, but I'll take the invite. There is nothing like a final dance to say goodbye.

RAUCOUS

They're standing at the end of the long dirty room, ten breeze block walls between us, each with its own empty doorway. They look like they have fought, Merrick standing, his back to the far wall, there's more blood on him than I thought. The kid downstairs must have been good. Merrick looks white, drained, but he still holds anger as he thinks. I can see the woman's back, her Parka still on, her clothes dirtied and scratched. She must have fallen because if Merrick put her down she wouldn't be standing now. Her left hand glistens, holding a knife, has to be because that is everyone's preferred choice of cowardice. Merrick's clothes have been slashed, I can see that much. The woman maybe had her chance and blew it, or maybe Merrick is done, one can only hope. The woman can't be a junkie, can't be a physical mess. She has run , caught only because of a closed door. She has moved Merrick round. He looks in thought. She's not what he figured her to be.

It had better be a knife, not a gun. But it can't be. I have the feeling Merrick would be missing a head right now if she held one of them.

They're staring, not wanting to make the next move. Merrick won't want another scar, and she can't turn and run. She knows I'm in the building, and Merrick will chase her down. If she's smart, she'll know she has to kill him, or put him down and hope he never finds out who she is. Would've been easier had Sally not died. She should attack. I know Merrick, he doesn't do patient. He has to be in trouble. Knives have taken their toll.

CHARLOTTE

I don't hear him but I know he's there. Merrick glances to the distance behind me. He makes no sound, mouths no words, just a look, nothing deep. Raucous is there.

I can't turn, a small break in concentration will bring Merrick sprinting for me. Raucous has overcome inertia and settled on the top floor. I wonder if he has my bag. I doubt it, he isn't on my side, he isn't on anyone's, not even his own.

I'm trapped and now I have two to take down. That should be the way. But I have more chance with Raucous, a past will do that for anyone.

Merrick knows, he's seen people who can and those who can't. He hadn't expected speed and movement; he hadn't expected to be cut. He stares at me, judging my size, my strength, looking for a weakness. He can't concentrate, I can see that. His left arm drags, his chest and stomach pour blood. His breathing is wrong as if a rib is cracked and pinching a lung. I needed this, I need him weak. I wish I had caused it, I wish the pain he felt now was all of mine to give. But I'll take it.

He looks at my knife, calculating. He remembers my move, he's regretting his decision to treat me with contempt. He should have taken the precautionary approach, should have assumed me to be better. He saw a skank and paid the price.

Raucous is making us both think. Merrick won't want to lose face, won't want to be saved by the big man at the end of the corridor. I can't hear steps or movement. I assume he is standing, catching his breath, hoping for a death to come. He can't like Merrick, he wouldn't understand Merrick's motives. Raucous won't have my bag, he'll have dumped it somewhere. I want that back, he won't have looked inside, not yet.

Would Raucous ever remember?

Merrick thinks I'm trapped, that I have no escape. If I turn and run I have Raucous to pass. He doesn't need to fight, not now. He can wait, wait for Raucous to stroll down to us, to trap me, to give me no escape.

I don't fear Raucous. I know I should, but history tells me he can do me no harm. But history can be wrong.

Raucous I could never handle physically. I could speed him, but I would need a lot of open space in which to run away. Merrick won't allow that, he won't trust Raucous, not now Raucous knows he killed one of us, that he killed Sally. Raucous can reason, there's more for him to know. Merrick wants death and he needs me to die.

But I need Merrick to fight. I want him dead, I need to be the one to kill him.

I raise my knife and step forward. Merrick smiles and nods. He accepts. We're on.

RAUCOUS

His head is gone and she is trapped. There is no reason to attack. I'm missing something because Merrick isn't dumb, It's no set-up, can't be. Sally dead, those boys and Darryl all genuine kills. There is no reason to test me, I am nothing but a collector. But there's a big piece of information I don't have, there has to be, there is no way to otherwise make sense.

Merrick and pride, which is the same as stupidity. He's damaged, some I caused, the cuts just an extension of that and his desire to attack. The kid downstairs got him good and deep. The initial slice and cut not felt because of shock and adrenaline. It catches you though, and your body adapts, it slows down to compensate for pain. Merrick is slow, but thinking too fast. He has handicapped himself in what would have been a one-sided slaughter.

The woman is no waster, she is no Sally, she can fight, she can run, she is not who we thought. She holds herself well, a stance to match any Tibetan fighting monk for balance and poise. Up on her tip-toes, the knife firm but loose in her hand. Merrick set to go.

I still have her purse, a bag for identification. I was going to make a visit on my own, find out who and why, nothing more, I wouldn't hurt or maim. Questions is all I had but now she fights and I have a decision to make.

CHARLOTTE

Merrick moves slowly to his right, he is circling, away from my right, away from the knife. He's still bleeding, but not a stream, only drips splattering the floor. His eyes constantly on mine, but his peripheral vision taking in what he needs. He needs a plan, a way to attack, better than the contempt he showed before. I doubt he'll charge, not again. He's not a man to keep repeating the same mistake.

He feigns all the same, a couple of shoulder twitches and forward momentum hoping I react and leave a gap into which he can run. I'm not buying, Raucous isn't coming anytime soon, and I know something about him that you don't, Merrick.

It's schoolboy stuff, circling and looking, waiting to see if a flinch comes, or someone runs. But I've done all my running. I need this to finish.

"You'll have to come soon, Merrick," I say.

He doesn't want to, but his shock flickers clearly.

"Yeah, I know your name. I know who you are."

"And who are you?" he asks.

"Sally's friend."

He fakes a laugh, a bad one, a hyena's cackle. His eyes drop. A mistake, the one I'll take. Not as big as I'd like, but the only one he'll be making. I step forward and slash.

RAUCOUS

Here we go, I'm not running. Merrick looks shot, and the woman moves well. She moved first, which was the way to go. Merrick looks and moves like the injured man he is. He parried with his left, got cut and moved back. He circles still, the woman not knowing what to do. She should attack, she has him not knowing. Merrick is buying time but I don't believe he wants me to save him. He knows she has to act fast and she knows I'm here. She'll think I'll want her dead or tortured too but she is wrong. But look at me, what else could I be? I'm an enforcer increasingly getting by on reputation alone.

CHARLOTTE

I slash his leg, more blood flows and he circles, knowing I'm quick.

I stutter step forward, on the balls of my feet. He sees me coming and backs away, mirroring my moves, always a distance between us like magnets repelling. Raucous is strolling, not making effort, I can see him now. He holds my bag, watching, not coming to his colleague's rescue. Merrick has no favours to cash in.

We circle, and I step, a swipe, I miss as Merrick moves. I knew I would, but I bet on which way he turns. I guess right, I step in, cutting a corner, closer than he wants. He reaches out with his left hand trying for my forearm. I slash across and cut through his palm. The pain doesn't register, not yet. He keeps coming and we're close. I drop my knife down, tip pointing out, pointing at Merrick's gut. He makes his grab, opening up his body to attack, he brushes at my right hand with his left, trying to get inside where I can't slash nor stab. I pull away, fast, but I realise too late what he's done. He brings his left arm down, hooking my right, the blade I hold in my right hand, flailing. He brings his left forearm against my elbow and pushes hard. My arm is extended, no way to bend, no way to stab. I reach across and scratch at his eyes. I dig my fingers and nails into the flesh on his face. He grabs his left hand with his right. He pulls, squeezing with strength. My elbow bends the wrong way, like a flamingo's knee, his ribs acting as a pivot as he exerts force. My mind works, as my nails dig into his face. He wants me to drop the weapon. My joint burning to the point of breaking, my hand losing grip and strength. Blood pops on his face as my nails slash in slow motion, dragging across his cheek.

I can't hold on and the knife drops. On the noise of steel against concrete, Merrick releases his grip and is climbing for position. He tries for an arm bar, but I fend off by slipping low. The feeling in my right arm coming **back**, the strength in ligaments and muscles returning. I try for balance, holding his arms, making sure they can move no further than inches. It is a Judo hold, grabbing at clothes, both of us close enough to kiss, each trying to bury our faces in the other's chest, away from punches, scratches and bites. His strength isn't standing up, he is my equal, we push and shove and cancel each other out. A school fight deteriorating into a matched hug. Only we can't stand and walk away with a tactical draw. One of us has to destroy the other.

I know what's coming, but I react too late. I'm off balance, not much but enough, manoeuvred over the edge of comfort by Merrick making a push. He fakes resisting my answer. He whips his right leg around the back of my left. He lifts me, a burst of strength he seemed unable to achieve. I'm on one leg, as is he, but the momentum is all his. He knew where we were going and I topple to my right. As we fall, in an angry embrace, Merrick looks for position. I wrap my legs around his torso. He'll fall full-weight on me, but I have to be in defence before we hit ground. I pincer, hoping I can hold on when the air is pushed from my lungs. I'm heading to the floor, back first, with a seventy-five-kilogram man coming crashing down on top. Grabbing at his head serves no purpose, I twist, hoping his shoulder will take some of the fall. He fights against it, but we twist far enough to reduce the impact. We hit ground with my legs around his waist and our arms free. He is on top, and I have no way of escape. He leans forward, I push him away as much as I can by stretching back and holding him distant with my thighs. He throws a short straight right at my face, not really believing he can hit. He needs to know how I'll defend. I push the blow away with my palm, grabbing his arm, pulling him in. I link my arm around his head and I slip my left arm under his right and lock my fingers together. I squeeze, his right arm pushes up against his head, he starts to hit me with his left fist. But he can get no power, nor speed, the cuts have weakened him. We are tied up, breathing hard, making cursory struggles to break free from an impossible grip. We are waiting for Raucous.

RAUCOUS

She's good, without me here, she'd have him beat. Merrick is only getting weaker as he bleeds. His strength and consciousness will go before hers. She wants him dead, she doesn't want to escape and she has more time than she thinks. I'm in no hurry, I need to work things out. The two of them locked up, two coiled snakes coming to the end of a fight, crushed up, waiting for the other to fade with no way to walk free. What is she thinking? She knows I'm here, knows I'm coming. She holds on. No escape. What can she achieve?

The easy way is to let her choke Merrick unconscious, leaving more choices in which I don't have to hurt a woman nor smooth her disappearance. He is still awake, every ten seconds he surges, but she has him tied, just like he has her. They're locked up till one gives up.

I stop and watch a test of muscle endurance. This woman is nothing normal, not a junkie, that's long been clear. And police doesn't fit. I look at her bag, still in my hand, I open the zip, feeling the weight for the first time. I look inside hoping for identification, knowing she won't have carried any. I find something I know.

The UK is not America, it is too small and has too long a history. There's no second amendment, no right to bear arms, guns come rare. Most guns found in gangs are left-overs from a long since ended World War, or sometimes a starter's gun modified to fire the smallest bullet. But this here is different. She wanted the bag, I now know why. Many things end with what's here. I pull out the gun, feel the weight in my hand and tears fill my eyes because memories can kill. I won't visit this long.

I know nothing of guns but I know everything of this, a Smith and Wesson 4506, a movie gun, Silver, flash, a real party piece. What everyone my age associates with how a hitman carries fear. It shouldn't be here, the owner is dead. That's what I know, two years now. I turn the gun over in my hand, I look at the handle, see the scratches and smile, I can't help it. A perfect piece of precision, cut and messed through stupidity. Tears fill my eyes. A gun. Something I never thought to see again.

I look at the couple on the floor, Merrick and the woman losing strength, never letting go, blood spread across them, mostly Merrick's. The gun in my hand.

"You need to stop, let go and get up," I say.

I speak quietly even with the chemical confidence of booze. I'm more sober than I've been in a year, memories of times when I was somebody take away my craving. My voice stays meek but the pair on the floor don't seem to care.

I should slide the barrel, flick a switch or create noise with a knowledge of guns. But I have no idea. I know how to take off the safety and pull a trigger. I'm not a hitman, I'm a glorified minder.

"There's a gun pointing at you, and I have some questions."

I try for Clint Eastwood yet in my head I'm woody Allen. The words work, something in my voice, a break maybe.

The two take tentative steps to look, small movements, eyes darting, searching out truth. Merrick breaks first, smiling. He lets her go, sliding away, looking ill and weak. He lies back, taking deep breaths, like a static shot of a grown man making snow angels of blood in the ground.

I can't see her yet, not properly but she is small and compact, muscly but aching.

She stands, weak, a struggle to straighten. Hands on thighs to make that final push to standing tall. She turns, messy, dishevelled. Her face dark through exertion and dirt. I'm going to ask, simple questions. But I see her, her face opening up, not asking for leniency, not asking for help, just telling me to decide.

Merrick laughs but I ignore him and stare at her. I step forward and stop, I drop the gun to my side, she smiles without humour. Her eyes are cold, her body loses the tense energy of the chase. She relaxes. I have to decide.

"Charlotte?" I ask.

She nods.

I look at the gun. I lift my head to look at her again. She shakes her head.

"He is dead," she says.

I nod because I know. But I had to ask. She was dead too.

She points at Merrick.

"He killed him."

"Darryl?" I ask.

"He was there too."

I stare at Merrick and his smile grows. He nods his head never taking his eyes from mine.

"Who did I kill?" Merrick asks.

"Michael Simmons."

Merrick takes his time figuring the connection. Her hair is short, her figure more muscular, but the likeness, the person is there.

"You?" Merrick asks.

"Me," Charlotte says.

"Quick?" I ask.

Merrick laughs, fake and in pain. "Slow." He drags the vowel for as long as his breath will allow.

I look to Charlotte. She nods, tears coming.

I click the safety. I hate guns. I've fired one three times, all at targets. Three times with this gun. I dropped it, it scratched. I never fired again.

Merrick lies back, closing his eyes.

"Today or tomorrow," he says. "I'm dead all the same."

I point the gun at his chest.

I pull the trigger three times.

The gun doesn't fall.

PART TWO

CHARLOTTE

I've been here before, never thought I'd come again. Raucous in his family home. A grandmother's flat. From what I can tell he has replaced only things that broke. The fridge, washing machine and television are less than ten years old. They built things to last back then. They remain here. Mahogany wardrobes straight from the 40s, and dark wood the material of choice for sideboards, tables and cabinets. A throw-back apartment to times when people believed in community. They had to, they were pretty sure they were all going to die.

I'm in the small front room. The thick red curtains drawn. I can't sit, although Raucous has offered. I drove him back in my car. We left separately, I had told him where to meet. He trusted I wouldn't run. We haven't spoken. What conversation can we have? We have nothing to say beyond death and loss.

Raucous is standing at the window, checking for arrivals and repercussions. He texted once that I saw. A message, the contents of which I have no idea.

He turns, looks at me again, the expression of a man who can't believe what he sees.

"Why aren't you dead?" he asks.

I inhale deep. "I wasn't there," I say.

"Then how do you know what happened? How do you know it was Merrick?"

Raucous holds down his anger. He has analysed and seen cracks in any logic. He used to do it quicker, but the day hasn't given him time to think. He's looking to test my story, find out any lies or misinformation through inconsistency.

I stare at Raucous, as he wants me to. The eyes tell it all, that's what he used to say. He could tell by looking. I never did believe him. But he never got things wrong.

"He made me leave. He put me on holiday. Bali. Of all places, hot and abroad. A month, he said. It would be a month. I went as someone else. New Passport, new history. But he kept in touch. Every day. A call. A chat. You know how he was."

Raucous smiles. Him and Michael as boys. The pair of them too smart to care.

"He was smarter than anyone I know," he says. "He could figure things that no one else knew needed figuring. He made those people a lot of money. There's no way Scully would have him killed. He had a hand in anything big?"

I'm struggling to answer. People knew Michael, knew his cool, knew his brains. Untouchable because he wouldn't allow connections. He always said they'd have to fabricate evidence to take him down. He never touched crime, just advised and cajoled. A man with enough brains to take a major wage and stay quiet enough to cause no one any fear. Only I saw his cool crash. I need Raucous to understand.

"He changed. His ease went. That cool, that calm that came from knowing. It went. He tried to hide it, fake it out, pretend he was the same old. But something had got to him. And he changed. He got rid of me."

"How do you know what happened?"

"Because he filmed everything. The whole house wired up and on film. He recorded the days. He would come back and watch through nights. His cool had gone. He was waiting to see something. And I think he did. We got burgled. An intruder. He told no one."

"What got stolen?"

"Nothing. But I saw the video. One man walking around, checking the study. Draws, picture frames. Not taking anything. Pulling things apart. It freaked him though, because he rarely went in there again. Never spent time in that study. It went fast from then. Speeded up. He got me to leave and he set things up."

"Set what up?"

"Me. Money. An exit."

"He was running away?"

"He was getting ready to quit."

"You don't get to quit. Not when you know as much as he does."

"Did."

Raucous looks to the floor, nodding his head, accepting he's gone. He pushes his clenched right fist into the palm of his left.

"You saw what happened?" he asks.

"I saw it all. They tied him up. Beat him. Stripped him. Cut him up. Sliced through flesh and kept on asking and talking."

"What were they asking?"

"No audio, just images. He screamed. I saw that much. But he didn't fight, didn't try and run."

"He would have figured it to be useless."

Raucous turns back to the window. He pulls back the edge of the curtain. He swears quietly as he turns to me.

"Was Scully there? I need to know. Was Scully there?"

I shake my head. He wasn't.

"Scully would have come to a killing. One that big."

"There were other men. Merrick led, but maybe took orders. He looked to one man a lot. But they never spoke."

"Scully's here now. He's coming up. He saw you, at distance. He knows who you are."

"I have a disguise."

"You're Sherlock Holmes now?"

I grab my bag, it's open, I pull out my wig. A long brown mane of ridiculous expense. I put it on quickly, look at the mirror.

"As great as that is, Scully knows you. A plastic mullet doesn't alter your face."

RAUCOUS

I gambled. An educated bet. At worst I thought Scully would send men but he's come alone. He's making bad decisions, putting himself at risk. But who am I to criticise? I can't figure things the way I once did. Look at this brilliant logic, Raucous. Hide her here, with me. Why would they bother to look in the 1940s flat of Raucous. No one but me and a boiler repair man have been inside this musty hell-hole since the late 80s. A woman in here with me? Not a soul would believe you. And now I have one, one I had dreamed of getting here alone, and I need to invent an adult game of hide and seek in a two room flat with no empty space.

I smile. A wig? What is she thinking? Scully knows her. Long fake hair isn't fooling anyone. I check the room, looking for signs of her. She moved herself and her stuff to the bedroom.

Scully coming alone is a mistake. He shouldn't do this. He doesn't know what's here. I messaged to say I'm OK and at home. A double bluff that fooled only me. Scully alone makes no sense.

Merrick gone, dead and alone in the attic of an apartment block. A woman on the run. He knows I'm here. He'll have information. He always has.

But he didn't kill Michael. There's no sense in that. Michael was the genius, the money maker. The man who could see through any weakness and patch it up to work. He made them money and kept them all out of arrest. Merrick alone, wanting revenge or a bigger place at the table. Scully would have gone for a killing. He'd have stood there and taken the credit, shown his balls and told no one. But everyone would know and Scully would just be stronger for it. The quiet Brummie who can kill. Scully didn't order that killing. But still leaves the problem of how Merrick stayed alive. Acting alone, killing a colleague, one as important as Michael makes no sense. Merrick would have vanished. I'd have taken that job.

The doorbell rings. I have no working intercom nor video. I've never needed one. If people were coming to steal from this house then it would mean they were coming to kill me. I push the button next to the plastic phone hanging from the wall. It worked once, I remember my grandmother telling salesmen to do rude things to themselves. But I've never used it. A simple job to wire it up, I guess. But I'm no DIY man, and no one ever calls.

I hear the glass front door pop. The air pressure changes slightly. My front door creaks in. I hear Scully step on the worn concrete, his rubber soled shoes squeaking on the shined linoleum. He isn't coming fast, just nice and steady. I open the front door and step away. Scully appears and steps through without pause. He feels safe, he checks nothing.

Scully takes in the room and nods. He's never been here but he smiles like he knew exactly how the place would look. A confirmation of how easy it is to pick how Raucous lives.

"How did Merrick die?" he asks.

I don't want to answer too quick. I give my puzzled look. Scully rolls his eyes. This is a game he doesn't want to play.

"Your police friends will have told you," I say.

"I want to hear it from you."

A simple test of facts versus versions. He trusts the police view, one he'll have had within minutes. A man taking hundreds to pass on information that causes no one harm. Not a bent cop, just a smart one.

"Got shot," I say. "Bled to death. Looked pretty beaten up too. Maybe stabbed? Can't say I stayed to do the CSI stuff. But he had it coming."

"Did you do it?"

"Nope, but I can't say I wouldn't like to be that person."

Scully stares as if his blue eyes would force honesty from me. A headmaster's threat of violence through powerful position. It never works and just means he thinks I'm weak.

"I don't have a gun and I hate knives. The lady did it," I say. "And she must have been good to take out that many men and finish off Merrick. As much as I disliked the guy, he was no pushover."

"And where is she?"

I'm sure he looks to the bedroom door. A glance that he tries to stop before it starts. That would have been a big giveaway.

"Too fast for a goon like me. She ran, and she got away."

"She took Merrick?"

"Easy to do with knives and guns."

Scully rubs his chin and taps his lips with his right forefinger.

"It's a problem for me. I needed Merrick. So now I need you."

"I'm not your guy," I say.

"I think you are."

I pick up a coffee cup from the low table in the middle of the room. I look inside and a thick semi-solid film has condensed on top of the undrunk liquid. Not even I'd sip that for a caffeine rush. Scully stares at me all the time. He wants my answer.

"Do I get a choice?" I ask.

"There's a car downstairs. You need to get in it now."

I take my turn to look at the bedroom door.

"You don't need anything," Scully says. "Just go as you are."

I wait, not making any move to follow instruction.

"You're safe," Scully says.

I give my blank look, the one I perfected at school.

"We all need our distractions. We need to go now."

I make no move. I'm Scully's man but I'm not leaving. If Scully knows and he wants a test of loyalty then I fail.

Scully smiles as if he knows what I think. He has that way. An ability to show insight when none exists. He turns to the door

66

and exits. On the landing, without looking my way, he says, "You need to come with me, Raucous. I need you to do something important for me."

I look to the bedroom knowing a teenage dream is behind the door, knowing just like then it's beyond me and something I'll never taste. Always so close in my mind but reality, as much as I ignore it, screams I am deluded. I follow Scully, shutting my apartment door behind me. I don't take the key. I leave that on the kitchen table. There is a spare hidden in the stairwell but I'm sure I'm never sleeping here again. I'm sure the likelihood of my life extending beyond the next twenty-four hours has diminished greatly. There would be a run of money on it if a book ever opened.

CHARLOTTE

I hear the conversation. I hear Scully's Brummie tones. Raucous reluctant to leave. He would have wanted more time with me, I'm not stupid enough not to understand his teenage desires aren't still strong. He hasn't aged well, but then neither have I. I'm hardly Mrs. Feminine now after the training and muscle. In shape, for sure; attractive, I wouldn't say. Raucous looks like he has lived the life, a man of muscle no longer able to drag himself to the gym. Strong but loose. We all get old, just some pretend they haven't.

I'm lost, I need to think. I've killed, had my revenge. What now? Go for Scully? Raucous didn't think so. Scully would be there for any killing of that magnitude. It was big. Michael was a founder, a man who made money. A man who never wanted to be number one. He didn't want the pressure, he knew he wasn't that man. He knew when it was right to kill, knew that the odds said someone was better off dead than alive, but he couldn't order it, couldn't carry that out, he had some type of compassion, looked after me, never did anything to hurt me. Other times he would know his decisions led to death. Maybe he reasoned it away with only those in the life, only those who knew the risks were able to be killed. No innocents, no bystanders. But then he was smart enough to make any argument work.

I look at my hands and they don't shake. Adrenaline gone, a peace come over me. I've killed three people in one day. Merrick

67

required help, and maybe he should have been my fourth. Raucous gave a little, the cuts he had were made by someone, probably the gang at the base of the footwell. A series of perfect events to have Raucous shoot Merrick. That's the way it went, the way it should be. Raucous getting the final revenge on a man who killed his friend. I tortured you though, Merrick. You went to another place knowing I had bettered you regardless of circumstance. I don't believe in after-life, but I hope this is the time I'm wrong. Michael looking down on me putting hurt on Merrick. The other man in the video I didn't know. Never seen before nor since.

Not Scully, but the other man who was there, the bag carrier, the man who talked and watched, the man Merrick looked to and asked questions and received only nods of encouragement. Another man aiming to become feared through the actions of others. You were there, but you are probably dead. A bag carrier is all, being told what to find and handing instruments to Merrick. The nodder. A man who did nothing but stand, watch and hold a bag as Merrick slashed, cut and spoke. Merrick did the damage, you were just holding his hand. I need my anger to be gone. I feel its strength has slowed. I'll wait because it has never been constant, strong then weak, apparent and then gone. But its base line, the level that kept me going, too high for me to ignore. I need that gone, I need me back.

I find myself exhaling long and hard. For the first moment in two years, I have time. I sit on the bed, thinking of a hot shower, and start to undress.

RAUCOUS

I saw Scully exit the car as I look from behind the curtain in my front room. The car is parked in the same spot, still running. An expensive saloon, electric, quiet and styled like a posh taxi used for exclusive clients. The front grille is huge, like a Land Rover but lower to the ground. A winged B adorns the hood. I should know the make but it doesn't come. I know it costs. It is easy to spot in the street. Too big for the narrow London roads of old, and too far from Chelsea to be the right price range for the area. It's black and one man sits behind the wheel.

Scully walks ahead, a tactical mistake if he thought he were in danger. He paces slow along the pavement, the opposite side to the car. I follow, no thoughts of violence or escape. Michael is dead. But Charlotte is not. I'd like to keep it that way, doing something stupid, accusing Scully, or condemning him to guilt does nothing here, nothing to help. I can't see Scully making that order. There is no sense in any of this.

Scully cuts left between two parked cars, crossing the street and I follow. Scully opens the back door to the car and invites me in. I slide across a leather seat, the space is huge, even I seem to fit. I slide across thinking Scully will sit in back with me. Scully stands, the door open, he is leaning forward so his head is framed by the space the door will fill. He stares at me, smiling, he looks to the driver and nods, the smile never going. He brings his attention back to me.

"I need to speak to the lady," he says.

I move quickly, sliding back to the door, but I stop as soon as I see. The driver has a gun pointing at me. Nothing fancy, I see the short barrel of a pistol. Scully lets his suit jacket open and I see his gun too.

"I'm not going to harm her," Scully says.

I want to surge for him. I think. The driver I have never seen, certainly nothing old-school, nor does he have the look of someone who can fight. I haven't seen his face, but his hand is still, no shakes no nerves, no emotion coming through. He's held guns on people before. I don't like not knowing.

Scully's show is all bravado. It isn't the Wild West, there is no quickest to the draw. Without the driver's attention, I could be out the car and on him before he could remove the gun from the shoulder-holster. He knows it and smiles the same.

"You sure she isn't going to hurt you?" I ask.

"I'm no threat. There are things you don't know nor understand, Mr. Raucous. She is safe. But I need to speak to her. And besides, I know she doesn't have a gun anymore."

Scully buttons up his jacket, takes one more smug look at me and closes the car door. No bang, or whack, just a simple sound of cushioned air as precise engineering seals the inside from out.

I watch through the window as Scully walks the way we came. I have a choice, and this could be the moment for it all to end. I brace myself, knowing I need to spring forward.

The driver leans back through the gap between the expensive leather seats. He presses the barrel of the gun deep into my left thigh. He waits until my eyes move from the gun to his face. He shakes his head. He knows my intention. He keeps the gun pressed for a second then eases back to his comfortable position. His gaze never leaves my face. I hear the thump of child locks kicking in. The driver nods again. I relax my muscles. The driver, without looking, reaches to the dash with his free hand, picks up a set of headphones and places one of the headpieces into his right ear. He places his left index finger over his lips, the universal sign for me to be quiet.

CHARLOTTE

I made a mistake. Never ease off, never take a break. Never assume. Never think you know. That's when they get you.

So I am here now, naked but a towel and the door is opened. It isn't Raucous, he would shout, make a noise and blush. The person is moving slow, not quiet. The door pushed open and two steps in. No more movement. A person, a man, standing in the room beyond the closed door. I reach for the clothes I have left on the bed. I have no gun and no desire to fight naked.

The voice stops me. I know who it is. We have spoken often but not in two years.

"You know I am here. You stopped moving. You know I'm in the middle of the room. I'm going nowhere and you have no means of getting to me. I'm armed. But I'm not here to harm you."

It's Scully, the Birmingham upbringing claws at his vowels. He knows me. But hasn't said my name. A disguise won't fool him at this distance. When he sees me, he'll know. My mind is blank. I wanted for so long to confront him and here he is. All the power in his hand. The gun, my gun, hidden away in the car because Raucous said so. I have a knife, but Scully will have a gun. No way I get to him without being shot. He'll have the thing out of his shoulder holster like a man on Miami Vice, ready and waiting for anything I do.

I find my knife and place it in the top of the towel, under my armpit, concealing it badly. No one makes a move.

"I'd come in, but I don't think I'll be welcome. I assure you, I have no intention of harming you."

Scully's voice hasn't changed. A monotone of certainty. He has power, he wants to tell me and make me understand.

The lies they tell. He doesn't want to harm me. No one has stayed unharmed. We all joined in a stupid game instead of aiming for mediocrity and middle-age. We have rules, most of them childish, most of them based on what we were. Too long been followed for us to break. The middle-aged men acting like high teenage boys in their local drinking den of rugby, football or hockey, drinking the same thing, acting the same way as when they were young and virile. That's who we are. Middle-aged has-beens who have not enough imagination or courage to break free of the youthful decisions on life. We won't die slowly from alcohol consumption on a grand scale, we'll kill each other so the youth who see us as role models can slip further up and the cycle repeats. Scully made it to the top long ago and now all he can do is cling on. I want to believe, but they have lured Raucous away, he won't be safe, and now he is here for me. But Scully alone isn't right. A second person is here somewhere. Scully doesn't take risks, certainly won't put himself in a position of weakness.

I look around the room, not sure what I am hoping to see. There is no escape. There is no gun. I'm caught and Scully needs to see it is me. Like a tired old beauty gone to seed, I need to play on nostalgia to save my life. I'm everything I promised myself I would never be.

RAUCOUS

The man is smooth. I'll give him that. A confidence that having all the advantages gives. He watches me but listens to his earpiece. If he is able to kill, I have no chance of movement. An inch toward him and the bullet passes through me. The gut or groin as that's where it points. No missing from this distance. I'm not quick enough to close the gap before he fires. No one is.

He listens, his eyes rolling left and right as if scanning the dashboard like it is the horizon. I watch him through the mirror. He sees nothing, a concentration, the audio obviously not clear. I hear nothing, no low hum, or teenage beat of high-speed throb that every headphone wearer on public transport loves to blast. The modern day equivalent of driving round in a supped-up cruddy little car tuned to a cutting edge and playing loud music with swear words. I used to be that kid, the passenger, the muscle. I only see demotion.

His eyes narrow, a concentration. His eyes stop moving. He has moved little, but he stills, waiting. I have to play this from his reaction. There will be no noise, she doesn't have a gun. I made sure of that. It was the right play. She'd kill him or make a mistake so some type of macho showdown would happen. She has killed today, maybe for the first time although she seems too good for a beginner. She won't have had the shock of realisation, the downer after the high. It will come and she'll ask questions about morality. She is no sociopath, but she can drag herself close. Scully knows her, he'll see her and say her name. She looks different, but I haven't seen her since I went away, Scully will have been in her company throughout the years. She has to play on this.

I can't rush from here. The gun makes me static. If they wanted me dead, I would be. I have no information they want. I'm not caught up beyond today, that is easy to show. Scully has no need for me, I bring nothing a gun can't replicate. I'm no minder, I'm barely fit enough to be a doorman. I don't want the hassle. For Daryl I could find the anger and desire. I wanted him. But I don't play the game anymore, I'm semi-retired living off reputation. I am no use to anyone, certainly not this man holding the gun. He has more than me. He plays, that much is clear. A power-player too. I've never seen him before.

I hate not knowing.

CHARLOTTE

I pull on my jeans and top, nothing else. Barefoot and bare shouldered. Bruises and scratches and aches. Scully waits, not moving, silent and still. The centre of the room, waiting. I move the knife to my back pocket. There will be no search, not one I'll agree to. I straighten, pulling myself up so I feel tall. Scully towers over me as most men do, I know that from memory. I've stood next to him so many times. Me and Scully. Alone.

"I have to call time on you," he says, "I hear you move, but you aren't coming to the door."

Scully sounds impatient, hiding the edge behind false friendliness.

I inhale deeply. I touch the knife handle with my right hand. I can reach it, not quick enough to beat a gun, but it is a comfort like a piece of blanket a child needs when staying at a new place. I clench my fists, telling myself I'm ready to fight. Scully, the man I wanted after Merrick. I need to speak, I need to hear him explain.

Will he give me the chance?

I walk to the door and grab the handle. It's glass and old, worn and scratched. Shaped like a diamond and so clearly not. Metal clasps, a lock that has turned a million times to exit a bedroom. It would be small in the hand of Raucous, maybe he just uses his fingertips. I turn the handle, it is loose and oiled, no squeak nor squeal, the door edges open, the only sound the carpet being brushed. I don't stand in the doorway, I'm not sure of Scully's desire to kill. Exposing myself would be stupid. I need him to see me before he makes a decision. I wait, nothing happens. I see him there, he is looking, his left hand empty, his right holding a gun. He holds it down at his side, but not relaxed, a little raised like he is ready to draw.

I inhale, I step out, the light clear on my face. I watch his expression. Recognition drifting in, disbelief fighting back.

"Charlotte?" he asks.

"Scully."

"Fuck."

RAUCOUS

His expression changes. Nothing drastic, not like a pantomime actor in the village hall. He wants to remain calm, knows faces can be read. But his eyes tell it, as does the pulse on his neck. Stress of a different kind filtering through his nerves. I don't know the words of the conversation he hears but I know the participants. Whatever is said makes him falter. At a high stakes table, the would-be cool head gives too many reads for success.

I need to know.

He senses me move. He smiles a little like he knows my thoughts. He is wrong, he has no idea. Information is key no matter what game you play and he lacks the pieces to put it together. He is no Chauffer, and that's where I am lost, a guess and thought at who he is. Scully in a pyramid of power and I have no idea if he fits in.

I need to plan. He listens and can hear the words and actions. A device to have the information I need. He knows I understand, a boast of sorts to tell me to acknowledge power, to accept my place. He is ahead of me and that's where he'll stay.

I don't mind being considered the fool, it has happened all my life for the right reasons. I'm no academic but I know enough not to be caught, or at least be ready to run. The moment is coming if this doesn't go well.

His cool is collapsing around his smooth skin. He doesn't want to hear nor react but he does. Charlotte talking trash would bring a smile even to him, there is more and the plan, whatever that may have been, has gone. Charlotte won't go easy and Scully is no killer, not of women, not of her. Just like every meat eater will scoff the final cooked product but have nothing to do with the butchering. Scully is no trigger man. He made it here with others doing that.

I move, a slide, nothing drastic nothing to get me shot. I need to push and test the boundary. It has moved. Losing your cool always moves the edge of possibility. I need to see where he is.

He feels the change, glances my way. Anger drifts across his face and he does not try to hide. His perfect plan, the control he thought he had, is chipped away and he needs to get it back. He pushes the gun barrel forward, still far from me. An indication to sit still. I don't, I move a little more in slow-motion and he understands I'm playing.

He needs to make a decision, and rank priorities. A big dumb lump in the back of his top-of-the-range car or a conversation in a flat between a woman he doesn't know and a man in Scully he doesn't trust. I'm an annoyance, and that's all I can be. I'm building credit for future punishment, but the here and now is my time. He steadies the gun and decides to listen. Were he a speaker he'd scoff at the insignificance of my challenge. But he has given me information, enough for me to use.

CHARLOTTE

Scully doesn't do surprised. He expects people to believe he knows all outcomes. He smiles, a genuine curl of his lip, nothing nasty or sinister. He smiles because it is me. I have to use this.

"Michael always said you were one to watch. The only one he could never truly figure."

I shrug like this is what everyone says. Michael figured me as a teenager. He knew me, knew what I'd do. Smart enough to put long-term objectives in motion years before they happened.

"But you made a mistake here," he says.

I don't like these words nor the raising of his gun.

"He spoke of you often too," I say.

"He didn't know me like he knew you."

"He knew you well enough."

We pause, I'm thinking of Michael, his words, the fact he was always right. The fact he never made mistakes. Maybe an autistic trait, he kept emotions in-check. But he loved, that I know. He saved me, and wouldn't leave me harmed. I stare at Scully, in his silence. I need him to be thinking of Michael. If there is anger I can use it, sympathy the same. Indifference and I'm done. But there can be no indifference. Scully, Michael and me. Not exactly the three pillars of unbreakable friendship, but our lives, our entire career based on each other.

I need to ask.

"Did you kill him?"

Scully stops raising his gun. He looks at me, twisting his head to the right, like he has only one good ear and he needs it to understand.

He opens his mouth, ready to spout. He closes it again. He looks to a picture frame of a Constable copy. The Hay Wain. Everyone had it at some point, like three ducks flying on a wall-papered front room. He looks back at me. He shows anger, nothing overt, but I know him, I've seen Michael speak and have the same effect. Anger is good. I can work with anger.

"You need to leave here. Not this flat, not this city, but England. You need to get out quick," he says.

"This is my home, where do you expect me to go?"

Scully smiles, he doesn't want the game.

"Bali is always good," he says. "A lot of things to do, a lot of relaxing to be had. Lovely place. You should try it."

There's no coincidence, he knows. He knows where I've been.

"You've been away awhile, "Scully says. "No one has seen you for some time. Vanished there, didn't you?"

He waits for a reaction, some words, anything.

"But you pop up again forty-five days ago. And here we are. You've done what you came for. There's nothing left. You need to go."

He knows. I shouldn't be surprised. He always knows. A small-time crook with a network that big makes no sense. But he knows. I've been back forty-five days.

"Did you kill him?" I ask.

He looks to the painting again. There's no inspiration. He holds eye-contact always, now he looks away. A person of psychological study could tell you the answer to what it means. I'm not one. His concentration comes back and I'm centre of attention again.

"I had nothing to do with it. I wasn't there, and I had no say. It happened before I knew."

"You would have stopped it?" I ask.

"I was not in the decision process."

He shifts, uncomfortable. He shouldn't but he does as if someone might hear.

"The decision process?" I say. "You sound like a businessman letting someone go."

"I am a businessman. I was not involved. At all. Michael made a mistake. He did the wrong thing. Was going to the wrong people. Someone else made the decision."

I step forward.

"Would you have stopped it?" I ask.

Scully looks down at the floor. He shrugs to himself, no theatrics, an answer to a conversation he is having privately in his head. He looks up and I know I'm in trouble. His eyes sheen, a look of destruction I have seen before. He has been set a challenge and he knows he is going all the way to the end.

"They didn't tell me because I would have. Merrick was fooled, but that is easy to do. He did what was done on the orders of another. Michael made a mistake and paid. He got you out. Not hidden. He would not want you here now. You need to go."

"Do I get that chance?"

"Depends on how smart you are and how fast you move. That's as much as I can give you."

"You aren't going to explain?"

"I don't have time. Neither do you. And frankly, Charlotte, I have no need. You used to listen to Michael. Now you need to listen to me. Run. Away. And stay away."

"Raucous?"

Scully almost laughs. He smiles as wide as he can and while it isn't far, it is enough to know he is tickled.

"Raucous has nowhere to go," he says. "There is no escape for him. Like there is none for me. The only thing he has is how long he gets to drag this out. Childhood makes bonds. Don't get killed by them."

We stand for a second longer than is needed. He relaxes his right arm and the gun lowers. He nods at me, and walks toward the door. He doesn't turn his back, he crabs as if this is how he always moves. He trusts no one. He leaves the door open.

RAUCOUS

Blood pressure can't be controlled by thought. The man is struggling to contain the anger. Something is wrong and Charlotte's death is not it. I sit still. No more games from me now. The boundary is blurred and he is looking for an outlet. Inside, prisoners give off signals of the most base type. You learn to read quick or face violence. I can read him, he needs to release disappointment caused by anger through inflicting pain. Some self-harm, but the manicured look of the shiny-headed man, makes it seem his object of resentment will always be outward. I need to know, I have only intuition to tell me. But I'm sure Charlotte is safe.

The same intuition tells me Scully is not dead. I would be too if Charlotte had killed. They have spoken, just as Charlotte needed. Maybe she showed flesh, maybe she showed anger. Michael and Scully were people of deep connection. Scully wouldn't have killed unless Michael made the ultimate betrayal. I can never be sure of principals of a man, they change with time and money, but Michael had it too good to bleat. Scully wouldn't have killed. There would be no benefit.

The man in front pulls the headphone from his ear. He stares as if the white plastic ball has called him a liar. He turns to me, ready to speak, ready for easy confrontation. An uneasy stand-off in which I know I must stay quiet. I do not move nor speak and he stares into my eyes. I don't look down, I never can. I never was one to be bullied, and no matter what, principals hold.

He picks up a phone, nothing fancy, a simple old-school phone-or-text mobile. He presses a button and I hear the ring. It lasts once. I have heard many voices in London. Many accents and languages. You can tell from most what people mean. The emotion is evident. The Latins are the funniest, every conversation sounding like an argument of insults. But the language he uses I can't get. Nothing sounds right, all monotone and cold. The words I don't know, nor can I follow. It is brief, five seconds at most. Three sentences maybe, but it is difficult to tell when one ends and another starts. The conversation closes without goodbyes. He opens the phone at the back, he removes the card inside, and snaps it. He opens the door next to him and drops the card and phone on the floor. No nonsense, no noise. He looks at me throughout.

He nods and turns to look at the entrance of my apartment block. I move now and look too. Scully has appeared, smooth and clean, doing up the buttons on the front of his suit jacket. He looks like a businessman, there's no doubt, but he looks like one who is sneaking away from a lunch-time tryst with a married woman from the office. His attempts to hide guilt condemn him to an obvious read. Whatever has happened was never the plan, and now he faces the next step in the consequences of change. The car door opens, Scully slips in, he sits in the front and the car dips on suspension so slightly. The car is one of the smoothest I have seen. Scully looks ahead but feels the attention from the driver. Scully turns to face him. Serious now, no smile nor one-upmanship, he tries for a bored expression of underlying anger. Amateur theatrics for a play in which I am the only audience.

"What?" Scully asks.

This is late-night pub talk between two drunk men who have taken an irrational dislike for each other over the choice of songs. A nice warm-up to see who genuinely is on top.

"You speak too much," the driver says.

"Words are never wasted,"

"Neither are threats."

"She isn't one."

"Because of life-long bonds? Or simple desire?"

Scully smiles now, as if he has latched onto the winning card.

"Because I say she isn't."

Scully keeps staring, asking, almost pleading for confrontation. I can't see if he holds his gun, or if he is genuinely asking to be shot. Does he think I am with him? Was that some type of shout out to my better nature. We know her, we protect her, we are in this together? Could be. Me and him and a man with a gun in a small space. Someone gets hurt, more likely killed. Decisions to be made by everyone.

Scully stares at his driver but says, "She holds up well, doesn't she, Raucous."

"More than well. Tough Lady. Was nice to see her."

"For a final time?" the driver asks.

I look to him.

"In her inevitable long life," I say, "I can't be sure I'll see her again. But I'll certainly make sure I check in to find out how well she is doing. Anything happens to her would sure make a lot of people unhappy."

"I like the way you speak," he says. "She must set many hearts racing."

"She's capable of many things," I say.

79

Scully looks to me and speaks. "She won't be doing any more."

I move. He holds up a hand. "She's alive."

The driver stays silent.

CHARLOTTE

I don't close the door Scully left open. I stand, knowing that my chance has gone. The desire was to kill, Scully the target. Now I have let it go. He didn't need to lie. Can I read him well? I don't think I ever could. He gave the information he thought I needed. Raucous would have attacked if he thought there was truth. Raucous sacrificed his life, went away for reasons only he knows. Michael's mistake that's what he said. The only one he said. The second killed him because there was no friend to take the shot. Not Raucous, nor me. Michael gone. Daryl too. Teenage boys and Merrick. I stand thinking, not watching, not paying attention. Raucous telling me to go and now Scully insisting. They know things I don't, and I know nothing because Michael never spoke. I hadn't vanished, that much he made clear. Always on the radar, always alive because Scully decided killing me was a waste. He knows what I have done, he knows I'm here. He didn't act like a B-movie villain and give me a ticking clock for a leave-or-die ultimatum. But I know he means soon. There will be no protection, not here. A place in the sun to wonder about what would have been had I taken Scully out. I'm going. I know that's right. Raucous to vanish again. Many things to say, many things to remember, many things for me to know. I would find nothing from Raucous. A man that silent doesn't need to share secrets.

I walk to the window, I don't know why. I need the light, need to let sun and air into the room. I need to see the view, see the city and my place in it. I'm not sure I'll be back. I'm not sure I ever should have come back. I'm a killer now. Revenge can explain, not excuse. I can create a narrative in which I'm the heroine eradicating evil from the world. None of those men were kind, none of them deserved to live. I have protected future victims, taken away the possibility of further harm. I pull open the thick curtains. I see a dirty white old-ladies net. It doesn't need washing, it should be

80

thrown away. I reach across my body with my left hand and pull it open enough so I can peek out. I see Scully in the front of his car, staring across at his minion that is driving. There is a man in the back, I can't see him clearly, but it must be Raucous. I look back to Scully. His mouth is moving but the words are lost. I look across at the driver.

I don't register at first. It's a bald man driving Scully's car. The car he uses for posh occasions. But it starts to sink in. I'm glad I didn't drag the curtains open to be in full view. It is him. I know it is him. I watched this man. I know his height, I know his hands. I know his face. Smile now, I think. Smile at me, speak away like you chirped away at Michael. It is him, I'm not inventing. I'm not creating a killer so I can keep on chasing and never give up. I'm not inventing a mythical creature to satisfy my own needs. It is him. I know this. I watched the film. I watched him give instruction, pass tools and laugh. I turn and run.

RAUCOUS

Scully's car and Scully's town. But this driver, if that is what he is, has a level of control. Nothing too obvious, nothing to mark him out as the number one, but his manner, the way he speaks, indicates power. The lack of threat and anger in response from Scully tells a story of underlying fear. No man I have ever seen had the balls to treat Scully so, no man that ever lived long after. But this guy drives and speaks and argues. Scully has him in his car but not under control.

I barely feel the motor slide up into power. No sound. The smooth roll of hardly worn tyres on old asphalt. The bilingual driver a cautious man at the wheel. The loudest noise the repeated click of the indicator. We pull out and go, heading north because that's the only way the streets allow. I know the area, know all the roads and systems. I feel safe here when most others don't. I've seen the place change, the people grow diverse, the shops open and close and change business and type. But it is my place, just as it always was.

"Do I get to know where we are going?" I ask.

No one answers, and I hold back on the desire to look back through the rear window and watch my home vanish gradually into nothing. I'd like to see Charlotte, I may never again. A woman who has changed but kept what defines her. Then there is me, dumb old Raucous. An adult with a child's nickname and nothing of his own except that which was given. We turn left, and we are heading toward the motorway. The signs not yet blue and no mention of which M we will take. But I know that's where we are heading. There is nothing this way but an escape from London.

The music plays and annoys. Five minutes and I break.

"I guess conversation is at a premium," I say. "I'll keep quiet, let you two brood. But I'm not listening in silence to radio Four."

Scully leans forward, presses a button, and some irritating Tory blow-hard is silenced in the nicest of ways.

CHARLOTTE

I run down the stairs and out into the street. They're gone, but the street system says they headed toward the turn. I run, not knowing what I'll do. Scully with the man and Raucous in back. Raucous made his choice, a killer like me. Merrick ours and a revenge shared. Is he one of them, is it just some large stupid game I don't know how to play? I run, sprinting, pumping arms, feeling the anger again. I've been fooled, but I don't know by who. Maybe myself, maybe everyone. A life full of liars and cheats and I don't know who anyone is.

I turn at the corner, the one-way system tells me this way. The road is long, but not endless. It is empty of cars. I pause, ready to burst into sprint again. A decision, but I have none to make. The road splits in a hundred metres. Two ways to go, then more and more increasing in complexity. I could run but never find, sprint into roads and never see them again.

I wait and look, staring at space. Cars cut across streets, people move, trees blow and my ease has gone. It is him. The man. Scully promised he had no say, his business mind accepting the outcome of a decision made by others. Merrick, Darryl and this man. He will know the who and why. Raucous is with him, he didn't go with pleasure. Does he know him? Know who and what he is? I have no way of knowing. Scully told me to leave but I can't, not now. One more man because Michael meant that much.

I look at myself as I walk back to the flat. Slow pace as I think, not looking where I am going but knowing the place. This saves me. I'm a lost local heading home, no reason to be on the street other than a safe passage to a local flat. If I had my head up I would have seen, would have reacted. I would have known.

I saw them but didn't register. Two men ambling along. They vanished and my peripheral vision didn't feel the need to find out where.

The entrance to the block is open and I pause. A break in my step. I look at the base and it is jammed, fighting against the hydraulic release with the help of a wooden wedge. The door fixed open, no one wanting to be trapped. This is not the time to drop guard. I step through, needing to know. The man driving Scully and Raucous, an unknown, a driver, a henchman, but one I had never seen.

I hear them before I see them. The door to the flat open but not fully. Whispers and movement inside where no one should be. I'm not dumb enough to race in and confront. I'm not smart enough to already be a million miles away. I walk past, slower than before, walking toward the stairs that take me up. I reach their base and hear them. I don't turn, not immediately. That will come when I take the first step.

The door remains the same. No one in, no one out. The noise has gone. They will be going room to room, playing a killer game of hide-and-seek. But I'm not there. I take the stairs to the next floor. I stand and wait. I hear a click as the front door is closed and locked. They know I am not there. They sit and wait. So do I.

RAUCOUS

The clock on the dash, all illuminous and green, a large screen, a tablet of sorts, tells me I've been sat for an hour. The silence not complete. Expensive tyres on roads of varying quality. Rumbles and bumps but not many. The leather seat warm, the air fresh from a quiet but not quite silent air conditioning unit. The click, click, click of an indicator breaks our mutual meditation.

The motorway stop advertises posh supermarkets, cheap food, and fuel. We slow on the pull off, hitting a running speed as we flop over speed bumps.

Scully looks to the driver as we reverse into a space in a half-full football field of a carpark.

"Unscheduled stop? Things not going to plan?" Scully asks.

I've never heard Scully like this.

The driver had been looking at his watch. Furtive glances, as it periodically lit. My eyesight not perfect but not blurred, couldn't read the text. A watch that shows you messages on a smooth black surface. He looked, the car kept running but now we stop.

"Plans rarely go the way they are written," the driver says. "You need to have flexibility and reserve strategies. There is no panic."

The driver looks to me.

"The woman. What do you think of her?" he asks.

I smile, I don't know details but I know emotion.

"I think you need to leave her alone. That way only frustration lies."

"She is just a wife? The woman of a man with forceful friends?"

"You already know that isn't true," I say.

He doesn't answer, he nods. He looks down, I have known him for two hours at most, and I see this is his tactic for thought.

"There is no reason for me to ask if you know where she would go," he says.

"None at all."

Scully watches us, looking back and forth, his smile widening. He laughs at the end, proper amusement.

"Comfort breaks, people?" Scully says.

He leaves us and heads to the food hall. The driver waits, realises I am not moving and pulls out a phone. He dials, there is an answer and he speaks the same nonsensical language in monotone. Ten seconds, answer and response. A final phrase and the phone is placed away.

"Not burning the phone this time?" I ask.

He stares at me, looking directly into my eyes like he thinks I can see the devil in them.

"Mr. Raucous, you are involved now in something important. The rules are ones you have never read nor heard. This is not a prison culture of macho posturing and sneaky attack. This is the grown-up world. Every time you speak all I hear are childish words. You are not doing yourself proud."

I smile, hoping to reach a level of irritation only the truly pathetic can achieve. A man who likes his own opinion and expects his words to be accepted with deep reverence is spouting lines like he is reading God's own thoughts.

But all I hear is a man in panic turning his nose in the air.

CHARLOTTE

They are still inside, still waiting. They are expecting a return, or awaiting order. They are nothing official, nothing sound. Raucous lives in a dead block of flats. An hour I have stood and waited on the landing above and no one heard nor seen. The hum of TVs in the background, occasional noise of flushed water and pipes creaking as heating kicks in. No people, no movement. No action. I am stuck. I need back in the flat for keys, clothes and peace of mind. How long can they wait? They do not know I am here, if they did I would be dead. There comes a point when they know I will not return. Their trap I discovered by chance, my delayed return an indication to them that caution is my first step.

I wait in a half-trance, processing information but finding few conclusions. I think of Michael, Raucous and Scully. I am folding the image of the driver and storing him in a mental space for later use. Having that man bash around my brain will only lead to mistake.

My monotony is broken by a creak. A door opens on the floor below me. Footsteps, two people, that is clear. They do not speak. I can't risk a look, I can't walk past. They did not recognise me in the street, but they would not have been looking. They were told I was inside. They will have a description, and I wear no disguise. I walk to the window at the end of the landing, the one that looks out onto the street. It is no perfect vantage point, but the only one I have.

I wait and watch, an ear to catch if they double back and choose to look upstairs rather than walk out. The window has no cover nor curtain, only dirt that blurs like Vaseline on a movie camera. I can't press my face against glass, I stand a step back, like an old woman with nothing to do but watch street action and invent gossip.

I get lucky. I think how long can good fortune last? The two men, as much as my mind remembers, cross the street. They walk quickly but not enough to be seen as rushing. They walk and my eyes follow them.

They are moving away, not returning. There were only two. I do not rush to the flat, I stay and wait, another hour, I'll wait another hour. Be sure, because they were there to kill and I have all the time in the world to think of what to do next. I lean against the wall and think of Raucous.

RAUCOUS

We wait for Scully in silence then move on quickly. We drive, away from the city and toward the coast. I watch signs and the names mean nothing. I remember them, but they are random words with no association. A city I have heard of, and then signs for ports.

We take small roads, too small for heavy traffic. The trucks and articulated lorries of cross-continent haulage go another route. This is the way in for employees and those who don't like to announce an arrival. The dark has set in and the full-beams bump and highlight trees and animals who dash for cover. The road is smoother than a country road should be. But rough all the same.

We drive toward a closed fence. The gate slides open as we approach. We drive through and it slides shut behind us. The view changes from country to industrial site. A central storage warehouse that seems huge to such a small car, but tiny in the grand scale of international customs. The place is quiet. I see two security guards as we slide along the edge and pull up outside the centre garage to a line of twelve sliding doors. Each big enough for a truck to back into. The motor stops. The lights inside the car come on. The driver turns to me.

"You have no idea what we do or how we do it," the driver says. "Mr. Scully here is a bodyguard down. You are that man now. We work together, which means you work for me."

I stare and say nothing.

"You will need this," the driver says.

He produces a hand gun.

I am no expert. I don't know what make, or how many shots or how to use the thing.

"The safety is here," the driver says and clicks a lever. "On and off. Then you point and pull the trigger if you so please."

"I don't do guns," I say.

"You do now, Raucous." Scully says.

I take the gun and feel the weight. I roll it in my hand. It looks smaller with me, but perspective is a subjective thing. It is heavy, like a quality cast-iron toy. But nothing more. I've seen such things on films and TV. I should do something now, slide or click and have the bullets and their casing pop out from the handle so I can check and nod at the quality. I can't do that as I have no idea how such things work. I hold it on my lap like it is a cup of coffee.

"You aren't too familiar with guns," the driver says.

"I've only ever killed without them," I say.

The driver looks at me with a rapid answer on his tongue. He holds it in and smiles his knowing smile.

"Let's go," he says.

CHARLOTTE

I worked quickly through the room. Aware that traps are set and people return. I found what I needed, dressed as I should. Took keys and what I could in a bag too small for it all. I left slowly, I checked, I looked, I walked. I needed to be sure. No one waited, no one came. I stayed alive.

I walked past my car, down the street, turned and walked back. I saw no one following, but I am no spy and copied the move from a TV show I watched as a child. I got in my car, started it up, and refused my father's advice to get it running warm. I left, and drove and turned and wound through streets I knew as a kid and into streets they built once I had gone. Familiar and unknown in repetition. Dark came and I had nowhere to go. I pulled up in a carpark. There was activity, but not much. A supermarket near housing estates never stop except Sunday nights.

I switched off the radio and sat, staring at my windscreen. Lights glistened and there was movement beyond, but nothing I saw made sense. I couldn't focus because my eyes filled with tears. They didn't break, they didn't roll. But my eyes filled. There was no end, there was no way out. Who do I kid, who can I fool? I want it all and I want them dead. I am never reaching a conclusion.

I sit and think, not knowing where to go. I can't kill again; I can't be the person they are. I have to end this for me. I killed Merrick. That's who I wanted, that's who I needed. Darryl was an extra, a way in. The two young boys, the would-be gangsters. Who was I to take their lives? I can't do this. It is not for me to do. I have done my part, more than I should. A woman was killed, Merrick killed again because of me. I killed her. Collateral damage to one without a heart, but not to me. I am someone. I feel. Michael loved me for being someone who feels. The only one with empathy, the only person he knew who could understand the feelings of others. What am I now? I'm a female Scully, a would-be Raucous, a killer trying to right the wrongs of others through their own methods of torture and death. A black widow trying to attack something I do not understand.

Scully there in my room, giving me the chance to escape. Go quickly, he said. Leave now. No waiting, he made it clear, he told me, and I got lucky. The man in the car, the driver, if not for him I would be dead.

Scully told me to leave, he knew what was coming. He gave me a heads up to go. He didn't order it. Why ease an escape from a hit you ordered? Raucous saying the same about Michael's death. Scully didn't order it, wasn't the man to have Michael killed.

I know nothing. I was a peripheral figure in their lives seeing only what I was allowed and knowing not enough to have me as a dangerous voice.

I'm no grass, I'm no snitch. I'm nothing.

I rest my head on the steering wheel. I stay that way for too long. It would have made no difference if I had looked up. They

gave me no time to react. They worked just like professionals do.
They came silent and quick. I had nowhere to run.

RAUCOUS

The place is empty and huge. A container that could hold the
contents of Ikea but sits empty. There is sparse light, strips of
glowing tubes not providing enough to uncover corners. The twenty-
one doors enter one space. A place for trucks to back in and pick up.
Each door has a number above, each in order, each one closed except
number 11. I watch as the door is lowered, and listen to the clunk of
metal shutters hitting a smooth concrete floor.

"What's your name?" I ask the driver.

He looks at me, like he holds the winning cards in a game in
which he has cajoled me into laying all my money out.

"You don't need to know what my parents named me. You
don't need to know anything. What you can call me, what I will
answer to is Christoph. I don't need questions; I don't need what
does that mean. That's what you call me."

I nod, knowing the man has too many secrets, and I'm too
tired to ask.

We are standing around the car, waiting, I assume, for others.
The place is silent. I am the only one with a gun in his hand. The
other two are concealing. Scully stands like he has spent a youth in
the army. Straight and patient and still. Christoph leans against the
car as if he has watched too many Italian films and just needs to be
cool. He is a lounger and nowhere near as smooth as he wishes. He
is watching his phone, reading messages, waiting. I watch his face.
It changes quickly, the glow from his phone telling him he has good
news. He smiles and nods. A problem resolved. He doesn't answer,
he slides the phone into his pocket. He looks at me as he turns to the
doors. He smiles that knowing smile like I am not in on the
information he has. I don't like the feeling it brings, a mild panic,
and a palpitation of the heart. Anxiety or heartbreak. I don't like it
and it won't leave.

Christoph claps and whistles like a common man on a
building site. Two men in yellow aluminous jackets appear from a
door at the back of the warehouse. They walk toward us quickly but

not rushed. One carries a case, the other carries pure size and intimidation. He is as old-school thug as a man can be. In the distant past his appearance alone would have forced me to challenge. But not now. Fighting to prove you are the biggest meathead in the building is no longer my life.

The men arrive and the thug is my twin. Easy to tell us apart through the youth he has on me and the glowing jacket. He stares like all good hardmen must. I stare back briefly then move on to other business. A victory in his head, and I'll give him that. I just don't play anymore.

"What have we got?" Christoph asks.

"Everything is delayed," the case carrier says. "Normal events, nothing suspicious. An hour behind cos of admin and customs."

"Nothing wrong in any of it?" Christoph asks.

"Not a thing. General nonsense. It is on its way as it should be."

"Unopened?" Scully asks.

"Obviously. Opening would mean the end of it."

Scully nods.

"When will it be here?" Christoph asks.

"Fifty minutes from now."

Christoph pauses, awful acting, a performance to fool us. He is not making an ad-hoc plan. He knows what he is doing, there is no off-the-cuff thought here, he is playing for time and attempting to look street-smart.

"This is Raucous," he says.

The two men nod and I'm still getting the eyeballs from the big man.

"He'll be with you, representing Mr. Scully's interests. He'll be acting on his behalf. Treat him well."

Scully places his right hand on my left shoulder and squeezes.

"Do what they say, within reason. Do the right thing. No messing about," he says.

Christoph looks to the window in the office from which the two men came. He nods and points up with his right index finger. The metal shutter on number eleven rises with its screech and clink.

Scully nods to me, Christoph ignores me. They enter the car. The engine starts and they drive away.

I stand there with two men, watching the metal shutters close.

I have no idea what is happening.

I know something isn't right. I can feel that much.

CHARLOTTE

I can't time it. It's quick, I move before I know I've been touched.

My driver's door opens fast, a man crouched down, with others stooped behind. The effort is redundant; I am not paying attention. Shouting, so much shouting. Instructions and demands. "On the ground, on the ground, on the ground." They look and sound the part, but I can't see clearly as I am hustled and pushed and manoeuvred. Bright lights shine into my face and I am on the ground giving no resistance, my right cheek pressed into the tarmac, my arms behind me, my wrists bound. A large hand pressing against the back of my head, a knee half-way down my spine.

The noise settles, their objective complete. They have me, my car and a gun. A gun that killed. I look ahead seeing booted feet and the cars. It is all official, or if not a perfect copy. Six police to take little me down. Why do I feel proud? They are armed, recording everything with body-cams, and waddling around in anti-stab vests that restrict movement and cause difficulty for graceful dance. There are a mix of males and females. A nice touch, seeing as they know it is only me.

One of the women identifies herself, a male hauls me to my feet. I don't catch the name nor the words she says, but I guess it is my rights. I am arrested under some type of act. No crime, no suspicion, an act of which I do not know. Anything I might say. I'm shaken, marched into the back of a van, all bare and white.

I am watched but alone. Three uniforms stand as a human barrier where the back door is open. I am not making a run. Why waste energy and annoy? I'm not drunk, I'm not looking for confrontation. I want the quiet, but now I have this.

So many questions. How? Why? And When? Too fast to be picked up, where was the mistake? They can't know who I am, what

I have done. But a woman alone in a carpark does not draw a special team nor a special assault. How is this happening?

The suspension dips with added weight. I look up and a police officer sits opposite me. He is not uniformed. He can't be a criminal as there is too much respect for him, but he wears a suit not body armour. He is olive skinned and lithe. Shaven head, and skin with fine lines. He sits and stares, saying nothing but giving me the serious eye. I hope the station is close. A policewoman says something to the man. My ears are shot as I hear nothing but muffles. The man nods. The wire interior door is shut and locked. The main door is slammed closed and within seconds we are jolted as the van accelerates away.

RAUCOUS

The smaller man explains. He speaks like a History teacher on the verge of retirement, reeling off the same facts he has for forty years, and no longer trying to add excitement and enthusiasm to his voice. This is the way it is, listen, learn and be able to repeat.

I'm not Scully's bodyguard, I'm his eyes. They left to be far away and free from incrimination should anything go wrong. The small man, who insists he is called Dave, reiterates the fact that they never get caught. It is fool-proof. Inside, I met a lot of men who cursed their luck and couldn't believe they were caught. Stupidity and arrogance combine in everyone to cause capture. The police aren't a group of super-brained genius, they just rely on the knowledge that criminals are dumb and repetitive organisms of risk-taking and mistake-making. Dave and the Big Man are clearly the weak link in this chain and I'm just here to make sure Scully's interests are kept in check.

A simple smuggle, an easy drop off. They don't tell me what or how large. But it is coming and I need to be here.

The two leave me alone, which makes no sense. I'm an unknown quantity and they are leaving me to roam freely. They check, and watch, but not with intensity. I could walk and leave and they would be oblivious until too late.

They retire to their office and I stay, uninvited, in the warehouse.

I'm sitting up on the ledge of loading bay 11, dangling my legs like a bored child sitting on a wall thinking about jumping. I don't look at my watch. When the time comes they'll tell me. I'm in the right place, it all happens here. Time after time in a way that leads me to believe they'll get caught. Just because something works once, doesn't make it fool-proof.

Activity starts with Dave walking back. He carries a clipboard, his gun, if he is carrying, concealed on his body. The Big Man walks with him. His hands are empty as is his mind.

"Go time," Dave says.

"Go where?" I ask.

"Nowhere, we are about to have delivery."

"And what do you want me to do?"

"Have your gun ready, anything out of place, make sure it goes back into place."

I want to answer, say something to point out his stupidity, but I don't. What would be the point? Dave wouldn't understand, and the Big Man would attack. I nod like I understand what would not be in place. The whole thing is a joke. Low-level morons operating as if they are high-level bosses on a Miami coast. And I'm the henchman. I actually feel the pain. Even in this low-league world I am a bottom feeder.

Dave presses the green button on the wall. It has a black arrow pointing up. This I assume is to help those like Dave realise that green means the door opens. Dave presses and the roller door clanks and grinds and makes its slow roll skyward. There is light, the angle of the beams indicate a large truck is outside. The door rolls and the large truck reveals itself. A single driver, a shipping container on back. The cabin is large and white. Gears grind, power hits the wheels and the truck slides smoothly in.

Dave doesn't close the door.

The truck manoeuvres, Dave and the Big Man take their positions. They stand either side of the container. Their view taking in the door and the driver. Sensible, clearly not instinct but learned behaviour. They have been told where to stand.

They look at me, I am as far back from the closed container door as I can be without my back against the wall. They stare and I get their meaning. I slowly reach behind me to pull out the gun. I let it hang to my side on the end of a loose arm. Dave squints. A communication. I smile inside. I could drag this out for minutes. A confused crunch of the forehead, a mouthed, "What?" but I don't. I'm tired, I haven't slept in a long time. I'm old and can't do the long days. I want whatever this is to happen as quick as possible and leave me in peace.

I lift up the gun, both hands like I know what I'm doing. I point it directly at the container doors. Dave and the Big Man smile like they've made me their slave. The Big Man walks over to the container door, he pulls a small cable, lifts a steel handle, twists it so it points out at ninety degrees. He walks and pulls the cargo door open. He speeds up, the container dark inside. The door is fully open. Dave and the Big Man edge away. There is a bang, as the container door smashes the side. Nothing happens. Two seconds of silence coming as the vibrating metal subsides to nothing. And then the whole game begins with a bang.

CHARLOTTE

The detective stares. He's good at creating uncomfortable. He is trying to read me, or give the impression he can. I've been stared at by scary men all my life, he has nothing different. Being male does not make you dominant.

"What do you know?" he asks.

His voice controlled and attempting deeper than his norm. He's been taught something somewhere, and he is using it now.

Silence is the safest option at any point with the police. Nothing or no comment is the easiest route to legal representation and a bigger chance to get out. But they won't know me, they won't know who I am. I am not coming up in any database. I know this. Michael gave his word. But he said to stay away. Being someone abroad is better than being someone who never existed at home. Problems only come that way.

"Know about what?" I ask.

The detective leans back. He physically acts like he's hooked a Marlin. As if I'd be that easy to reel in. One question? He doesn't know me.

RAUCOUS

They rush out, walking that strange walk. Their guns raised, their knees bent. All in black, faces covered, vests on and looking the part. They cover every-which-way, shouting and calling, I count eight of them. All jumping down from the container. Dave and the Big Man race away. No one shoots, screaming continues and I watch. I lower my gun, not all the way, just to waist height. I watch the pantomime play. The team are dressed as policemen should in such situations. All covered, all black, all carrying equipment that has a use, but is never put into practice. Walkie-talkies, clips and what-not. They look too big, too wide, too heavy. But they fan out, pointing their weapons and shouting their instructions. The Big Man makes it to the door to the office, Dave has backed away to the open front door. I stand where I have been, and pay attention to detail.

I wait, knowing the next step, knowing that the chaos is just not going to finish.

Dave reaches the door, still no one shoots. They don't need to bring him down, there are two more here. Me and the Big Man. Maybe they have people outside who can scoop Dave up and the carnage of a shoot-out in confined space can be spared. Who knows the thinking? But they all act in unison. And I wait, and I watch, and I feel the weight of the gun in my hand.

Dave reaches the door, not surprised by his stealth and ability to avoid being a target to eight men with assault rifles. He doesn't run for freedom, doesn't chase the darkness outside and the fresh air of momentary relief. He does what an imbecile does, he stops, turns, raises his gun, and fires. Not once but five times. The muzzle explodes in sparks and flames and smoke. Bullets fly too fast to see. No one drops. Dave can't kill anything with his gun. The eight men return fire, the fire, noise, smoke and shouts make the warehouse small and the ability to pick out movement increasingly difficult.

The goon squad fire but miss their target. Dave escapes through the door and away into the night. I keep my gun at my waist. I turn to watch the Big Man. It is his turn now.

He is backed up to the door, he reaches behind him and opens the door out. He raises his gun in his free hand and shoots. Five shots again as if this were a new rule in shoot-outs learned from the good old cowboy films of John Wayne and Lee Van Cleef. The goon squad turn as one, guns raised, and fire away as the Big Man ducks into the back room. The show, of smoke and fire and flashes less and less impressive.

Now it is my turn.

The group slowly divide. Three go to the office door, three go to the front door. All the time doing their bent knee low walk with their guns raised. The two that are left point their guns at me. I smile, I nod. I raise my gun. I've seen enough, I know where this is going. Only two makes it easier, and not impossible. They shout something about getting down, dropping the weapon, about giving me the option about giving me time. These are not the words of truth.

I watch their movements and they aren't quite right, how their nerves are there to see. They won't come too close, they hover at the edge of range.

I have thought as I watched. I know most of it, I can see through some, but not all. The holes in information I fill with guesses. I'm good, but the further you go with estimates the less likely the far out reaches are true. But there is no long story here. There never was. I look at their shoes, their brand new shoes. Their black trousers with the crease and the perfect thread. All new, all unused until now. They have been dressed for the occasion. This the biggest and best bust of their careers so they all went to the store and bought new. I look around the warehouse, the smoke drifts and there is a vibration of echoes from bangs and shouts, I look at the walls and the floor and the cases and the chaos and see, or rather don't see, all that I need.

I look at my gun and smile. I love these things, how this is, how they should always be. Were the world filled with this there would be so fewer deaths.

I raise my gun, point in the direction of the two and pull the trigger until all the explosions finish and the click, click, click of empty chambers seems louder than any other noise.

CHARLOTTE

He waits now, thinking I'm hooked. I look down at the floor, bouncing and swaying to the movement of the truck. I have no plan, no real idea of how to escape. I'm caught and heading into a situation Michael told me to avoid.

I'm no longer a real person. Records gone, my identity unknown on any computer. That's what he told me. Not fail-safe, he said. There are always ways to get around the problem, always information to be gained through means nobody knows. He knew, that was his job, that is what he did. He gathered information, put it together, made plans and advised. The smartest man in any room. But they got him. He knew they were coming too. He made one mistake he said. Just that one. And it cost him his life, and gave me this life to live.

"My name is Siri," the officer says.

I don't look up. I don't care. I'm not bonding with him, not talking, not telling him who I am. He has moved from aggression to trying empathy. He is going through a mental list of tactics to try and get something from me.

"Like the phone thing," he says. "But I was named first."

I stare at the floor. Always follow your gut, that's what I say. Always. And mine is rumbling, tying in a knot. The whole experience is off. I have no idea how, but the whole thing is gone.

I look up.

"What's the deal?" I ask.

He smiles like his tactics are working. And maybe they are. I'm not fresh, not thinking as cool as I should. Who knows who is winning?

"Who are you?" he asks.

"I'm nobody. You have my details, my documents. You know who I am."

He smiles that little knowing smile. If he is married and his wife faces that then she should smack him hard.

"I know details about your existence, but I don't know who you are. Strange things have been happening and you seem to be there."

"I'm here. Nowhere else."

He smiles again. Different this time. Forced.

"But you don't know where we are going," he says, "or what waits there for you. Speaking to me, probably seems the last thing you want to do right now, but believe me, I can help. I can make things smoother."

My turn to smile.

"I'm arrested on terrorist charges? That makes no sense. You have intelligence on me? I don't think so. Mainly because there is none. Why did you pick me up? Why the extreme?"

He uses a pause again. An irritating tactic.

"Because you are dangerous," he says.

"I'm no danger to anyone. I've done all there is to be done. My threat level doesn't exist."

He smiles again. He bangs on the side of the van three times. The van slows, thirty seconds of a crawl and then we stop.

He leans forward into my space. His hands clasped together. We look each other in the eyes. His are dark, mine I can only imagine are bloodshot from exhaustion and physical impact. Adrenaline or some other magical force is keeping me going. I try to remember the last time I slept well. That was before Michael died. The last time I slept was a long time ago. I don't know what time it is now. But it's late, and too long since I rested. I have to keep my calm, my cool. This man has something I need. He has revealed that much, but he thinks I have something more. He needs me to confirm or deny something. A policeman that knows too much before they tell you what they want is not a person you need in your life.

"I need to know," he says.

RAUCOUS

They haven't fallen. They stand, untouched as I knew they would. I wasn't pointing at anything specific, pointing out a target or looking to double tap their chest. I just raised and fired. They didn't run, or dive for cover. They flinched, but who wouldn't? They didn't return fire. They had no need. Not with good old Raucous pulling the trigger.

They shout now, on my knees, down, face down, and I shake my head. It isn't happening because that would make me look weak, make me look like a quitter, and I can't look that way. Not now, not ever. I won't quit, can't quit and these two are heading for trouble.

I walk forward, and they shout again. Down, on the floor, we will shoot.

And I smile. I know they won't. And even if they do, they won't hit me with anything. I know. I've seen, and the game is going to end how I make it end.

The one on the left raises his gun and fires into the air. I flinch, because it wouldn't be normal not to. But I move forward the same. If he had brains, he'd point it toward me and let me see the flash of the muzzle. I'd stand my ground to that. But they back away, two men with big guns backing away from me. They know, but I don't think they understand I'm in on the game. I walk, arms spread wide, shoot me, a suicide by attack. But they can't, they can't do anything but panic.

I'm close enough to rush them. It would be a dumb tactic normally, giving up an advantage of surprise and confusion, but it matters nothing here, it will have the opposite effect. Whoever watches will see the madman I want to be and draw conclusions about what I am and the lack of intelligence I possess.

I can't let on, not yet.

CHARLOTTE

I have no idea what he wants, who he thinks I am, what he thinks I know. I have no idea if he knows who I am. Who I really am. I don't think I really do anymore.

"You need to open up and speak, to tell me," Siri says. "There is a way out. I can give you that. I can protect you."

I rub my eyes.

"I have no idea who you are," I say. "You have me as some type of important being. A central part in something huge. You have it wrong."

He leans back. Rests his head against the side of the van. He places his palms together as if in prayer and brings his index fingers to his chin. He stares at me.

"We are on the edge of something here. Something important. Bigger than anything bad you may have seen."

"The World War?"

"You were not alive for that."

"Rwanda?"

He sighs. "The western world, the world you and I live in. Something is about to happen. Soon. Something bad."

"And you know this how?"

"Intelligence."

"Clearly not yours. And I fit in where? I am not, nor have I ever been, a terrorist."

He is alert now. He thinks he has the hook. It is a small difference in his eyes, a sparkle as if he is about to enjoy the game.

"I know who you are," he says. "I know who you married."

"You know nothing."

"Your name is Charlotte, and you were married to Michael."

He knows, and the charade is gone. He knows and he doesn't need me to tell him basics. There is more. Michael was no terrorist, not even close. He was a crook, a brain, not brawn, and a crook. One of the best.

"Don't need to deny or confirm. But you do need to tell me what you know. You shouldn't be here, you shouldn't be involved in any of this. Dead men and revenge. Why are you back?"

I smile, he doesn't know enough. Someone has seen me and said who I am. Raucous? Would he speak? Give me the heads up and then talk to save himself? Who knows? I haven't known Raucous in years. He was honest, for a crook. Honest to Michael.

"I'm not back for anything anymore. It's all done."

"What's done?"

"The very little I came back to do."

"I need you to tell me what that is."

"It has nothing to do with terror, nothing to do with that at all. And it's done. Look at me, I'm done."

I've had enough. The game, the people, the men, all of this. I'm too tired, my mind has gone. I don't want this anymore.

"I need you to tell me what your husband told you, and why that has made you come back now."

RAUCOUS

I charge them and they know it's coming. The one on the right swings his automatic rifle like a baseball bat. Shooting, it seems is no longer the way to use them. It comes at shoulder-height and I duck, not too low, but crouching enough for it to swing over my head. I stand as it passes and stomp out with my right foot against his knee that holds all the weight. The pop is audible before his scream and the ligaments, cruciate and anterior are all snapped which means he drops. There's no walking that one off, not for many a month. I turn, and I'm not as quick as I used to be, and I was never that quick in my youth. The other guy rams his rifle into my gut. The biggest target, so it makes sense. I feel the air rush out of my lungs and I hate that feeling. Too many times, too many people taking that shot. I know I won't breath, I know I'll want to crouch and take the ten second count, but I can't. I ride the pain, and the explosions and the inability to inhale. I ride the desire to kill him. But I can't do much, can't do much at all. I lunge forward and he moves to his right. I was expecting left and I'm off balance and going the wrong way. I'm moving like Frankenstein in a hammer horror, and the guy with the rifle is floating on air like the young Ali.

The rifle butt hits my shoulder blade from behind. I drop to a knee but come back up immediately. I turn and the rifle butt is heading for my nose. I sway right and it misses. But I'm slow and this guy is scared he'll get hurt.

He swings the rifle again and I catch it under my arm. The crash against my ribs will do me no favours for a few days, but my lungs are bruised beyond repair so I go with the flow of pain. I snap my arm down and the guy's weapon is now no longer effective. He lets go and starts to turn.

There's no running away, not now, not from me.

I trip him with a kick to the heels. I loom over him, I raise the rifle. I wait, because I need to. I wait for the voice. It doesn't come. This man can't be important. I smash the rifle down into his chest. The worst place if he weren't wearing a Kevlar vest. But he is and the pain will be spread and dull. The guy is smart enough to play dead. He's no actor but I choose to be fooled. I drop the rifle and look around.

The guy with the busted knee is writhing, the guy with a bruised chest is playing possum. I walk to the roller door at the front of the warehouse. I walk slow, there's no need to run. I won't get far. There are others out there and some I haven't seen in a while. They'll stop me soon enough. Maybe even explain the whole mess.

It'll be lies mostly, but the truth will be hidden somewhere. It's what they do. A constant test. As a kid I wanted this life. I'm too old, too slow, too sad to be here now.

They won't let me go.

CHARLOTTE

It just comes without warning, anger, a need to hurt.

I leap forward, aiming with my forehead. He's quick and blocks me as I fly. He wraps his forearm around my neck. He drags me down. Choking me, and putting on pressure. I gag and spit.

"What do you know?" he asks.

I can't speak. He knows this but squeezes harder.

"What do you know?"

He releases pressure but not the hold. I can breathe but I know he has the potential to take this away.

"Know about what?"

"What is going on, the plots, the plays, the plans for whatever it is they are going to do."

I can't understand, I know nothing of anything. I know Michael was a crook, I know I was his wife. I know he kept us separate. If I know nothing then I can't say anything.

"I have no idea what you are asking," I gasp. "I know nothing. I knew nothing when I was in the life and even less now I'm out."

He releases me, pulls me up by my shirt and sits me down. For the first time in twenty-four hours I feel compliant, used up, ready to fold. I need sleep. I don't need to know what is going on.

He leans forward again, and I brace for an attack. He has me conditioned because I'm weak. I feel weak.

This morning I would have walked through him, taken him apart and smiled. Had he been in with Daryl and those two boys, he would be dead. Now, I just want out. I have had enough.

"Did Michael ever speak to you?"

"He was my husband, he spoke to me all the time."

"About what?"

"Anything and everything that wasn't work."

"You know his work?"

"You do, I do, everyone did. But he was smarter than you all, so he lived a life."

"And then he was killed."

I pause. It's such an obvious ploy. A stupid police ploy, the brains went to the dark side or onto careers with more money and more ease. There isn't a single genius in the police. Not one, just mass stupidity among criminals. Only a few have enough smart to survive and Michael was one. They all clung to him for the magic to wear off.

"I know he was killed. I saw it."

I'm playing, but playing wrong. I know this. I see the reaction in his face. He tries to hide it, but the surprise escapes before he can reel it back. I shouldn't speak, I need to keep quiet.

"How did you see it? You weren't there."

I don't answer, silence is best.

"You've let it out, and now you regret. That's OK. It is a start. How would you know?"

I stay silent.

"You saw it? But you weren't there. So a recording exists, or at least did."

He stares at me trying to read, seeing if he has anything of truth in his hypothesis. He sees what he wants to see.

"A recording. That you have seen. Did you watch it all? He died badly."

"I know how he died."

"And you'll also know who was there, who did it."

I don't speak, there is no point, the story tells itself, and the big brain inspector whatever is about to tell it back.

"Merrick, who is dead. Daryl, who is dead – along with a couple of kids that no one will miss. A favour to society with those gone."

"I have no idea what you are talking about."

"You know the truth. You were back for revenge. Seems you have taken it. Anymore on the list?"

"There is no list, there is no revenge. I have no idea what you are talking about."

He smiles, content in his knowledge of victory.

"All you people know is revenge. An eye for an eye. I understand. Michael was a good man, died badly. There's always love to consider. Strange you did it alone. I imagine you had help."

I know he is looking to include Raucous to see if I'll give him up.

He waits for an answer but understands it isn't coming.

"Who else was there that you need to avenge?" he asks.

"I don't know what you are talking about, but if I understand the story, then while others might have been there, they wouldn't be known, wouldn't be involved. It sounds like your story ends there."

He nods and smiles.

"Yes, the story does end there."

He bangs on the side of the van, the idling engine kicks into gear and we move off.

RAUCOUS

I thought they would appear behind a wall of uniformed men. But they are confident, they have watched and the only man they bring is Dave. Good old Dave, the go-to man who can't be as dumb as he seems. There is no place for the mentally weak right now, not here. I should be the dumbest, and I hope they think I am. It's a disguise I wear with comfort and ease.

Scully is the first to speak. He is stood at Christoph's side. They are smiling, like they've played the greatest April fool of all time. I stop my walk and stare, trying to look confused instead of bored.

"Quite the show, Raucous," Christoph says.

I can't answer quickly, that would show too much. I need the perplexed silence of a man who doesn't know what's going on.

"It's all over, Raucous," Scully says. "We needed to find out something, something about you."

I continue with my low-intelligence stare of Neanderthal understanding. It's something I perfected as a kid.

"It's Ok, Raucous," Scully says. "None of this is real. We needed to find out something. We have the answers."

I look around at the carnage in the room. The two men lying in pain, the smoke. But I see what isn't there. I am not going to tell.

"None of this is real, Raucous," Scully says again. "The two guys you took out on your attempted suicide are definitely real. But nothing could have killed you. No real bullets flying here."

I had seen the lack of impact craters from the start. The flashing muzzles and nothing hit, people nor walls, was as obvious as could be. The flash was enough to put me off. An old novel I once read about a detective and bodies in sump oil warned me of a blank in the face.

I continue with my dumb blank stare.

CHARLOTTE

He doesn't talk. We sit, bumping and swaying as the van moves through traffic. The stops and starts decrease and the ride becomes smoother. The idea we are moving from the city is clear. The whole ride is wrong. It should be short, we should be at a station. We should be where we need to be.

Siri stares into space. A certain meditation on events unfurling in the past present and future. His eyes flicker every few minutes as if the problem moves away for another to contemplate.

He knows what we are doing, knows what he needs to do. A confidence that he possesses can't be faked. The whole situation is wrong. The take down, the interrogation, the length of the ride. Everything is a red flag, everything is screaming get out but I'm trapped in a moving van with a man who has the better of me.

"Where are we going?" I ask.

Siri acts like he hasn't heard, staring at the fascinating space in front of him. But I know he has taken the words in. His concentration slips away. He looks at me.

"We're going to meet some people. They are unsure of you, unsure of why you are here, back in the UK. Bad timing is bad timing, but coincidences are just a little bit too much to comprehend for many. Your word and my own thoughts. Who knows how it will go."

"That means nothing."

"It is all there is to say. It is the only answer I have."

"We aren't going anywhere official?" I ask.

Siri looks into space. It looks like he won't speak. But he does.

"No, nothing official. Too late in the day for official."

RAUCOUS

"Mr. Raucous," Christoph says. "An interesting reaction. You have an ability to be something less than you are. I'm impressed. Soon, I'll have another piece to figure you with."

I am lost. The man is smarter than most, smarter than me. Scully is nothing in terms of insight. But the act I have is one I stay with. Dumb and then increasingly dumber is the only way to be when faced with an intelligent man looking for an intellectual debate.

"See what you want to see," I say.

"Just as you do," Christoph says. "Mr. Scully has vouched for you. But then he would as you are his, how would you say? Minder?"

Scully smiles but there is no humour only an edge to crazy.

"Doesn't seem like you need one, I'm certainly not the man to go up against all this," I say as I indicate the room.

Christoph smiles.

"But you just did, Mr. Raucous. You just did."

"I'm not being caught and I'm not saving anyone. I was getting bored of not being killed."

"Looks like that was what you were trying for."

"Seemed no one wanted to do it."

"They were under orders not to."

I nod, look around

"I wouldn't have hurt your men," I say. "All you needed to do was ask."

Christoph shakes his head.

"Actions, Mr. Raucous, as you very well know, are a much better indicator than words."

"What do my actions tell you?" I ask.

106

"They tell me little, as I believe you are smarter than you appear. But suspicion is always with me. No reason so far to no longer want you around."

"Just say the word and I'll walk."

"There's no walking away now, Mr. Raucous. No way of walking at all."

CHARLOTTE

The van moves in silence. Siri stares and his mind is either whirring at speed or empty of thought. He gave little indication of which. I sit and stare into the space he watches. There is nothing to see, nothing to hear, nothing to understand. This trip is wrong and the destination I hope is days away.

"You need to tell the truth," Siri says.

I look up at his eyes staring at me.

"Always," he says.

"That old thing of never having to remember what you said, you know?"

"When we get to where we are going. You need to tell the truth. I can only help so much."

"You aren't with me," I say. "You are the one bringing me to wherever or whoever is waiting."

"That's my job."

"You are no policeman," I say.

"Not as such, no. But only a few know this."

He pulls a phone from his back pocket. His fingerprint lights up the screen. He slides his right index finger slowly down the screen after pressing. He stares and reads, nodding.

"It seems we are ready," he says.

He bangs three times on the side of the van. Nothing changes, we move along as before.

RAUCOUS

We wait in the office, for what reason I don't know. It is about me, I know this from the smug content on people's faces. I am not in the loop and the surprise is on me. It is a step up from kids at school playing practical jokes and waiting for the victim to open a bag and find something nasty. But it isn't too far. They are excited and waiting. A huge TV screen covers most of the far wall. It is off, but Christoph, Scully and Dave glance at it too often for it to be nothing. There is no conversation. We are all sitting in basic metal frame chairs. The door to the office is open, and the clear up outside is taking place at speed. The fake police are now over-dressed, clumsy janitors, racing around picking up debris and evidence. They move with ungainly efficiency like a timer has been set and an outcome required. They work like a big financial bonus is coming their way.

"What are we waiting for?" I ask.

I am bored, tired of silly games, tired of being treated like a moron. I deserve it, I know that, it is what I want. But it grates that they believe my act.

"A couple of things," Scully says.

His words are followed by a stare from Christoph. He admonishes as if Scully has given away his trade secret.

"Want to let me in on those? Sure looks like we are waiting for the pilot episode of something important."

Christoph looks my way, an eyebrow raised because he can't control it.

"We are waiting for news, and word and a start. Tonight is important. As will the future be," Christoph says. "Patience is an aspect of life that needs to be built."

"Patience is easy when you know what is coming," I say.

"Fear of the unknown, Mr. Raucous. I would never have placed that on you."

A word game, a test. I shouldn't join in. But I do.

"If you aren't afraid," I say, "you will never avoid ignorance."

"Is that a quote?"

"Could well be, sounds like it was. The truth in it is what matters."

Christoph looks at his watch, then the clock on the wall. 9.25 late evening.

"Not long now," he says.

CHARLOTTE

The van slows twice but doesn't stop. I hear voices, brief conversations from outside or up front. I hear metal against metal as if gates are closed, poles hitting each other. The van never stops, its way never halted, but it slows enough for people to check.

Siri sits, no expression, no muscles tensing, no emotion shown. His eyes look left every ten seconds. I can't read what it means. He looks to the cab up front. But we can't see as the panel has only one small window and it is shut with a metal flap.

I hear the clank of metal again from outside, longer this time, a noise of thirty seconds, then a thud. The van moves forward, pauses and then reveres as it turns. We sway with the motion. The van stops. Siri looks at me a final time and stands. He pays no attention to the fact he has turned his back on me. He knows I have submitted. He steps to the rear door and waits. The lock is turned. The door opens and I see nothing but a wall at least 15 metres distant.

Siri steps out and looks around. He sees who he needs to see from out of my view and nods acknowledgement. He turns to me, he reaches out although he is too far away to touch and motions me forward moving his fingers toward himself. I inhale deeply, I stand and I step out of the van. Siri does not offer a hand. My natural instinct makes me turn to where Siri looked. My plan is to nod a hello, cool and calm. But I don't. I look and I see and I know and I am scared.

109

RAUCOUS

I can't react. Eyes on me are waiting for the wrong emotion. I watch with the others.

Christoph had told us and we walked into the warehouse to wait and watch.

A door opens, a man appears. Police. And real. She comes next.

A person I had hoped to see again, but had wished I never would, stands there. She stares at us all. Her eyes not focusing on me, not giving me any more attention than the others. I see her fear, I see how she can't see an escape.

We had watched the van reverse to a stop inside the warehouse. The same place the same smell. We had watched a man step out. We watched Charlotte step down.

She looks tired and beaten. I have anger for the man, although he treats her with calm. A simple wave to bring her out. He shows no aggression.

Charlotte shows fear.

I want to protect her, I want to run to her aid, to get her out and free, but I know I can't. I know now is not the time and now is not possible. But I have to make the calculation. Is she here to be executed in front of me? Do they need her alive? Why do they need her at all? She is Michael's wife, she is back, she knows something, and they know she has killed. The man who stepped from the van first might know everything they need. Christoph has the final say, the executioner's word. I do not look his way; it would only tell him what I feel. Charlotte didn't make it and now she is never escaping this life. No one speaks, no one moves. We wait for Christoph to decide. He doesn't move, he watches Charlotte as she is led toward us. She stops as the man who came from the van first holds her upper right arm.

"Charlotte," Christoph says. "I haven't had time to talk to my colleague. You know most of us, Raucous in particular. But now unfortunately is the time to talk."

He looks to the clock, he looks to his wrist watch.

"So little time," he says. "What do you know, Charlotte? Why now, why today, why the killing?"

110

He is calm as if he expects the answer. No one denies his charm.

"She doesn't know," the man from the van says.

"Siri," Christoph says, "I appreciate your judgement and skills, but coincidence is a horrible thing, and today it makes things that much more difficult."

Siri holds his palm out pacifying.

"She came for revenge, she knows who was there, she has had her say. She knows nothing."

Christoph looks Charlotte up and down.

"So you have seen me before," he says.

He looks to Siri.

"A recording exists," Siri says.

"And do we have it?"

Siri shakes his head.

Christoph turns, chest-on to Charlotte.

"Does it still exist?" Christoph asks.

Charlotte smiles and is smart enough to know that the answer will keep her alive.

"More than one copy," she says. "Insurance is something everyone needs for those catastrophic days."

She smiles now. She knows she has bought some time to live and plan.

Christoph inhales deeply. "Revenge," he says. "Always dig two graves. I've always liked that."

He pauses, he isn't thinking, he knows what he is going to do. He looks at his watch again.

"We need to go and watch," he says.

CHARLOTTE

I bought myself time with the recording lie. Three exist. One on my phone. The original and a copy in a safe. He needs me to give them up. I have a film of him involved in a killing. He wants and needs to know. I have something, leverage of the weakest kind.

We follow him into the open office. The TV is on, the quality high definition. We watch the middle of an action film, a balding has-been of an action star smirking one-liners. I can't hear the audio but I know the film. I know the life experience.

No one speaks, I do not look at Raucous as much as the film reminds me of him, the film goes on. A laptop on the table is open and on the national news webpage. We wait. Christoph looks to his watch. He looks to the clock on the wall. He looks to the TV. The film stops, a weird cut to a studio and newsreaders. Only images, no sound.

The TV shows panic and devastation. Videos made on phones show people running, buildings on fire, windows blown. Everyone has something to film. The calm types documenting a moment they will never forget. A film is rocked by a further explosion. The bar along the bottom of the screen, a ticker tape of Birmingham under attack. The grainy video wobbles and falls to the floor as the person holding the phone is blown off their feet by another near-by explosion.

Firefighters not yet arrived, panicked people in the street, people running for exits. I recognise nothing famous, no buildings to bring back memory nor monuments that scream out England. Streets, normal streets, shops and pubs and houses, destroyed, on fire, collapsed and rubble. People with blood covered faces and bodies lying still on the street. Tears and shouts and anger while people film and stream live chaos. We all watch as Birmingham suburbs, and small communities are awash with death and fire.

We cut to flames in a city and a reporter talking to the screen, we see devastation. Buildings with blown out windows, we watch. Another explosion, then another. Screams. We hear further explosions, the reporter not speaking to camera, but ducking and staring, and looking for shelter. Another explosion, no one speaks. I look to the laptop, the page a mass of red writing, I lean closer to see.

"No need, Charlotte," Christoph says. "This is what we are here for, this is what we do. Birmingham is now the first of cities to be bombed. Repeatedly. Twenty-seven devices. How many have been successful?" he asks.

Siri looks to his phone.

"All of them," he says.

"All of them. Twenty-seven suicide bombers. Small bombs, but strategic places. Birmingham burns and your country panics.

Twenty-seven bombs, unprecedented. And a half-a-million for each successful one."

He turns to Charlotte.

"Why are you back and why are you killing men?"

Charlotte opens her mouth but says nothing.

"Birmingham is not your problem," Christoph says. "It is this country's problem. Right now, I need to understand if you are my problem and if you have spread a word to cause concern to my plans."

Charlotte stares at him as scenes of destruction repeat like gruesome holiday pictures on digital camera. Images that define people's lives.

"Coincidence," Christoph says. He waits but receives no answer. "I always hate coincidence. I don't believe such a thing exists. You have something that you know I need. Information. You will tell me. But you bought your time. Congratulations. But this is a start and there is an end. I need to know if Michael told you, and if you have passed on word. So you don't die, not now. And we will speak."

He turns to Dave.

"Lock her up in the store room. Get someone to stand guard. Tomorrow is another day and this one needs her beauty sleep."

"I'll stand guard," Raucous says.

"Of course you will, Mr. Raucous," Christoph says. "Of course you will."

RAUCOUS

I sit all night on a metal-frame chair outside the storeroom. I sleep in spurts – a trick you learn inside. Small noises wake me, movement, knocks and shuffles. I sleep deeply but can wake when needed. A survival mechanism for when surrounded and housed with men without morals or ethics.

No one comes, the night passes quietly. I hear nothing from the room. I hope and wish Charlotte to have rested. They gave her no blanket, pillow nor mattress. A bare floor in an unlit room without windows. Barely enough space between cleaning kit and long forgotten boxes for a cat to curl up. She looked gone when she stumbled in, a state in which any type of sleep would be natural and welcomed with passion.

My cheap Casio tells me it is 6.30 a.m. I have slept little in two days, certainly not enough to recover from exertions. I feel weak, I know my eyes will hang and colour black. I need caffeine and I need a breakfast of meat and protein. The corridor I sit in has a strip light. A door sits at either end, both with push-bars to open. There are no windows here, and the walls are thin and plaster with wooden frame. Nothing solid, nothing permanent. A post-build addition for whatever reason this place exists.

The door to my right pushes open and Christoph, Siri and Scully walk through. Siri, as wiry as he is, presents as the muscle. Anyone that small with that much confidence is psychotic or trained. The calm he holds hints at the second. A man trained in hurting, a man not used to being taken down. I don't want to fight any more.

I don't stand or move. I watch them take the few steps needed to reach the door. I watch them as they watch me.

"Heard anything from our lovely guest?" Scully asks.

"Not a thing," I say. "Either escaped or crashed out. Nothing at all."

Christoph gives Siri the nod to proceed. Siri produces a key and opens the door.

I stand as I want to see. I peer over the heads of the three and look into the room. Charlotte sleeps deeply, her chest raising. If she is faking it is the best I have seen. She is curled, her right arm acting as a pillow, her knees bent up to her chest. She looks peaceful, like a drunk sleeping off the night before. She looks like she could sleep forever.

Siri looks to Christoph for conformation, as if they have discussed all possibilities and Siri just needs an OK to proceed to the next step.

Christoph nods and Siri kicks Charlotte firmly, hitting her feet. Charlotte stirs, and for a brief moment I can see she remembers nothing. The knowledge floods in quickly and she starts to attention. She doesn't stand, she sits up and stares at four men looking down at her.

The stupid stand-off ends quickly.

"It is time for us to talk, Charlotte," Christoph says. "I would offer you my hand to help you to your feet, but I have heard from reliable sources you are likely to snap it off."

Charlotte stares and says nothing.

"You need to answer truthfully," Siri says. "It is the only way this works."

CHARLOTTE

I slept well. For a moment, just the briefest of moments, I was awake and unaware. It all came back quickly and I saw the storeroom, the floor and the four men watching me. Raucous is there. One of them, one of the people who kill and destroy and deceive and manipulate. A terrorist attack, who knows how many dead and they chase me for killing a few men who killed Michael. The recording is my saviour, my piece of comfort, the only way I am still alive. My life is that. Information they need, evidence they need burned. But how much? A lifetime? I doubt it. He has an urgency and desire, but ultimately it matters not. I have bought time but not my safety.

They look at me waiting for an answer to his idiotic talk. He speaks words as if scripted for Goldfinger. A James Bond villain of the old-school, wanting to talk like the big man he desperately believes himself to be.

I sit up and think about standing. It makes no difference and staying where I am is more comfortable. They loom over me if I am on my feet or not. I put my hands on the floor behind me and lounge as casual as I can be.

"The recordings we will come to later, Charlotte," Christoph says. "But what is paramount is what we are doing now. "

"Blowing shit up?" I ask.

Christoph runs his tongue along the inside of his bottom lip. He smiles. All fake.

"Slightly more complicated than a teenage would-be terrorist, but yes. Blowing things up is what is the concern. Last night was a success, Birmingham and the country as a whole are in somewhat of a panic, you might say."

I tilt my head back and look at the ceiling.

"For what exactly? Politics? Revenge?" I ask.

"All valid reasons, for different people. But we aren't finished. This is a start. But we need to know how you and the information you have fits in. We need to know how you alter the plans."

They expect me to speak and join in? I shake my head.

"I know nothing," I say.

"You never spoke to your husband?" Siri asks.

"All the time, but not about terrorism. That never came up."

Christoph stares again as if reading my face is a past-time he loves.

"Your late husband knew everything," he says. "Ultimately cost him his life. He spoke to the wrong people, people who are mine." He looks to Siri and smiles. "But we all make mistakes. His just ended up with his death."

I am expected to react as an angry wife. I have done all that. Anger is gone. The grieving process is long and there are many set-backs, but I am where I need to be. Words from a killer mean nothing.

"I know nothing about what happened last night," I say, "nor what happens in the future. I know Michael wouldn't have been involved, wouldn't have wanted in to that."

"Then you know why he was killed. And you come back at the moment we start. I do not like coincidence."

It is time to roll my eyes.

"Deal with it, because that is all it is," I say.

He looks to Siri. Siri shakes his head. He produces a knife.

"I have no time for a back and forth game of words. I need information."

"I don't have any," I say.

He is holding the knife, but I can see he has no intention of using it. A show, he is not a man to cut. He is a man who orders people to do so. Raucous is watching the knife and nothing else. Siri stares into space and Scully grins like he is watching a comedy. The situation, the combination is wrong and sending out the strangest vibrations. Nothing seems real. There is the piece of information I lack to make sense of it all and I don't have Michael's ability to make the leap of imagination to place it all together.

116

Michael was killed because he knew of their plans. He died because he made the leap of imagination to see where they were heading. He spoke to the police is what he implied. They are the wrong people, the only ones for us. Michael spoke because of what happens now. To protect Birmingham, to stop these men. There is more, because they stay here and wait. They are not running, nor hiding, they are carrying on as if they have made the first step toward a destination. A terrorist attack on Birmingham suburbs brings attention and high alert. They have shown they are capable. They have shown others it can be done. A new list of martyrs for a cause I have no ability to define.

He walks toward me with his knife, anger acted onto his face. Siri grabs him. I see Raucous tense and Scully grin.

"Now is not the time," Siri says. "It serves us nothing to hurt her now. We have time."

Christoph stares at me with anger forced onto his face. He nods in answer.

"But it will come soon, Charlotte," Christoph says, "that much I guarantee."

RAUCOUS

I spend the day waiting. Walking, pacing, sitting and thinking. The place near sea, I can inhale that much, countryside, a working farm producing big bales, and crops. A big warehouse and four smaller buildings for accommodation and work. They have Charlotte locked in a storeroom. They do nothing but check laptops and phones. They talk in languages I don't understand but there seems no rush nor panic. They have a room, open-plan, desks and phones like a call centre for a cheap insurance company. Bouts of activity among the long hours of nothing. No one explains to me, and food is brought in every few hours. Nothing healthy, all processed and sugar filled. I eat it up for energy and something to do.

I replay the morning in my mind. Nothing makes sense just like nothing ever has. A terrorist group, ready to be caught. Siri an insider, with possible police connections. He is the only one to vanish for the day. He left with uniformed officers. Real or not, I do not know.

They have caused chaos in a country through an unprecedented attack. The news speaks of nothing else. There have been arrests and police raids and suspects taken in, but nothing here, nothing at all but men who look calm and ready and in the know. There is no fear nor panic. Everything is under control. But I am here, part of it. A minder to a man who sits at a corner table alone, eating doughnuts, sipping tea and looking into space with a smile on his lips. Scully does not speak to anyone, certainly not me, and no one seeks him out for conversation. Christoph appears every hour, looks into the room and no one tells him a thing. He stays for a minute then leaves. Charlotte is unattended, she has no escape. Were she to unlock the door, she has to come through this room or the warehouse, and there is no way to remain undetected.

I want nothing of this, I would have walked and not looked back, but she is here, and while my life is worth nothing to anyone but me, and then not much, my history and my life tell me to stay.

Christoph needs the recording, and there are more attacks to come. I want nothing of this but I can and will not leave Charlotte. Christoph's act this morning, Siri holding him back like a barely believable tag-team in American wrestling. Charlotte didn't buy it, just like I didn't. A rouse to set up something. Fear maybe? Or the clear possibility of violence. He killed Michael, something I would like to speak to him about, but he will not harm Charlotte, not now, not with me alive.

Escape is difficult. To walk outside is possible, I have done it twice. We are far from civilisation. A large warehouse in countryside. A large road in, well maintained, and a storage facility. An industrial sized farm, still operating, still growing, but a sham of a façade to hide the real operation.

There is no patrol outside, but there are cameras, pointing in not out. There are men doted around, dressed the part in farmer wear, and doing farmer things. Heavy vehicles move and work takes place. Walking away is not possible, and the vehicles inside are locked. A truck, three white vans, and two black cars. One of them can lead to escape. But getting in one, and getting away would be a challenge to even the most superhuman superhero. I am the only one thinking of escape, and there must be holes in their system. I can't find any, certainly none to exploit and get me and Charlotte out.

There are more attacks coming. I do not know where or when. Scully might know but he seems to not care, he seems as if his job is done, and he is hanging around because he has nowhere to go. The big crime king reduced to nobody in the presence of people he could never beat.

I don't know how much time I have. I don't know anything, and I don't know a way out. I have to wait, watch and react. The time is coming, because we don't walk away. Scully is not going to be left alive. He knows this, he must know. I am a minder that cannot fight against the force I see.

We are small, nothing in comparison. Low-level crime with an ability to import in secret. Our muscle and fear tactics are a joke to Christoph. We are all tagged to be killed. We just don't know when.

CHARLOTTE

Locked in a storeroom with artificial light. No soft bed, nothing but cleaning products and an occasional opening of the door for food or a simple check. I could attack but where would that get me? Into a corridor with another group of men to fight through. Now is not the time.

The morning's performance was not something that sits well. There was no genuine threat of violence, not then. A forewarning of what could come, a slash, a cut, a little torture. He knows I have seen him participate in my husband's death. I have seen how Merrick hurt and killed, and how Christoph watched and smiled like an insignificant psychopath loving the show. He knows those memories are what are running through my mind, but he knows I am aware that the information I have is the only thing keeping me from being very dead.

They think I know something about their plans, about what is happening and what happens next. Michael never told me. You don't believe in coincidence? Neither do I, but I have no reason to understand why I am here. If it is to die, then so be it. But I'm taking a piece of you with me, Christoph. A big chunk.

Raucous flinched when he saw the knife, tensed ready for action. But he relaxed on their first words. He knew it was fake. There was no way nor need to be hurting me. I can't figure Raucous. He is wrong for it all, he is playing too many roles. They clash and make no sense as a pair. My saviour and now my prison guard.

I am locked here until the next attack, if that is what they plan. Another bombing, another twist and added leverage to whatever they are trying to achieve. I'm dead, I know that. Escape from here is not possible. They will not let me free, no chance. I know them, I have seen the glee in their achievements, their love of the death and destruction they caused. All I can do is bring as many with me as I can. I would bite out Christoph's throat, Siri I would do the same. I'll stay alive for that, I'll stay alive even if it means I only leave them with a scar. A piece of their cheek, an ear or nose. Anything that would show them who they killed every time they look in a mirror. I'll stay alive for that, I'll take any punishment for my chance at that. Michael left them with no memory other than victory. I'll not leave them that way.

RAUCOUS

Siri returned and spoke quietly with animation to Christoph. Like two Italians holding down volume but unable to keep gestures in check. I watched them from across the warehouse, Scully watched them too, his maniacal grin never leaving his face.

I tried to speak to Scully. He smiled and told me now was not the time. There was nothing to say nor explain. You'll see, Raucous, he said. And that was that. He went back to leaning, sipping and smiling.

Siri walked away from his boss. The room watched and the men stayed silent. A fear of one man and none for the consequences of a planned attack.

The TV buzzed all-day, silent but with a strip of news running non-stop at the bottom of the screen. A Twenty-four-hour news show. The aftermath, the deaths, the fear the confusion all on an eternal loop of misery. Birmingham was in panic and the country all but at a standstill through fear. I watched the same speeches and the same information over and over again. Politicians talking but answering nothing. Police were searching, clues were found, but no one had an idea. If they had, the attack wouldn't have happened. The deaths kept increasing and no one in the warehouse cared to count.

The evening came and the light outside faded and went. Nothing of importance happened, and no panic set in. The calm of maybe twenty men sitting and watching laptop screens a constant bore through endless hours. I was alone with thoughts and images of Charlotte.

They gave her the last meal of the day. Fried chicken from whatever small take-away they thought dumb enough to ignore who buys. I glimpsed her briefly, as I became ready to sit guard outside her door. No one had asked, no one gave an order. I was stepping on no one's toes as no one was coming. It would be me alone. They knew she had no way out. I knew that too. I was thinking of who would want a way in.

I pulled up a chair, the folding type, something to be used for brief spells and one I would use for a bed. I rested my back against the wall and waited for a half-sleep to come. I knew it would, I knew it would take time, and I knew I would wake in starts. That's the way it works. I have an alertness to anything happening, even sleep doesn't take that away. Feelings from many years before, honour and friendship and sacrifices and promises I made to my only friend. A friend who was killed, and his wife who I loved as much as I loved him. I thought my debt had been paid in time given to keep him innocent. I was wrong. The debt is nothing I can repay in full. My debt, my guilt will never be balanced, not fully. And here I am, placed in the middle of crazy fanatics following whatever insane ideology when all I want is my simple life and to be free of madness and the burden of loyalty.

If Charlotte dies, I will have failed. If Charlotte dies, I will kill.

CHARLOTTE

I try to sleep on the cold floor. No one came to take the paper box of fried chicken away. The grease and left overs of gristle and fat fill the air with smells of late Friday nights. The particles cling to my clothes and throat. Another night of fitful sleep until morning. Another night of trying to place logic on what is happening, another futile mental exercise into how the hell I ended up here with these men.

Maybe someone is guarding the door, maybe Raucous, who knows and who really cares? I can't escape. I haven't tried. The door has a handle on the inside and a lock. It wouldn't take long to smash through, but then where do I go? There is no escape and no way out. I am trapped, a prisoner to people who care nothing for anyone but themselves. Siri, a monster with an underside of weird. A player at heart, a man trying for mystery. Christoph, a man who has no core. Nothing there but a black hole of energy sucking hate. I have nothing at all to survive, nothing at all but a hope in miracles and chance.

RAUCOUS

I wake. But I am too late. I glance at my watch and see the time as 1 a.m. I have slept and not been disturbed. But now my peace is not their concern.

I am hit by a bar. The man swings it with force from above his head. I reach up and deflect a large part of the energy away from my scull and onto my left forearm. I feel the sting but know it is not broken. There will be an egg of a bruise without ice, but that won't come till this fight is over.

I fall back and sideways and roll away. I get to my feet quickly and see I am faced by three men. They are wearing black but their faces are bare. Siri and two of the men who arrived in his van. The police, they say. Bullshit is my call. Siri stands in the middle, and he holds the bar. The two men flank him and come at me.

"We aren't here for you," Siri says. "We are here for Charlotte."

"Why the bar?" I ask as I crouch ready for defence.

"Spiriting away and we don't need onlookers."

I look at the two men, I have a chance to take them both. The tight space of the corridor gives me an advantage. It becomes more a test of strength and short blows. This I can do. We are all getting hit, but I know I can take the most punishment. They are empty handed and without guns. They needed stealth and quickness, they have neither now.

The two jump me as one. A wrestle now. Me against them. They are trained and know leverage and moves, and twists and holds. But so do I and I am still stronger than the pair. My cardio lags behind so I need to make this quick. They are going for chokes and holding my arms. I fling myself against the right wall, using one of the men as a bumper. He deflates like a popped balloon and releases his grip. The second is on my back and has his right arm hooked around my throat and locked in with his left hand.

I hate the sensation of no breath.

I turn and he reaches his legs around my waist. I have a human tortoise shell. I run backwards and smash him into the opposing wall. He grunts on impact but his hold stays strong. I look at the door to the store cupboard that Siri is unlocking. Two turns and the door opens. He holds up his hands in a defensive surrender. He says something but I don't understand. The blood is pumping in my ears. I reach up with my arms to try and grab the man's head. I haven't stretched in years and my large arms get nowhere close. I bend forward hoping to slide him off. I look up and see Siri raising the bar. I move, but I'm slowed by the weight I carry. I turn but not fast enough. The bar crashes into the side of my forehead. I drop to one knee and feel warm blood flow. It trickles past my eye, but not in. I am buzzed and slow. I look again and Siri is leading Charlotte through the door at the other end of the corridor. The man I smashed into the wall is stumbling and following. The man on my back is not letting go. I fall forward, and feel the blood lacking oxygen in my brain. A dizziness and loss of clarity. I am about to pass out, the cut not helping. I make a choice, I scramble at his forearm, a beginners mistake and not something that will help, I slow, I breath long and slow, and I weaken. I fall forward, and stop all resistance, I am limp and not moving. A sack of bones and flesh. The man still holds. He waits and squeezes and then finally releases. He stands, he must be looking at me, he must be staring. I know it is coming.

The impact is heavy and strong and in my ribs. A toe-punt of hatred and it hurts. I hear his steps, the door open and close. I look up and I am alone. I try to get to my feet and my balance is gone like I have downed tequila with abandon. I stagger to the door they did not use.

CHARLOTTE

It all happened quick. Raucous jumped, Siri my saviour, a hand and escape. Smooth, but with a hitch. The violence, the fight. Siri not concerned with the men he left behind. He took my hand and we moved fast, short of sprinting. He took me through a door I had never used. It led into a small room of Farm tools and tractor parts. He rushed me through to the far side and a large sliding door, it was open enough for us to squeeze sideways. A white van sat idling, the driver I could not see. Siri rushed me to the rear doors. They were open. We jumped inside, Siri slammed the doors shut, he banged the side of the van and we accelerated away.

"What about the others?" I asked.

"They are already dead. And we will be too if we don't get out right now."

The van makes noises and slides, accelerating. The driver is pushing, and fighting against the poor traction on the terrain. We crash into nothing and keep heading away. Siri is breathing hard, and my adrenaline is putting me on high alert.

"You are dead, you know that," Siri says.

I don't answer. I don't understand.

"The recordings you have, they kept you alive for a moment, but not forever. He wanted them, but now he doesn't believe they exist."

"They exist," I say.

"I believe you, but he doesn't. And that means he'll kill you without problem."

"And you broke me out because you don't want me dead?"

"I broke you out because I'm as dead as you when this is over. He figured me out."

"Your boss not happy with you?" I ask.

"Not my boss. I'm police. He knows that. He gave himself away. "

"The inside man."

"That's right."

"Who let Birmingham burn. Your official boss won't like that."

Siri pauses, looking around the van.

"I was kept out. I think because he knows. I have received less and less information. I need to know what you know."

"You know where he is now, send them in."

"They are coming in, right now. Heavy handed. Anyone in there is dead. No prisoners, they will all die. We are out. But I need to know what you know. People can die."

"I'll die. I need a safety net, a protection. I need the recording. I know nothing of your plans. A lot less than you."

Is it safe? I remember those words. Is it safe? I want this to be real, I need this to be real. It feels real, the panic the violence the chaos. But this isn't what I feel. Everything is off. The recordings, my only protection and now this man, Siri wants access for his own well-being. I call bullshit. And I call it loud.

"Bullshit," I say.

"Bullshit? I've just got you out, I have just broken cover, I am getting us out and somewhere safe."

"Who's driving?" I ask.

"What does that matter?"

"Other people are in on it. A Driver and the two you left with Raucous."

"Raucous is dead."

"I doubt it. If this is real, he'll be alive, if it is fake, he is alive."

"You think that much of him?"

"I know that much."

"Where are the tapes?"

"Get me out. I'll take you there."

"My turn to call bullshit."

"Call what you want, but the tapes are where they are and need to be. Not where you can have them."

RAUCOUS

I walk into the main office. I walk to Scully's seat. I open the top drawer and pull out the gun. Too easy. But my mind, a headache, a scream, but I am awake enough to have my plan. I know too much, have seen it all. I walk to the exit, through the warehouse. Out into fresh air.

The cold brings added pain. I wince, I'm not OK. Unstable on my feet and the uneven ground is no excuse. I can see what is happening, feel it and know it. I walk to the gate that leads out into the world. Two men approach, I stare at them, not hiding my gun as I walk on forward. I hear a cackle, a walkie-talkie, garbled conversation and I am left to walk alone. No one follows, no one challenges, I am free to stagger with a loaded gun out into the world.

I follow the road, the only one in or out. I walk for what feels like hours but is only minutes. I stop at the first real bend. It is not 90 degrees but close enough. A blind corner that can't be taken at speed. I stay the farm side of it and sit and wait and think and listen. One of two things has happened. I'm betting on the second, even if hoping for the first. The first would be a miracle and the idea only sticks in my mind because it is scrambled and bruised and aching and hurt. I want to sit, but know I'll struggle to stand. I relax and wait and hope. I am still waiting when I hear.

CHARLOTTE

The van moves at speed, corners taken quickly and with danger. In the back, Siri and I brace ourselves against the rocking and physics. Siri braces himself against the side and the ceiling. I fall and stumble and bang against the long wooden seat as well as the panels. Extra bruises to a body that can't take more.

"Where are they, Charlotte? I'm risking everything here. I need the recordings."

"Get me to a safe place and I'll tell you," I say.

"Do they actually exist?"

"You'll find out," I say. "As soon as I am out of here. There is no rush. Your boys are coming in. All done. Relax."

"Do they exist?"

"You'll have to trust me."

"I don't trust anyone."

"It's a trait I admire."

"You need to tell me, I can save you."

"You already have, right? Just need a bit more distance and I'll send you a copy."

"This is bullshit," he says. The cool evaporating.

"It always is. All of it."

His face changes. Anger or disappointment or failure, I can't understand. I don't care. I need this to be true and I know the recordings are important. Not as much now as before, I can see that. But something, a little chip. My only way to bargain and beg.

Siri makes a fist, a frustrated face and bangs the panelled side of the van three times.

Boom, boom boom.

I'm not stupid. I know.

The van slides and skids, and moves fast and we rock and roll. And fall. A ride for fun and kicks.

"You need to tell me, Charlotte."

"You need to prove who you are," I say.

RAUCOUS

I hear it, the whine, the screech, the tyres on a surface that won't grip. I try for alert but there is a fog in my mind. I shake my head as if it will physically splash away like a dog just out of the sea. Nothing happens other than a headache that hurts. I feel my brain slap scull, a nausea rises but I don't fall.

The noise is louder. I step into the road.

The lights, on full-beam, illuminate the road and the trees either side. The vehicle has slowed and is not as crazy on the revs as it had been. Do they not think we haven't seen the same films as them? Is it safe? Marathon Man. Yes, it is safe. Fools everywhere and I am the biggest one.

There is a danger, but natural reactions work in panic. It is just the way it is.

The van is close, not a hundred metres away, it takes the blind corner slower than it had on the way out, that I do not doubt.

I am lit up and visible, but I'm ready to dive. I am closer to the left edge of the road, and that's where I'll jump. The Van will be sliding the other way as it takes the corner.

The Driver sees me and hits the brakes. It's inevitable. That is the way it works. No one ever decides to run through a living being when confronted in an instant. That has to be premediated and the driver is not thinking of death. The brakes are on and the swerve arrives. I move left all the same. I hold the gun, but I do not fire. The van stops as it heads toward the trees on the right. The engine stalls. A sound I needed to hear.

The driver I leave. Maybe not the best decision, maybe not the one a cold-blooded killer would take, but it is mine. I know what I want, and I want the driver to run.

I walk to the back of the van, hoping it is unlocked. But as I step forward, the back doors fly open. I raise my gun aware that it could be Charlotte, aware that it could be anyone. The door obstructs my view, but only briefly. I see him, I see Siri, and then I see Charlotte. Both step down, and both look shocked. Siri, I have you. A cheap trick from a great film and I'm sure he played it badly. Charlotte sees me, she looks over my shoulder, she sees the farm. She twists her head toward Siri. Siri pays no attention, his eyes are on me and the gun.

"Raucous," he says.

I raise the gun and fire twice as I step toward him. There is not even two metres between us. A double tap to the chest, and he drops, as he flies backward. Up close the bullets must hurt.

Charlotte steps toward me.

"What is happening?" she asks.

"A set up," I say. "Did you tell them anything?"

"Nothing."

I turn to the driver's door. It opens and Scully steps out. He has his hands raised but a grin on his face.

"Don't shoot," he says. He smiles all the time. "Killing me is no solution. Keys are in the ignition. I'm not about to play silly buggers by throwing them in the wood."

Charlotte steps quickly to the driver's door and gets in.

"She is making the right decision," Scully says. "You don't have much of a chance, but driving away at least gives you a shot."

128

I hear something behind me, I turn but keep the gun on Scully. I see the back of Siri darting haphazardly into the woods. I don't aim my gun, I let him go.

"Word of advice, Raucous. Next time a double tap to the head," Scully says.

"Why are you in this?"

"The classics. Greed and stupidity. Sprinkled with arrogance. I'm as dead as you are. Only my life expectancy is a little longer. I'd get going. Enjoy the little time you have left."

I won't shoot him, he knows that. He smiles and there is a weirdness in his eyes as if he wants a bullet. I walk past him. Charlotte has the Van in gear. I walk round and get into the passenger seat. Charlotte accelerates backward as we turn a circle to head out again. I watch Scully watching us. His goofy smile and a wave. A man I do not know.

CHAROTTE

Raucous jumps in and we go. I don't know where, or for how long, but we go. I press the accelerator, moving up through the gears quicker than is healthy. Raucous looks in the mirror to see Scully pass into distance.

"Where do we go?" I ask.

Raucous keeps looking in the mirror.

"We go fast as far as we can," he says.

He looks at his gun, shakes his head. Stares into the wing mirror.

"We going to make it?" I ask.

"More chance out here than back in there."

"More than none," I say.

"Not much more," he says. "Did you tell them anything?"

"Nothing at all. They wanted the recordings. And my knowledge."

"Do they exist?"

I look at him.

"Don't tell me," he says. "I'm not one of them. This isn't part of it. I don't need to know."

"They exist," I say. "But they mean nothing."

"It would be better if they did."

I drive as fast as I can on roads I don't know. Country roads with high hedgerows. There are choices of left and right. I alternate, taking only the rights will put me in a circle. The headlights illuminate animals and trees, and roads with holes. We drive and bounce and Raucous watches the rear. No lights coming, nothing to be seen. I keep the van at high speed. More and more distance is best. I need the scenery to change, I need the city again. I need to vanish. I want out.

There are roads and lanes that lead into the street we are travelling. Small farm tracks and occasional wider spaces. No one to see, and nowhere to go but straight. It has been minutes since Scully waved goodbye, but time is relative now. Minutes seem like hours. Adrenaline pumping but forward progress slow.

I drive, bouncing, we are not wearing seatbelts. I reach up and over my right shoulder to where I assume the belt is. I don't look, simply feel and grasp the buckle. Raucous senses my movement and looks. He nods and reaches for his own belt. In unison we pull. For the briefest moment my eyes leave the road. And that's when it happens.

I don't see anything, there are no lights. I feel the impact on my side of the van. It hits behind where we sit. By design or miss-timed I don't know. We rock up on two side wheels, we balance for the briefest of moments. I watch Raucous and his large mass bump up out of his seat, the seatbelt grasped in his left hand. We topple and tumble, and roll. It seems like an infinite, never ending horror fairground attraction. I have no idea where I am in relation to the van, and no idea where the van is in relation to the road. I feel the van flip, but I know it can't be. We roll, and somewhere in there, hitting dashboard, wheel, roof and floor the ride ends its visual trip. I'm out and feel nothing more.

RAUCOUS

I didn't see the car that hit us. The opposing side and I assumed they would come from behind. They didn't follow because there were already people ahead. It must be big, a Land Rover or some such, because it hit hard and sent us rolling. No belts to keep us in and no airbags to hold us tight. We roll and topple and scream and crash. I see Charlotte fly, rag doll in vain attempts to resist everything Newton discovered and kids hate at school. Difficult to stop, but stop we will. Neither of us conscious when we do.

I can't tell how long I was out. Charlotte, isn't moving and the van rests on its left side. Her left leg rests on my chest. She is breathing, and so am I. I look around the van. I can see my gun. Up front, behind the seats, closer to me than I could have hoped. I move Charlotte's leg, I sit and feel pain everywhere. I look down and notice blood trickling from my right forearm. There will be other cuts, maybe some bone damage. I hurt everywhere, isolating anything right now isn't going to work. I crawl toward the gun, I don't know why, standing just seems dumb in such a crowded space. But I realise quick that I've been out more than seconds.

"Don't bother, Raucous," the voice says.

I try to squint at the windscreen that is no longer there. It is dark, a little light, I don't know where from, but it is enough to give me the idea of a figure. The man stands and peers into the van. I recognise him as my head clears enough for my vision to formulate real images. Siri smiles, nothing friendly, just a smile to tell me who has won. He makes sure I see the gun he is holding.

I can't reach my gun without being shot by Siri. And if he is here it means others are too. The people who rammed us, the car that brought Siri, the people, whatever number they thought would be required to keep us safe and causing no trouble.

CHARLOTTE

I wake up outside the van. I don't know if I was thrown free or moved. I come round slowly, my head throbbing, I'm on wet grass. Lights and figures move in a blur as if my eyes are covered in raindrops. Noises begin to become clear words, images become objects that I recognise. Raucous is sat two metres from me, cross-legged on the floor. A male, middle-aged Buddha. Siri stands behind him, a gun in his right hand, a gun that points at Raucous.

"Sleeping beauty," Siri says.

I sit up and move to stand.

"On the ground is fine," Siri says. "I've had my fill of escapades today. Sit and be quiet."

Raucous nods.

A crane on the back of a truck is backed toward the van. The van is smashed up and tangled, blown glass and tyres. A crumpled can tossed aside by a giant. Two men I recognise from the farm hook up straps and pull levers to tighten grasps.

I watch and wonder. No escape and will we return? A last chance at freedom, a low one and we blew it. Two failures sitting, being punished by the school bully waiting for the truly important man to arrive and sign off on our death.

Raucous looks at the grass, in thought. Thinking of the mistake he made in siding with me. Thinking about how his silence and apathy would have kept him alive and out of this. I have killed him, and he knows, and he can't look me in the eye.

RAUCOUS

I don't want to look at her, I don't want to cry. I failed. I didn't save her and now there is no need to keep us alive. Maybe Charlotte can gain hours, but there'll be torture for information. I have no use, nothing to bargain with. I could be used as a means to force her to speak. Threats to my life and safety, tortured in front of her, to make her give up information, but I doubt it. Too late in the day and not important enough, not in the grand scale of terrorist attacks. We are dead. We aren't yet because the main man isn't here to call it and watch it. Siri wants me gone and he wants to do it himself. He knows I know and we wait as his excitement builds and my life ebbs away. A failure to finish the life of a failure and I can't help the only woman I have loved.

What does she think of me? Why do I care? I know what she thinks, because there can be only one thing. I am nothing but the person who accompanied her to death. A failure and a shame and the man who was never good enough.

"Your time is almost gone, Raucous," Siri says.

I don't answer because I have nothing smart to say. My answer is yes, I know. I have no gun, no plan and no hope.

"You're probably thinking about what happens to Charlotte," he says. "But it matters not. You are both dead. You are both never seeing the sun again."

I feel the gun press into the back of my scull. I feel the cold metal and the small circular pressure point. I inhale because I am afraid. But I know not to fight, not to try and twist and pull off a miracle move. At least have dignity, at least have my head opened while I sit stoically and keep all the pain and sorrow and hurt and fear inside.

The pressure lifts, the barrel is removed.

"Not now though, Raucous," Siri says. "Way too easy and fast. A bullet to the back of the head and all gone as your lady friend watches. Not good enough. Not good enough for me."

"I guess you won't accept a fair fight," I say. "Seeing as you are a coward."

I should know which side it comes, but I'm not thinking, not trying. The barrel slashes across the back of my head from left to right. A back-handed slash. He must want to fire, want it really bad. But he held back and hit me.

My head lolls forward, but I pull it back.

"Pretty cheap shot," I say. "Cowardly, some would say."

I smile because I want the pain.

"If it were me, you'd be dead already," Siri says.

"But it isn't you, is it? You are nothing. An insignificant piece of a bullshit puzzle. Nothing famous, nothing to. . ."

I can't finish because the pain explodes in the base of my scull and lights shoot to my eyes. He clipped me again and this time I'm not pulling myself back. I slump forward and breathe heavy. Not out, but nowhere near conscious.

It feels deep.

CHARLOTTE

Raucous is looking for death. He has given up and wants the manly way out. A provocation to have a quick and easy death. They won't give him that, not now, not after betrayal. But we can't stay here too long. It is the middle of nowhere, I paid no attention to signs, the names of small insignificant villages mean nothing to me.

But there is too much light, too much activity. A crane, a destroyed van and three cars. Too many people doing too many things for this to be quiet and safe.

A fourth car arrives. It is Christoph. Everyone stops and everyone waits. Siri moves away from Raucous and walks toward the parked car. He replaces his gun into his hip holster. He walks casually, a movie-star knowing he is king.

Christoph steps out and they speak. Siri nods often and smiles as he turns to look and point at us. Christoph asks a question and Siri shakes his head. Christoph loses himself in thought for five seconds. He snaps to the present, observes the scene. He states something, he stares at me, he smiles. He pats Siri's left shoulder. He steps back into the car and they leave. Everyone watches and as the car vanishes, only its headlights showing where it is going. They start to work.

Siri walks over to the crane driver. He gesticulates and points, and receives the information he needs. He steps down from the cab and heads toward us.

He knows now. He knows what happens. He is confident. He strides. My heart beats fast.

RAUCOUS

Siri ties my hands behind my back. I feel the tightening of the plastic cords. He pulls them tight so they bite into my flesh. I can't resist. I can't think. My head throbs and my mind is cloudy. I want to vomit but nothing comes. I am a ragdoll. Siri man handles me and I am embarrassed. The blows to my head as bad as those to my broken ego. I don't struggle. No fight or flight. I'm playing dead because that is what I am.

I watch him tie Charlotte the same way. He is using white plastic ties. She resists a little but only for show. She doesn't want to be broken and refuses to submit, even now. Siri enlists two men to get us to our feet. They march us to the destroyed van. We are pushed inside, and Siri follows. He uses another plastic tie to attach our legs to those of the seat. We are not going anywhere fast. Siri shuts the broken doors and vanishes from sight.

134

CHARLOTTE

I hear the groans and moans of the engine outside and the van begins to lift, and sway. We are hovering above the earth and moving. I stare at Raucous but his eyes are concentrating on other things. He tugs at the ties but he knows they will only cut through his flesh.

We are in a situation we know nothing about. Tied up in a van, one that cannot drive. Swaying and tied. There is no reason for us to be here. No reason at all.

I feel us being lifted higher and higher. Ten metres maybe, the crane was tall, attached to a truck. The noises and movement tell us we are trudging forward at low speed. Low speed, high torque, fairy-steps ahead to a destination that can't be far.

I hope we are being lifted onto the flatbed of a truck, but there's no logic in that. If we need to be moved, this van is not the way.

My gut jumps up like it will push through my throat. It's like turbulence. A sudden drop on a long-haul flight but no oxygen masks fall.

The swaying hasn't stopped, but the forward momentum has. We are a pendulum, back and forth in the breeze. Raucous senses something and I see the blood dripping from the torn flesh on his wrists. He knows, he understands and I just don't make the connection.

We drop. I don't hear the click as we are cut loose. But I felt the nausea of a roller coaster ride. We fall and spin. The back doors open and for the longest of seconds I see the water below, the rocks that sit breaking its surface and the rush of shrubs and brown and rocks on the sheer face of the cliff down which we plummet. Raucous tugs at his ties, adrenaline and fear and power ripping flesh. We fall forever but no time at all. I see everything in slow motion but time speeds up. Nothing makes sense and the van tumbles and spins as we rock back and forth, stopped from flying and crashing by the ties to our hands and feet.

I watch the water rush toward us, I feel as though I have all the time there has ever been to brace myself, but I don't. The water comes to meet us and we smash, a sudden stop, my body smacked against thin metal panels and I feel the speed slow and settle to gentle sinking. The back door, busted beyond repair is open and water rushes in. I look to Raucous whose face is red and neck bulging as if dying from the most painful of poisons.

RAUCOUS

Charlotte looked so calm and then she didn't. She couldn't understand what had happened. I knew, I saw. And it came too quick.

My wrists are bleeding, the plastic ties cutting deep. I have pulled and squeezed muscles. The plastic holds just like it is designed to do. But I feel the stretch, the gap extending, I feel the skin razored and shaved as I pull and slide my hands further and further into the grip. The free-fall came and I pulled again. I can feel the blood popping in my face, my neck bulging in muscle and veins. Many years ago I could lift weight and throw plates of serious size and with chemical assistance. A man on roids with rage to match. I want that power now, I need it. The strength of someone who won't give up, who has that extra rep, that extra sinew to break. We fall and tumble and hit water, the impact breaking my force. The water seeps in, quicker than I hope. The van sinking, Charlotte thrashing to break her own ties. I sit, concentrate and pull. The pain of the top layer of skin being removed from the top of my hands as I wriggle again. The stretch in the plastic not yet enough. The water rises or the van sinks, whichever is not important. They both mean death.

The water is at my waist, and it rushes in faster. I can't look at Charlotte, I have to fight, and force. I feel my hands slipping, lubricated by blood and broken skin. The ties slipping toward my knuckles, where they stick and I force once more.

My hands pop free, the pain not yet come. My ankles tied so I can't stand nor move. I am not yet free and the water rushes in. Charlotte's chest lapped by small waves, no bubbles, just water rising without stop.

I dip down at the waist, ducking my head underwater. I open my eyes and the water is dark, dirty and my eyes sting. I see the tie around my ankles. I sit up and gasp for air. The water higher, Charlotte's neck only above the surface. I look around, the destroyed van, the broken panels, torn and twisted. I grab an edge and pull, the metal tears, my hands bleed, the edge slashes at my fingers but a piece the size of a cleaver blade rips free like thick paper.

I duck down into the water, I see the tie on my ankle, the piece of metal in my hand, I slide it between my ankle and the white plastic. I pull and slash and the tie separates like it has no strength at all.

CHARLOTTE

I watch Raucous get his hands free. It's too late. The water is up to my neck and coming faster. I think of the times I have read or heard people speak about death by drowning. The most peaceful or the most painful. Contrary accounts of the same demise. I will find out but I will never be able to tell. It hits me then and I smile. How can people speak of the comfort or pain of this death if they do not die? It seems absurd and it is, and I laugh. The water at my mouth. I stretch my neck higher, clawing at those extra seconds of life, I look at Raucous but he is gone, under the water, doing whatever he can to free his legs. It is too late, Raucous. Way too late. I laugh, but not long, the water enters my mouth and I hold my breath. I don't feel fear, but it is not relief. When it comes to the end, I just have to hang on.

RAUCOUS

My legs are free and I push up through the water. My head in air but the rest of my body under the surface. Charlotte is under, no escape. Her height not enough. I inhale deeply, I know where she is. I would like bigger lungs, longer breath, a fitter me. But I have all that I have and I dive under the water. I see Charlotte, not clearly but enough to know. Maybe I see what I want to see, the water too dark to tell if expressions are real. She is holding her breath but for how long until now I do not know. I grab the seat of her chair and pull myself down, holding myself under, fighting the need to float. I let go and grab her left ankle, I hold myself under. She is not moving, nor fighting. I hope she is calm. I force the metal shard into the plastic. I have no time for nuance nor finesse. I cut, not knowing if her skin breaks or if she bleeds. The metal slices through quick, she is free. I let go of her ankle and push up looking

137

for air. My head hits the van's ceiling. There are two inches of air. I see and hear Charlotte gasp, alive, choking and looking for more air than we have. I cut through the ties on her wrists.

"Take a deep breath, as much as you can," I say. "We have to get far from the van before we come up."

She says nothing but gasp and choke and inhale and splutter. She has heard, she has to have heard. The water comes up and I take a deep breath, a little of the quarry water enters my mouth, but I don't spit. I hold and dive and pull Charlotte with me.

CHARLOTTE

Raucous pulls me under. I have heard him. Away from the van. They will be watching, checking, making sure and smiling. If they see us, have any idea we are free, they will come and kill the classic way. The van is sinking, gurgling under. Raucous holds me back, waiting for the light we can see on the surface to darken and go. He makes a decision and pulls me as he pushes free. He is no swimmer, and neither am I, but adrenaline and fear are the strangest of things. He is cumbersome, and I lead. Swimming ahead, dragging him now. He has no grace, no style, no idea. All he has is the desire to reach far from the van. I see the edge of the water, the rocks. Raucous is heading out into water, into more open space. I pull him toward me and the water edge.

I can't breathe, I can feel the need for air. I understand I need the sanctuary of the edge. There is no light anymore. I don't know if this is because I am checking out or because we are in dark.

Raucous is flapping, struggling, moving to the surface. I pull him, kick in the water. He follows but his movements drag rather than push. I pull him, his mass, his resistance. We want to work together but we have no experience of such things.

My left hand touches the edge, like a rough swimming pool, I grab what I can. My head breaks into air, Raucous behind me. I gasp as quietly as I can, look around, and stay low in the water.

RAUCOUS

She pulls me to the edge, she is making better decisions than me. I am dragging her down, I should let her free, but she holds me. If I float to the surface here they will see and come running to kill. I can't leave her and she can't leave me. She has a plan, she is making me move away from my idea. I have to trust her. Fighting will leave us nowhere but where we are. We need to hide. Just one glimpse and we are dead.

I don't know where we are, but an old quarry is the guess. The sheer sides, the tumble gave me enough to see. The water, the shape of the lake. Natural or not, we are in a water pit.

Charlotte drags and I follow. My lungs bursting, the desire to inhale so strong. I hold out, but I know I can't much longer. I feel her surface, I know I will. I touch the side, I hope we are hidden. I break through the water into air. I gasp, I want to be quiet. I force myself to be quiet. I need air and I gulp it in. I look at Charlotte, her face strained, wet and wide-eyed. She inhales too, she stays quiet. I can't hear properly; my ears need to pop. My head ringing, the thump of blood pumping. We need to be hidden and quiet. It is all I can think.

Charlotte pulls me close, not a romantic embrace. We need to be as small as we can be. We cannot move. The smallest of movements get seen by even the most blind of beings.

"Stay quiet," she says.

I look at her face, all white, and shiny and reflective. She understands. She scans the cliff top for where we fell. She turns her back, buries her face in the mud. I do the same. I smear my hand brown and wet, I rub the dirt on my head. A boulder for a skull. Not reflecting. We wait and breathe and hope.

CHARLOTTE

I start to shiver. I understand we have to wait and hope to be hidden. They won't come down and search without reason. We are inside a van, under water without hope. But they will wait and watch, they need to be sure. I am cold, a painful chill. I feel my teeth crack against each other. We wait. I see nothing but the mud and rocks my face is pushed against. I feel nothing but the freeze of my body heat being drawn out by the water. Raucous is tense and shivers too. His large mass trying to stay still, trying to move as little as possible. I strain to hear for movement or conversation up on the edge of the quarry. I do not want to look, nor check for search lights. I hear nothing. I move my head slowly, looking for Raucous, seeking his approval. We are safe and we can move. There is nothing now but the cold and the water and the silence.

"I don't think they are gone," Raucous says.

I can't speak. I try but nothing comes. A shake in my voice.

"There is someone up there, waiting," Raucous says.

"How do you know?" I ask.

"Because they have to leave someone. Someone alone, someone to wait to see if others come. But we have to move. I can't stay in this for much more."

We move slowly, trying to make little noise and few ripples. We move along the edge, looking for a way out, a way to climb. We edge further and further, we look and see nothing. But we know there must be a way, a path or road. Someone had to get here at some point. To die now, like this would be the dumbest of ends.

We edge and look and see. The steep wall broken and flat. Like a tourist beach on an island, a smooth shallow slope into the water. A road for trucks, wide and inclined as it edges further inland.

We move slowly and our feet touch the bottom. We walk, then wade, always as close to the edge as we can. We walk expecting to be seen and chased but no noise comes. We walk up the road for five metres and stop, we sit, our backs to the steep sides and gasp and hold each other. We need warmth not love.

"Are we safe?" I ask.

"We are dead," he says. "And the longer we stay that way the safer we are."

"What about them?"

"They are for some other time. If you want revenge, you do that, but not now and without me."

"We got lucky," I say.

He doesn't answer. We sit, holding each other and wait.

RAUCOUS

I am holding Charlotte. We are cold and shiver. We can't wait long. They won't come, not now. We are dead. They have killed us, and staying that way means we will live for a long time.

I have wanted to hold her for an eternity. And here we are, holding for body warmth, nothing else. No emotion, no closeness through shared experience, just a basic need to survive. We have to move, we have to find shelter and warmth. Staying here will only lead to death. We have to go quiet. It is likely someone or some people have been left.

I stand and drag Charlotte to her feet. We are wet and cold and suffering. We walk forward, keeping close to the edge of the road. We have no cover, but walking in the open is stupidity. The road opens up into a flat area. There are two wooden sheds, old, abandoned, locked and broken. We head to the smaller one as it is closer. The glass windows have long since broken and been boarded up. The door, padlocked to the main frame, is weak and swollen, and ill-fitting. I pick up a rock, look around, check for light, a torch, a movement. I see nothing. I bring the fist-sized rock down, and the screws keeping the lock in place fall out with ease. The bang echoes loud, I should have checked and pulled with strength. The wood is rotten, and wet and weak.

We wait for a reaction, a call, or a beam of light, but nothing happens. We want to believe they have gone. We need to believe we are free. Inside is a dusty small space. An empty storeroom, with remnants left. There are dust sheets, and empty hessian sacks. They have sat, untouched since the quarry died. I remove my wet top, shake it out and hang it from a hook on the wall. I grab a dust sheet and dry my body. I wrap the dustsheet around me, I feel warmer, better. I know this is in my mind but the comfort brings calm. I remove my other clothes, hidden under the dust sheet. I shake them out and hang them to dry. Charlotte follows my lead. I look at the inside of the door, I slide the bolt across to fit into its hold. The door doesn't move to a push.

"We'll stay here," I say. "Onc night."

"A fire?" Charlotte asks.

"Not now. Not safe."

Charlotte throws hessian sacks into a pile in the corner. She crouches then lies down. I move to her and lie next to her. We move close and she wraps her covered arms around me.

"For warmth," she says.

I say nothing.

PART THREE

RAUCOUS

We wake and dress. I don't watch her putting on still damp clothes. I glimpse flesh and it is bruised. Like blood has exploded under her skin in multiple points, a patchwork of red and purple, with yellow edges and tinges of green. I see myself too. A wreck of a man, all loose and blubber, bruises of my own.

"We are dead to them," I say. "We can walk away, all over."

"And when they attack again?" she asks.

"It is not our fight. We can do nothing."

"If they come after your home, where we are from?"

I know this will be possible. But it makes no sense. London is too big, too important for that to work.

"They have done their attack," I say. "Everyone is on high alert. There is no more."

"You don't believe that," she says.

And I don't. But it isn't my job.

"Let it go," I say. "You did what you needed to do, we are out."

"You can let this go?"

"I've been insulted, beaten, hated and discarded by people I cared about. I did nothing. These are nothing. I got you out, and now I'm out. Whatever happens next in my life will be away from where I know and be something different from what I am. That's it. Messing with them, as you know, means death. "

"We aren't dead."

"No, we're lucky. You don't get to escape twice."

"That's it?"

"That is it, for you and me. What do you suggest we do?"

"Grass, police, tell them where, who and what."

"Do you have a phone?"

"You know I don't."

"And a payphone will be traced. Siri in the police. A call from anywhere near here and he knows we are alive. Think about us, our lives. We walk away as the ghosts we are. When we are safe, where we need to be, we can decide then."

CHARLOTTE

I know Raucous is right. It is selfish, it is us first. But this is what we are.

He spoke in the hut, us damp and bruised and cold. I listened, knew he was talking to keep us alive. We walked out of there in silence. We were still cautious, still alert to what was around but we heard and saw nothing. We walked through lanes, aware that there were people posted, look-outs. We kept walking, hoping. Nothing happened, no one came and we walked for forty minutes. It was cold, but we created our own heat.

We hear the noises of motors approaching, more than one, a noise from the sky too. Raucous stops and grabs my arm. He looks around, he drags me to the opposite side of the road. There is cover, trees and hedges. We walk in, not deep, not truly hidden, but not conspicuous, not out in the open like two idiotic trekkers without the right gear.

Within moments, cars whip by. Dark sedans followed by marked police cars. They have lights and noise set to nothing. Their speed, all in unison, all barely holding the road on bumps. They fly past, the noise of approach and departure the Doppler effect gone mad. Raucous looks to the sky and two helicopters drift by. We watch them and the cars all going, all heading to where we came from.

"We don't need to make any calls," Raucous says. "Someone already has."

"You think it was the van last night?"

"If that's what you want to believe, then go with it. Good an explanation as any. Whatever it is, we are out."

"I don't feel like walking back to London."

"The closest car and I'll steal it."

"Still have those skills?" I ask.

"Only if the car is old. The new ones are all computer and too tricky."

"You remember when-"

"I remember," he says. "I remember everything."

RAUCOUS

I don't want to, but I need to.

We walked too far. We are tired, and I don't want anymore.

We hear it long before we see it. Drunk voices travel fast. A country pub, attached to a village. Not much more than a hamlet, and not nearly big enough to accommodate all the cars. A function of sorts, not a wedding. A birthday maybe. Someone popular. This many people and this quality of car, don't turn up for a nobody.

My birthday left me alone. They always do. I never celebrate, why would I? Another year, Raucous. Another one gone and still you have nothing.

It's early, and the cars keep coming. We watch, looking for the one that fits. It takes a while. A diddy woman, in a small, crappy car. No power to it, certainly no more than 1000 cc. a few dents in the burgundy paint, and the MOT isn't going to be passed.

She parks away from the pub because there is no space near. A small road, already filled with other cars. She rushes, fumbles with her keys. She is wearing a shapeless, flowery gown, and carrying a shoulder bag. She also carries a larger bag, but she opens the boot and puts it inside. If we are lucky, and I can still boost cars with ease, we have a couple of hours before the alarm is raised. Probably more. People are going to be here for a long time.

We watch and wait as she might double back for something. We wait ten minutes and she doesn't reappear. I go to work. It's easy, and I hate myself for doing it, but she was the obvious target just like she will be at the party.

The car is old enough to be classic, but young enough to be normal. We drive out slowly, stopping, a few miles from the village.

I get out and pop the boot. I grab the bag and get back in the car. I hand the bag to Charlotte.

"See if there's money," I say.

There is, sixty pounds in twenties.

"Back up supply," Charlotte says. "She'll be ok."

"No, she won't. Not ever if she doesn't change. But we come first right now."

CHARLOTTE

We drive, not stopping, not eating. Too many cameras at service stations, and too many people. Under the radar is what we want. Raucous has the radio on, looking for news, looking for information. He doesn't pull over when the news breaks, but he slows, like everyone on the road, and listens while moving forward.

They speak in hyperbole of success and capture and strength. They don't say they failed, that the atrocity could have been stopped. They speak of triumph and how they had put an end to it all. The reporter speaks of a co-ordinated raid. They describe the farm and the buildings, they describe the set-up and how twenty-three men were captured. They speak of their origins, of where they were born of how they were in no way British. They speak of how the farm housed a terrorist cell of incredible sophistication. They speak of British bravery and foreign stupidity. They talk like we live in an all-conquering Victorian age of National invincibility. We are one as a nation, united against a common enemy.

The details worked, but were limited. I filled gaps with my knowledge and hope. Twenty-three men, I couldn't remember how many I saw, couldn't pick their faces out from any crowd. I wondered how they knew, what mistakes they made, whether Siri escaped, and was on the run. Twenty-three men. The farm gone, the game over.

I am lost in thought, my own mini-triumph. I turn to Raucous, his face showing nothing but thought. No happiness, no smile. He stares ahead, watching the road, but on auto-pilot, his brain working over-time.

"You don't seem relieved," I say.

He doesn't answer, he drives, watching the road, looking ahead. He continues for minutes. We start to see signs for where we want to go.

"They weren't that stupid," he says. "They weren't stupid at all."

RAUCOUS

I drive slowly and within the law. Always indicate and always give way. An extra ten seconds gained through a risk on a road is not worth a thing. Slow and steady. We wind through roads, ones I know. I'm heading home but cautious. There are always things you need, and always things you want. If my flat burned, I know what I'd want to keep. It wouldn't be obvious to most because they haven't lived my life, they didn't know who brought me up and how it was done. Memories are fine but objects hold it all.

I drive slowly, turning into my street. There is minimal traffic and no one walking. I have to ditch the car, but we are in London now. So many places to leave and so many more cars to steal. A paradise for so many people, no more than a crook. I see a space up ahead, big enough to drive into without reversing. We are moving slow, I start to press the indicator when I see.

"Shit," I say.

Charlotte looks at me. "What?" she asks.

"Two guys in the blue Ford."

"Where?"

"Don't look but we passed them," I say.

"Who are they?"

"I don't know, but they are watching my flat."

"You can't know that."

"I know. They were looking at the entrance."

"Did they see us?"

"We'll know if they follow," I say.

"You're sure?"

"The dash had four coffee cups. They fall off if you drive. Two men, two cups each. They've been there a while. No reason to sit and wait for any other people other than us."

"They know we are alive?"

"They want to make sure there's no one else."

"Police?"

"I doubt it. The police are not that dumb."

CHARLOTTE

Raucous drives nice and slow, an eye on the rear view as I watch behind on the wing mirror.

The car doesn't follow, no one does. Raucous drives like he knows where he is going. He joins a queue of cars, he indicates left and slides into the parking area of a rundown shopping court.

He drives left, moving toward an auto-centre advertising cheap MOTs on orange signs. He pulls into a space as close as he can find. Cars of all ages and types parked in a row. Pretty smart, what we have will look like a car waiting to be fixed.

We get out and Raucous leads me down the side of the auto-centre, around the back to a loading bay, he walks toward the green hedge that looms large and provides a barrier to the road on the other side. There is a small break in the green where lazy people have walked a shortcut. We slip through, the branches scratching at my sleeves. Raucous leads me right, and we are walking next to a red cycle path.

"Do you have anywhere to stay?" he asks. "Because I have one place and that is currently done."

*

We find a café and spend some of the sixty pounds. The woman returning to a car that had gone. I feel a moment of guilt, but it drifts away quickly.

"We have nothing," Raucous says. "And no way of getting anything."

"Wait it out?"

"Wait what out?" he asks.

He takes some of the money from the table. "The same?" he asks.

I nod agreement. I have a solution, an idea at escape, but nothing concrete. I don't know if it exists, if the bolt-hole survived or was lost in time. Nothing makes sense and old security is not what it once was.

I drift away thinking about times I loved, with a man I loved, in a place I knew nothing about. It all feels a long time ago, and it is, I guess in terms of years. Three now, or maybe more. But three years, I don't know if that is an age or a brief step back. I think of Michael and how he would see me, how he would react. He would trust Raucous, as much as Michael could trust. Childhood bonds are difficult to break for reasons that make no sense.

I think of those times, younger us, dangerous us, the lack of fear and the belief in who we were. Michael smarter than anyone, seeing everything at once. Knowing what others do, putting random acts into comprehensive patterns and predicting moves. Always ahead, always smiling, seeing where anyone was going. Raucous the angry young man, smiling with a person who understood and never judged. Maybe Michael needed the muscle, maybe Michael never cared, only used. But I can't believe that as it makes me question everything about us. A trophy wife in a cabinet, brought out to boost an ego.

I snap out of my head, Raucous hasn't returned. I look around to see where, expecting him to have bolted with the money. He is standing, holding two cups of coffee, staring up at an angle. I follow his gaze and he is watching the silent TV hanging down from the ceiling. A news reporter talking about terrorism, the tape at the bottom of the screen looping information and facts about the day and year's top story. Terrorism on the UK's shores. There is footage of the farm, I recognise the buildings and layout. I see where we ran, where we jumped in a van, where wheels left marks in the grass.

Raucous watches, almost waiting for something to appear. A gallery of faces, names flash by, footage of capture. I can't see detail from this far, but Raucous stares and doesn't move. But no one does, the other nine people in the café stare too. The names and faces mean nothing to anyone. But we all stare the same as if being given the meaning of life.

I stand and walk to Raucous. I want to see the TV clearly too. The faces vanish as I walk the couple of metres, Raucous still stares ahead but his focus seems on the inside of his mind rather than the screen.

"This is going to run for a long time," I say.

"You sound proud," he says. "Did you see the faces?"

"Only when I was there. Couldn't see the screen too well."

"Wait, they'll come up again. They keep looping the same thing as if this is important."

"Why? It's over. They have them."

Raucous turns to me. "I didn't recognise a single one of them," he says. "Not one face."

I start to speak. He cuts me dead.

"Don't give me the whole, they look alike, you didn't see them well, nonsense. Not one of those faces were there when we were."

"So what?"

"This isn't right. This just isn't right."

RAUCOUS

I don't recognise anyone. I saw faces, talked and sat among them. I recognise no one. I am not going mad, not mentally disintegrating. Not. A. Single. Face.

We sit and talk, I interact and speak but nothing is right. I feel it rising, I know it is coming, the rush the need the desire to do. Rationalise and then forget, know what is wrong but do it the same. An addict's rush to do what they know will hurt.

"It doesn't add up," I say.

Charlotte looks at me.

"We can't do it," she says.

Futility in the attempt, by I try all the same. I see it in her, she doesn't hide. She'd love to talk herself down, the conversation is happening in her head, the same as it is in mine. A back and forth of bullshit, a false debate believing in reason when the answer, the outcome is certain and decided.

Charlotte understands and knows. The consequences are real and obvious. Talk and we die, our death revealed as fake and people come to see, to speak and to kill.

"Why are we back here?" she asks.

"Because it is where we are from. It is all we know."

"People will see us, people know."

I turn to her, the TV showing the same.

"Where do you suggest?" I ask. "We have nothing. My flat watched, yours, I presume is the same. They were Scully's men. No doubt in that. Waiting for someone or something."

"Us?"

"I don't think so. Watching the house for someone, anyone to come by."

"But why?"

151

"Information, the recording? Anything. Loose ends. They know it is just us, but they don't like coincidence. Nothing left to chance. They'll watch for a long time. And I imagine my place is shredded. Taken apart piece by piece. Destroyed."

She places her left hand on my right upper arm.

"I'm sorry," she says.

I inhale through my nose.

"No one's fault but my own," I say. "Your place, wherever that may have been is done too. They know where you were."

"I rented a small place. Hotels at first."

"On your passport?"

"On one Michael gave me."

I nod. Michael knew and was good.

"So we have nothing, and are where we should be. Any suggestions welcome."

"We need to tell the police."

"We don't know who is safe. We need to vanish, we need money, and we need to regroup and go. I can break in somewhere and hope for the result to be a big score. I can boost a car and sell it. But it puts me being alive out there."

We are talking too much and people listen. Information for cash is something we don't want.

"There is my old house," she says. "But Michael told me never to go back, not even in an emergency. It wouldn't be safe, he said. Not safe at all."

"Why not?"

"Michael didn't go for explaining. He just stated fact."

"What's there?"

"I don't know. There used to be a safe with a stash. There used to be jewellery. There used to be a lot. It has never been sold, bills paid from an account automatically. It is there. Unused."

"In the country?"

"Here."

I inhale, an old house that isn't a home anymore. A place she was told never to return. We have nothing else.

"We've been killed once already," I say. "We can look."

152

CHARLOTTE

The street is dark, lampposts glistening, no smog nor fog, just cold. My house, where I lived for years as a married woman without a care because I never thought about what my husband did. Here I am, back on a street of handy wealth but not filthy rich. Victorian houses turned to apartments, and we owned the ground and first floor. We bought it long in the past when prices were high but not killer. To sell it now would be a profit of eye-watering magnitude. But what would we buy with the money? Something similar for a similar price. It was no investment it was a quiet home. We were in the well-to-do, leafy suburbs with semi-safe streets away from the workers and where we grew up, but a five-minute walk back into our roots.

"It's not right," Raucous says.

He grabs my right upper arm gently.

The street is long, and curved, the end not in sight because the semi-circle styling takes houses around a slow corner. Cars line each side, and they are all of a high quality. An occasional Camper breaks the monotony, but the wealth is on display.

"Which one?" he asks.

"Thirty eight."

"Can we see it?"

"Not from here."

It is dark enough for us to seem a couple walking home. We don't break stride, but we slow.

"It isn't right," he says. "That van, the white one, the blue writing on the side. That doesn't belong."

I look and see and the van is tall, an extra section placed on top as if required for a removal company. The writing says Jones and son. The business less clear.

"How close to that van is thirty eight?"

"Two or three houses away."

"Same side?"

"Opposite."

Raucous stops and holds me enough to halt my stride. He turns me to him like we have just reached a magical moment, he leans forward and I am sure he is going to try for a kiss.

"I know you haven't lived here for a while, but you ever see something like that round here before?"

I think and I don't remember, I have no memory of Jones and son.

"Never," I say.

"So someone with a van has moved in here, right opposite your house in the last whatever amount of time."

"It happens," I say.

"Not this year it doesn't."

RAUCOUS

I walked us away. I don't like vans parked near anywhere, especially near my destination. I don't like vans. Charlotte doesn't know it and whatever business it might be, they don't make enough money to live here. Maybe they are working inside a property, but it is too late and too dark and the wrong day to be doing business.

"Where is the key?" I ask.

"Under the third plant pot on the left."

"Obviously."

"There's a brick patio, the brick lifts up and the key is under that."

"Better than average," I say.

"Not a good idea to go in," she says

I smile.

"No, but I'd like to find out who is watching."

CHARLOTTE

It takes two minutes for Raucous to find what he is looking for. A group of youths, teenagers or older, I can't tell. Young enough to be young and out and wasting time. Eleven of them. Eight boys. He approaches easy and calm, and they stand to attention. Raucous is big, but they have numbers and almost certainly knives.

"How are you at breaking and entering?" Raucous asks.

The question brings the leader to the fore. Smaller than the rest, but wide, blue eyes that sparkle.

Raucous is told to leave with profanity and gestures.

Raucous rides the insults out with a smile.

"I'm here because I need help," he says.

"You some type of nonce?" the leader asks.

They stare at each other, Raucous tall, wide and imposing. Not moving, but not tense.

"There's money in it," he says. "Or valuables at least. If you want the chance, it is yours, if you don't I'll walk away. Find some other group."

"You can pay for sex somewhere else," the leader says.

"I need someone to walk to a house, pick up the key, go in, stay for five minutes then come out again. When you come out, you can bring the most expensive thing you find in there with you. TV, jewels, whatever you find."

The leader squints, he doesn't want to be fooled.

"What makes you think I won't come out with a lot of whatever I want."

"The fact I'll chase you down and hurt you. But the deal is there. Walk to a house not far from here. Let yourself in. Wait and then come out. Simple really."

"What's the catch?"

"Someone might try and stop you."

"And if they do?"

"You'll have the key and you can come back later. Or as a group you can walk right through them. An easy score either way."

The leader looks back at the other ten. No democracy but he needs to judge opinion.

"Someone?" he asks. "And what stops this someone getting one of us."

"I'm no tactical genius, but if say three of you go, then that's three against whoever might turn up and three times what you can bring out. But obviously if you can't do that, not a problem. I'll find someone else to do it."

The leader looks back, four nods that I see.

"What road?" he asks.

"Longdale."

The smile appears like it should.

"Lot of money on that street."

"You might even find car keys."

"Why?"

"I don't want nor need the house. I need something inside. And I don't want anyone knowing I've been there."

"Bullshit," the boy says.

"If you don't want it. Not a problem. Really expensive house. Lot of stuff inside that would sell easy, and high."

I'm making a guess these kids want easy money. The leader is ballsy, which helps. A show-off is easy to manipulate. A group who want the money without the risk is a persuasive voice to a boy who wants the bragging rights.

"Explain the set-up," the boy says.

Raucous talks.

RAUCOUS

We watch the boy and two of his friends walk the street toward thirty-eight. I have us sit on a wall in front of a house. There are small knobs of metal, where once a fence stood until the second world-war took them away. We are far from the house, a hundred metres, but close enough to see.

"If they run the other way when they come out?" Charlotte asks.

"Doesn't matter. This house is compromised. It is not somewhere we can stay, we need the money inside and we need to get away. That isn't your house anymore. Hasn't been for a long time."

We watch, from a spot that is dark. The street lights don't cover the area perfectly. The three walk cautiously, speaking, about what I can't hear. They look at numbers and check out houses, they find thirty-eight and walk the steps, all three look for the key.

I can't see clearly, but they must be moving the pot, and they find the key. They shuffle to the front door and try the lock. It works and they push the door open. The first steps inside, the second and third follow. The door closes and we wait.

I don't know what I am expecting but it isn't this.

I check my watch, minutes pass. Five minutes go. Then ten.

"We should go and see," Charlotte says.

"No, something is wrong."

"They are trashing the place looking for anything to sell."

"No lights came on," I say. "Looks like nothing is happening in there at all."

We wait and watch. Thirty minutes moves to forty. I have no plan beyond waiting. The three don't know we are here, don't know we are watching. We would meet back at the park was the plan I told them. They don't know where we are. They can't.

Charlotte starts to shiver, I place my arm around her. She doesn't move or push me away. We look like a couple, a stupid couple in the cold air. We can see our breath as we exhale out of time. We don't speak, we hold like we have known each other for ever. A comfortable silence, of small shivers and a painful wait.

The front door opens and we are too cold to react. We turn slowly, squinting at the door, looking for our way in.

CHARLOTTE

The door opens and I expect them to be carrying large objects. My TV, tables, anything they believe of value. They come out one by one, but they don't bounce. They are each separated by another man, each of them with their hands bound behind their backs. Their youthful faces battered, and the smile gone. They look nowhere but to their shoes.

They are marched across the road to the van. The side door opens and they are pushed inside. My attention returns to the front door. It is open, no one has locked it. A figure steps out, in no rush, he looks up and down the street. He looks my way, his scanning stops and he stares. I want to stand and run, to move. Raucous senses and he holds me tight, more than affection, a hold, a stay calm and don't move.

"He can't see us," Raucous says. "We are just a blur. We are in the dark, he is in the light. He knows there are people here, but he can't know who. We're dead."

"We just sit and wait?"

157

"For the best. They will be gone, and then we can walk and figure what to do next. That house is dead to us. They will leave someone inside, or someone to watch. We need another plan."

We watch him walk slowly down the steps and into the road. We watch him walk to the van and speak. We watch the van drive away. We watch him enter a black sedan and sit and wait, the car facing us. The lights ignite, the engine starts. The car pulls out and heads our way.

"Shit," Raucous says.

The car moves slow, but it can do nothing more as the limit is twenty. We are trapped and the headlights illuminate the street.

"Go on," I say.

Raucous looks at me.

"You know as well as I do,"

Raucous smiles, like a little boy. Cheekiness that only teenagers possess.

He leans in, covering me completely with his size, his back. I hide, my body in his large frame, his back a huge slab. We push our faces together, Raucous as nervous as the teenager he has become. We kiss, no tongues, a movie kiss for an audience of one.

We hear the car move past, the lights on us then not. We kiss, like James Bond hiding in a chase. The car doesn't slow nor stop, it rolls on by. Our lips pressed together but like we have never heard of tongues.

We wait, we hear nothing new. We unlock our faces and embrace, we look at each other. We know what we saw, we know who drove by. We have no idea what it means other than danger.

"That was Siri," Raucous says.

"And if he is free, what does that mean?"

RAUCOUS

She explains that it is a dumb move. Michael told her, made her promise, and that is that. Michael dealt in absolutes. It is a bad idea to go against his advice.

"He told me to forget about it, to not go back. Anywhere. And he was right," Charlotte says.

"It is a safe house, they had your place watched. They won't know everywhere."

I'm talking but fooling no one. Desperation and a need to find shelter.

"Michael said avoid them all."

"But who knows about this one?"

"Michael, me and whoever Michael told. I told no one. Why would I?"

I know it is dumb, I know we should walk on but we have nowhere to go. We have no more chances. Siri is about, and staking houses. We need an escape and we need it quick.

"We have to try," I say. "Otherwise we are on the streets."

I can see she wants to accept, we have nothing. No money, no place and no clothes. It is dark, and they have taken away our two places to live. We need something.

"If they have it watched, they'll be easy to spot," I say. "We've seen it both times. They are not being subtle. They are waiting for someone who isn't us. We are dead. Remember that. Mine was watched by Scully's men. Yours by the police. Two different groups, two different reasons."

"Michael told me never to return."

"He told you never to come back to the UK. He told you a lot of things. We have very few options."

As we walked away from her old house, as we thought about Siri being there and the three boys who had seen and spoken to us, she tells me about the safe house. Their old place, a storage of sorts, an escape, a way to have time and space to themselves. For them a private oasis. She thinks only they knew, but it would be stupid to think such things. Michael had told her never to return. He never explained why, nor said it was dangerous. He told her never to go back, the place was nothing anymore. Never go back.

"Could be for any reason," I say.

"It would be for the right reasons."

"We have nothing left. No options."

CHARLOTTE

It won't work out, it is pretty certain, another place to go and see, and leave disappointed. Maybe Raucous is right, maybe we have to try as we have nothing. Two dead people walking with no recourse to supply or survival. I want this to work out, I need this to be true. But I know, deep inside, that we are wasting more time. We have nothing other to do, a long shot with risk is better than a high street doorway and the cold of night. Maybe we used up all our luck in the back of a van with plastic ties. Maybe we are dead and this is just ghosts walking through a city that can't see us. Nothing makes sense.

We walk a street, I grab his hand, we interlock fingers, a disguise of sorts.

"This is the street," I say.

Leafy, green, trees not stained as dark as others, a low traffic area for the pretty damn rich.

"Which one?" Raucous asks.

"The one opposite the tree that leans across the road."

I look and see, a tree not quite falling but a few storms short of collapse. It has been there a long time, and we are on no type of bus route. The tree would never survive. The street lights illuminate as they should. It is dark in many recesses and corners, but light enough to see. I spot nothing suspicious, no cars out of place, nothing unusual, no one in the front of their cars drinking coffee and watching.

I look at all the houses as we pass, curtains closed, people locked inside. I watch the first and second floors as this is where the best viewpoint lies. No movement, no light, no face peering. We walk. The leaning tree opposite us now, he squeezes my hand. I glance at the front door, large and black and still. The lights off, the flanking windows dark with shutters drawn. I don't stop walking, pulling Raucous forward, like we have somewhere else to go.

"We get in from the back," I say.

RAUCOUS

I smile like she's told me she loves me. There's a whole load of the younger me that wishes she has.

Here I am walking with her to the secret hideaway her and Michael had.

I went away for him. A guilt he never acknowledged. He would have died had I not killed them. I would do it again.

Drunk men fighting over nothing. An offense at physical contact. A scuffle, knives produced, and I made sure they died and not us. I took the fall because I committed the act. I killed the men. They brought the knives. They wanted to hurt, not us. But the video showed me with my anger exposed. I couldn't take the insult and I couldn't walk away. Michael was there, but no fighter. He wouldn't run either. But I stood up, I walked forward, I was the one that drove the knives in. Michael watched.

I stood up in court and told everyone Michael had tried to stop me. I had refused to listen. He had wanted peace.

They believed me because Michael spoke too. He told them the same story. Some was true but most was lies.

I went down and he made great. It is the way it is. There was no need for two punishments. He looked after me, as much as he could. But when you want no help, there is nothing he could do.

Here I am now, Michael dead, Charlotte in my life and me too far gone to do anything different from the moment I was sent down.

I look at Charlotte, and I know I made the right choice.

CHARLOTTE

We walked to the end of the road, turned right, half way down the street there was an alleyway. I turned into the dark, unlit lane, pulling Raucous with me. I can see little, only the long grass either side of the worn mud path that runs down the centre. A dark alley no one should enter.

"I didn't see anything, anywhere. Nothing suspicious," he says.

I believe this, but I know he wants this to be true, needs it even. This is the last shot before we truly have nothing but us and criminal acts to get us through.

"The back door is about fifty metres down here. Back yard and back door. The key under the third pot plant if the place is still mine."

"There was no activity out front," he says. "We'll have a look from here."

We walk the small path, stumbling occasionally, hearing animals always. We get to the back gate, a solid wooden door as tall as Raucous, and the height of the wall. We have no idea what is on the other side. I hope for what I know, an empty paved area with steps up to the back door. An easy route into an easy source of cash. A safe house with a safe and an emergency fund for an emergency that I had never seen.

I push the gate after lifting the latch. It creaks because it always has. I push the door slowly and it scrapes leaves along the ground. There is no security light, there had been but hedgehogs, cats and foxes set it off on a continual loop. It went. We step in and the darkness remains.

Raucous pushes the back gate closed, the same creaks, nothing in reverse. The moon and residual streetlight gives enough for me to see the yard. It is as I left it, the paving slabs not as clean nor bright. The steps up to the back door are clean of debris, but not sparkling, not used. I walk trying to make no sound. I take the steps and see the plant pots, the plants, not dead, but not what was originally there. Weeds I guess, but maybe the winter debris of something summer beautiful. Three pots in a row. The third I lift, it is heavy, and the sound of porcelain on tile makes me wince. There is a clear circle of different colour where the pot had stood. There is a small tile in its dead centre. I place my fingers along its edge, digging my nails down the side, looking for traction and grip. I ease up the tile and it moves and tilts and I pull it free. The key is there, the door looks the same. It will fit. But it doesn't mean it is still mine.

"There's an alarm," I say.
"You know the code?"
"Always the same code. Every place we had."
"Birthday?"

162

"Random, but always the same unconnected numbers."

"Where's the box to switch it off?"

"Two metres from the door, in the kitchen."

"We go in, if the key works, get to the alarm. If it doesn't stop on the first attempt, we get out quick. Down the steps, out the gate and keep walking."

I nod, but I don't know if he sees me.

The key slides in, I turn and the door pops open. The smell of the kitchen says the place is empty. A dullness to the air. Stale. But I can't be sure. The beeps of the alarm distract me. I walk to the box, pull down the protective flap, and punch in the six-figure sequence. The beeping stops and we wait, holding our breath.

"How long would it take for security to arrive?" Raucous asks.

"Minutes," I say.

We stand, still, waiting, Raucous looking at the clock in the kitchen. A redundant exercise as it has stopped. Maybe he is counting. I'm not. We wait and nothing happens.

"We need to check the house," I say. "Just in case."

"Together," he says. "I have no idea of the layout."

We walk, room to room, neither of us switching on lights, or straying too close to windows. The curtains are all closed, our eyes adapted to darkness. There could be figures hiding, we would never see, but why would they? We are here to be caught.

"Are the recordings here?" Raucous asks.

"No," I say. "There's nothing here but cash and valuables."

We walk past the front door. No post, only flyers and promotional letters addressed to the homeowner. The rooms upstairs and down, are empty. We find no one, and no sign of a new occupant. A house left to rot for a few years, and no one bothering to look because it is owned and the bills come out of an account that would take ten years to run dry.

The safe is as all safe's should be, located behind an oil painting in the front room. I turn on a lamp, the light low. I hope the curtains block out everything.

I see the dial and enter the numbers, the same figures as the house alarm, but in reverse. The safe opens to reveal the cash. Bundles of twenties adding up to a whole lot of money. Four thousand is my guess, maybe a little more. A lot to spend in town, not enough to live off for a year. There is jewellery too, the value depending on the buyer. Retail price dwarves the cash, but the hassle of getting it sold.

Raucous nods his head. A result.

"Do we stay?" he asks.

"Hotels ask for ID and video clients. Walking streets at this time is just asking to be stopped. Siri is at large. This place isn't watched. I think we should stay. Keep it low-key."

He nods, it is best. We are tired, we need to rest.

"I'll lock the back door," he says.

"Keep the lights off, curtains closed. I'll take the main bedroom."

"I'll take the sofa."

"There are five bedrooms, Raucous."

"The sofa is mine," he says.

I understand. Still not at ease, near the safe, not wanting me to run. Instincts he has. Nothing malicious. Why trust me? He has no reason at all. He is here because of me. We know this.

"Goodnight, Raucous. You going to sleep?"

"Eventually. I need to."

RAUCOUS

I sleep well, but wake quickly. No Sunday morning crawl from a comatose state. I'm on the sofa, the room dark, but there is light from the cracks around the curtains. I hear nothing, but something woke me. I sit up and the blanket I found slips to the floor. I look up and Charlotte is standing, waiting.

"I usually wake quicker," I say.

"Me too. It's ten. I've only been up thirty minutes."

She looks at me, I imagine what she sees. Nothing pretty, nothing she would want.

"We need a plan, Raucous," she says.

I sit up and rub my face. I want cold water.

"Sell the jewellery and move on. We aren't safe here, outside. The country is on edge, your place watched, my place gone. They are waiting for something. They must know we are alive."

164

"I don't think so. They are waiting for someone to lead them to the tapes," she says "That's all. A loose end they never knew existed. They want it."

"They'll be making their escape too."

"They aren't," she says. "Siri about, Christoph not on TV. It doesn't add up and what we know isn't enough to make conclusions. They are free, walking around and we are in a place where we are known. This place was a bit of luck. But we don't have much to stretch. A mile from here is my home and I'm known. I don't want to be chased down, I don't want them to believe I am alive. Being dead is just fine."

"We need money."

"We?"

"I don't know how far we'll get before we part, but right now it is we."

I smile because I want the We to be forever. It won't be, I'm too old to believe in miracles, but the temporary sentiment is a boost to an ego that long since shattered. We know we need to raise money, we are in limbo. Stuck in a house that gives us nothing but a wall to hide behind.

"You can't walk into a place and just sell that stuff," I say. "You need ID, you'll be filmed, signed for."

"You know people, Raucous."

"Not safe people. Not people who will pay the price you deserve."

"The jewellery is all we have, and any price is good."

We talk, I explain. We agree I can't go. Charlotte is unknown to most, certainly the lower levels. She looks different, she can hide. There is nothing suspicious about sunglasses and hat on a woman trying to offload dodgy gold. I explain the routine, the place and the means. I explain how she needs to get a price. She shuts me down. She isn't dumb. I agree, she isn't. But I fear for her, I know why.

She leaves with the jewels but leaves the money. A sign of trust and faith. Probably four thousand pounds in an open safe. I'm going nowhere. It's like the old days. No way of communicating, no phones just a goodbye and a belief that she'll return on time.

CHARLOTTE

I walk to the bus stop and follow the instructions. I wait for
the bus with others. Old, young and no smiles. The drizzle in the air
and the greyness of sky can't hide the fear in people. Everyone
watching others. Everyone looking to the floor but looking for a
way to observe behaviour. The conversations I hear are about terror
and bombs and Birmingham. The country in fear, but they have
been caught. The group responsible have been caught. The fear
remains. People on edge, wanting to feel safe.

The bus stops and I get off with the two other people. They
are together but have tension. A young couple with issues. I walk to
the street Raucous named. I know it from childhood, I know the
reputation. It is different from then, but only in small details. The
fashions have changed, the store fronts have unfamiliar colours,
selling different goods but the black buildings and drudgery remain.
I remember being here thirty years ago, messing around, Raucous
with us, our friend and bodyguard. A big lad with an attitude.
Walking and talking and being young.

The store front is a model shop. The shelves filled with
remote control cars and drones and kits. They are overpriced and no
competition at all for sales online. A shop only an idiot would think
to enter.

I push the door open and the historical ring of a tiny bell
sounds out to announce my presence.

RAUCOUS

I wait, thinking about what she is doing. I think about the
four thousand pounds and the insignificant amount it would be.

I should have gone but I'm known. I don't know if word of
my demise is now a general fact. No one would lament because no
one ever gets close. I'm someone they knew but not someone they
love. Being dead, having a chance to start over is something I
should embrace. But she needs protection. A second body to look
out. She is smart and tough, taking Merrick showed that, but we're
beaten up and needing to get out. Haste and panic lead to mistakes
and pain. Take everything slow, take everything calm.

I walk the house, the curtains closed, looking in rooms and looking at art. The taste isn't mine, too old, too classic, too dark. It's an old man's house of antiques and age. Dark wood and carved shapes, a house in which a whodunit is set.

To have a life with this as an escape. Michael, with his mystery. An open man who spoke his mind but only when required. Smartest man I ever met. They killed him, and I guess I know why. He was no snitch, but he was no terrorist. Scully's man, the consigliere of old mafia films. The smartest man in any room, a reader of people, a man who knew. They killed him, and Charlotte had a revenge, got something that grated out of her system. But we lost too. Our home, our childhood, our lives are now away from the place we are. We paid a price.

My home, that of my grandmother before me, the place I grew up is now sat empty and watched. The guys were Scully's, I know that. One glance is all it took. Scully staking out my flat makes no sense. But he is a cautious man, loose ends are what will kill you. He needs to know if anyone else comes and sees. He will be searching for that holy grail of recorded leverage. A tape to have an insurance against Christoph just in case, just to bargain for your life.

Christoph is not going to walk away with a local gangster knowing the insides of a terrorist operation. Scully isn't dumb but he's been caught here. The mechanism, the reason, the desire I cannot explain. He is in, and he is never coming out. He has a shelf-life for these people, and it has all but expired. He doesn't need Michael to tell him this. He will have worked that out himself.

There are too many variables and too many unknowns. Terrorists and police and local hoodlums all in unison, all blowing up Birmingham for a reason no one explained. Scully destroying his place or origin for cash, because it can only be money.

I am back in the room in which I slept. The safe open, the money on view. I sit on the sofa, I lean back and I wait, ruminating on the past few days. I'm smarter than most believe, but I'm not Michael, those gaps in knowledge, the illogical progression of events won't gel together into a coherent whole because I cannot make the leaps of intellectual imagination to smooth out bumps and fill information gaps.

Running away, hiding and being someone I am not, is the only way to go.

CHARLOTTE

A middle-aged man who has spent a lifetime indoors walks from the back of the shop. I know his name and the description is right. Raucous described him perfectly. A skinny man with the gut of a drinker. The pale, pallid skin of a man who sits in an office all day under artificial light. His name is Peter. He is connected to Scully, operating under the man's permission. The cut paid, and the police kept away. An illegal operation that works because Scully is a man of respect.

"I have something to sell. Cash. Nothing traceable and not quite legal," I say.

Raucous told me there was no password, no secret way to approach. Open and honest. You say, you show and then you haggle. The official price, the one at high-street pawn, is higher than here. But that's why they exist. Some people just can't take that risk.

"What are you talking about?" Peter says.

I place the carrier bag on the table. A supermarket name stamped in blue over the white plastic. The red handles slowly collapsing open. Peter looks inside. He smiles at what he sees. It is a large score of necklaces, gold and jewels.

"This. I need a price, a good one. Cash and then I'm gone."

"The shop you are looking for is further down the road. Big sign outside telling you the price you get per kilo."

"I can't do that, which is why I'm here. A price, an agreement and an exchange. Easy."

Peter opens the plastic bag further. He uses a biro to push the bag open. No fingerprints left.

"I'm no expert," he says. "But it looks valuable. The shop down the road will pay big money for this. Looks to be thousands worth of decent ornaments."

"How many thousands do you think?"

Peter smiles again but his eyes are always into the bag.

"I'd say a couple of thousand."

"You really are no expert," I say. "Anyone with a little expertise would see there's a retail value of two-hundred-thousand at least in that bag."

"Seems like you know more than me," he says. "I wouldn't have that type of money."

"Not even in the safe out back? The one fixed into the floor? The one with all the cash and jewels?"

Peter's eyes are on me. They should be. I shouldn't know this.

"Who are you?" he asks.

"A customer. Someone whose husband is not coming back and someone who has limited assets and limited cash and needs to raise funds fast. Someone who knows that this isn't the only place to do business, but came here first because it is where I want to do business. I could pack up and walk two miles to the computer shop on Morecombe Street. Not the place I want to go, but I know the way all the same."

Peter rubs his chin, clean shaven, an effort made.

"What makes you think I'd let you leave?"

"The fact that if you try and stop me, I'll shoot you in the face."

I lift my shirt to show the gun. He smiles but his bravado is fake and the worry settles.

"We are on film," he says.

"And I'm wearing a hat, a wig and sunglasses. I also know the recording equipment is in your office out back. I also know I'd walk over your dead body and take the recording."

"It is automatically sent to a server," he says.

"No, it isn't. It is saved on a hard disc. One which I would take. Are we doing business or threats?" I say.

"How do you know this?"

"Because this is big business and I am not taking more risks than I need to," I say.

"I'll need to weigh it, need to check it. You will get more money officially. Stolen?"

"Not stolen. I don't think it actually exists."

"I'll have to break it down all the same. Minimise risks. That lowers the price."

"Check, be quick and make an offer. I know the value-"

169

He tries to speak but I know his point and I hold up my hand.

"I know the real value, I know the retail value and I know how much it is worth to you. We both need to make money and Scully needs to be paid. I'm not here blind nor dumb. Do your work, make your offer, and I walk away."

Peter pauses, thinks, he can't resist. This is a big score, but if Raucous is right, and he has been so far, the safe out back holds two-hundred-and-fifty-thousand in cash. A safety net for occasions like today. Dirty cash that can be laundered here, and nice pieces of gold and stones to be sold wherever the demand is best.

Peter knows his stuff, he checks the stones, he weighs the gold, he makes noises and talks to himself about numbers and quality. I watch, the routine precise and fun. He follows a script but tries for the world to ad-lib.

He puts everything back into the bag. He thinks even though he has long since thought of a price.

"Seventy-five thousand," he says.

He has to try, I guess. I inhale deeply.

"I don't have time to play, Peter," I say.

He flashes a look at me. He has never told me his name.

"I don't know your name," he says.

"You don't need to. But you do need to give me the right price. I don't have the patience for a pointless haggle. You know the worth as well as I. Make the correct offer, which is 100,00, and we are done."

He pushes his right palm across his scalp. I'm clearly torturing the man with unreasonable demands.

"I can't go that high," he says. "it just doesn't leave enough in it for me."

I grab the bag, smile and say, OK. I turn.

"Ninety thousand," he says. "Right now, in cash, and we are done."

"Ninety thousand from the two fifty you have out back?" I ask.

His face tells me he doesn't like that I have so much information. Raucous told me to be me, push it, don't be meek.

"Ninety-five," he says.

"You tell your boss that I wanted a hundred and ten. Then tell him you got me down to a hundred. Everyone is happy. You'll

170

double your money, maybe even more, might even triple. I told you my price, you know the worth, you know the killing you'll make. Someone else a mile away will see the deal as it is. Five thousand less won't save your face. A hundred. Yes or no?"

Peter smiles because his bluff is called. A hundred is too little, but I can't get much more. It is a deal that suits us both. He has to take it or watch a year of profit walk out the door.

"I need to call for confirmation."

"I don't have time. You call, I walk. Money and I'm gone. You know it is all genuine. You think it is hot. But it isn't. You can sell on as it is, and that's a lot of money. Or you can break it down and sell as you see fit with a smaller profit. Your choice. But you make it now."

"What's the catch I can't see?" he asks.

"There isn't one. You know I should get more than a hundred. You know you can sell for more than double that. And sure you might have to sit on it for a while and sell it off little by little, but you'll make your money fast enough. And it isn't your bankroll, is it?"

Peter nods. He rubs his face, and I know I'm walking out with the money.

"A hundred," he says.

I nod. He smiles again. Maybe he is thinking of skimming some gold. A hundred is too low for what is in the bag. He could take some himself and know the price he paid would be the right amount for twenty percent less.

"You don't have a bag for the money," he says.

"You do. A rucksack is fine. You not afraid I'm police?" I say.

"If you are it means my boss isn't as powerful as he was, and no police is walking in here with the gifts you carry."

"Your boss is still around?" I ask.

"He checks. He is around. He is very hands on."

"He'll be happy with this," I say.

RAUCOUS

I sit and think about a future. I idealise and fantasize like everyone does. A future with Charlotte. I'd need to get in shape. Hell, I'd need to be someone different. But I dream all the same.

She'll get the money and then we'll be gone. How long together. Her with a big oaf like me. As recognisable as any man. I think about my life. The wasted time, the prison years, my fights my beliefs the reason I went. Michael. I went down and he didn't. Maybe he fooled me, but I don't think he did. I came out and my life went as smooth as it could. Who I was got me my job. Michael made it happen, I'm not dumb. He gave me a path believing I am who I wanted them to think I was. We had no contact, he was a man I shouldn't be near. I heard of him because I worked for him.

He died, or was killed, before I was ready, before he was.

I heard the news. I sat in my cell and I didn't cry. I thought about him. I thought about her. Charlotte. I thought about wasted time and a life thrown away.

I came out.

I was in my grandmother's flat. I was a collector. I was me. No friends, no life, nothing. I was going till I met someone better or simply lucky, or someone sneaky. I was going until someone bettered me. It was coming soon, I wasn't making the effort to stay strong. I was making waves and causing hate. I see that, I know that.

My mind flies through a thousand memories and a million possible outcomes to events that already happened. I'm sat on a sofa. Lost, away from it all. I'm drowning in an emotion of self-pity and callous self-cruelty. I'm comfortable and feeling safe and I miss all the sounds and gut-feelings. I'm slow, tired and in a false sense of security. It happens before my eyes even open.

CHARLOTTE

I know I am being followed. I just sense it. Paranoia maybe, but the gut-feeling of someone's eyes. I walk with my rucksack full of cash. Raucous told me to walk to a shop, buy a new bag, transfer the cash and leave the old one to linger and rot in a bin or bush. It'll be tagged in some way. He didn't predict the tail.

I turn a corner and wait. My back against the wall, looking at the corner. The tail is no professional. A small man, wiry and old. Late forties but a smoker, so could be younger. He jogs round and sees me as I see him. He acts too late. The surprised jump reeled in too late.

"Why are you following me?" I ask.

He stutters and stumbles over words. He can't think. He is a low level man not ready to step up.

"I'm walking that way down the street, toward the supermarket. If you follow, I'll hurt you. If you don't give up, I'll shoot you. You get that?" I say.

The man nods.

"Good. Now you can stand and stare or turn and go. Up to you. I see you on the next street and you'll hobble home forever."

He stares at me, evil in his eyes. He wants to be a big man, but he is weak, under orders and smart enough to know he has no chance.

"No point with the stare and grin. Do something now or quit."

He does nothing.

"I thought so," I say. "Be seeing you."

I turn and walk. It seems a long way down the road but a hundred metres at most. I reach the corner and turn. The guy is where I left him. He is speaking into a mobile phone while he eyes me. A call to someone to tell them he is off the tail. Another man calling in the fact I beat him.

I'm cautious all the way back. I take streets I don't need, and loops that make no sense. I see no one more than once, and no one follows. I make sure, I am careful. I walk the lane at the back of the houses. I push through the gate and walk the steps. I relax, open the back door, and walk in. And I see. And I hear. And I don't know what to think.

RAUCOUS

Comfort kills. The easy life makes you dumb. It is fact, and I slid into lethargy like the giant gorilla I am. Sat lounging on a sofa waiting in comfort, dozing, feeling calm and dead.

The tap on my shoulder and I still don't react. Charlotte waking me from a golden slumber with cash and a way out.

"Raucous," I hear.

I smile, I actually smile like Charlotte is my newly-wed wife. I smile, all content and snug.

"Don't move. Turn around if you must. But just to look."

I know now. I hear the voice. The tap was hard and metallic. There is one person, I can sense and feel that much.

I turn my head, nice and slow. Quick movements are not needed. I see and smile the same. I don't do surprise, and never would show such.

"Charlotte isn't here," I say.

"No, but she will be soon. I'll speak to her then. Hear how you are still alive. You don't die easily, do you?"

"Going easy into the night just never did it for me."

"It won't be happening now. I promise you that."

"Then why the gun?"

"Because without it I don't believe you would extend me the same peace."

CHARLOTTE

I'm an idiot. I walked cautious and calm and alert. I shook a tail and walked my walk. I was free of it all. Cash in my hand and the jewels gone. An easy score. Then returning home like a content housewife to show the man what I had managed. Never safe and Michael said to never come back. Not here. Not ever.

"Charlotte," he says.

I look at the room. Raucous on the sofa, unable to move. The gun trained on the back of his head. The man in the middle, the man I didn't want to see, smiling a welcome and inviting me, with a gesture of his hand, to join Raucous on the antique couch.

"It hasn't been all that long, has it, Scully," I say.

174

"I could do nothing about your death. Nothing at all. Couldn't stop it."

"So you didn't try."

He blinks. He knows. An excuse is only ever that.

"Raucous knows there was nothing I could do," he says. "To interfere meant my death. There is no apology to make. I did nothing wrong."

I sit down on the sofa. Raucous watches me, his eyes say do nothing. He is calm, but then he always is. He is thinking, he is away from the room in his mind looking for something. There is no way to communicate, no touching, no tried and tested way of obtaining information. I would have touched Michael's knee. He would have known.

Scully sits down in front of us. He pulls at the seam of his expensive trousers. He has matching socks and real leather shoes. He looks tired but alert. His smile not quite the gleam of old.

"We don't have too much time," Scully says. "I'm guessing you have seen the news, the arrests, the farm?"

We nod.

"Good. I'm sure you have figured it all as bullshit."

Raucous leans forward. Scully raises his palm.

"Raucous, I'm not part of it," Scully says.

Raucous leans back. Tense but settled.

"You are in it all," I say. "You going to tell us it was you who called the police in?"

Scully looks at the floor and rubs his ears like he doesn't want the noise to enter. He looks up at me.

"That was part of their plan. I was needed for connections involving import. A slow build and a long con. They are good. They are powerful. They don't need that anymore. They certainly don't need me. I am as useful to them as you are. I am as dead as you."

We sit in silence. I sneak a glance at Raucous. He is staring straight ahead. No hiding the fact he will not speak.

"Why are you here?" I ask.

Scully wants Raucous to open up. He needs Raucous. He is seeking something, justification or an apology only he knows.

"Because I am still somebody, Charlotte. Your jewels set off an alarm. Calls came and the guy made the right decisions. You were followed and you warned him off. Not a problem. I got the

175

call. Didn't immediately believe it was you, what with you being dead at the bottom of a lake. I heard of what happened at Michael's place. A little lady turns up at a jewellers and then gets followed to close to here. I had to check it out. So I did, and I find Raucous. Now, I have no idea how you got out. No idea if you have the recordings, no idea of your plans."

Raucous leans forward again. He stares at Scully like a heavyweight staring down an opponent. Sonny Liston with a problem.

"We have none," he says.

Scully starts the smile. He has him engaged. A start, one that Raucous willingly gives.

"I don't care," Scully says. "I'm not here to kill or use you as leverage because you don't provide any. Offering you up to the man isn't going to do anything for my life expectancy. The tapes would be a nice revenge, one I'd take. But ultimately that is all a waste. "

"You aren't part of it?" Raucous asks.

It is Scully's turn to lean forward. He shows his face in close up. He wants Raucous to read.

"I was left for dead. Set up to be taken out. I'm not dumb, not trusting and I'm alive. Just, but alive all the same."

"They think you are dead?" Raucous asks.

"No, they know I am here. And I know I am a target. Killing me is going to bring whoever does it a lot of kudos. So I came back here, where I am known and wield some type of power to hide in the open as much as I can."

Raucous turns his head to me, I think he is asking if I believe the story.

RAUCOUS

Scully talks too much. He chatted before Charlotte came. Spoke a little but not much. He wanted to wait for her, to tell us at the same time. No games, no tricks, just talking. He has me and Charlotte on a sofa, with a gun. He has spoken, dragged me in. Told me he is a dead man too. I look at Charlotte, she believes the story. Maybe I do too. It seems the only way to explain why Scully is here and we are not dead. But I'm too old to trust.

"Why are you here?" I ask.

"Because you aren't dead. Because I'm not running. And if I know you are alive, Christoph does or will. And that means you are dead too. They will hunt you down and kill you. Just like they will hunt me down."

"We are out. We are dead. They don't know," Charlotte says.

"I know. They will know. But what you lack is knowledge of what is coming next."

"There is no next," I say. "A bomb and gone. There is no sense in hanging and trying again. No sense at all."

"No sense, but a lot of money. They bombed Birmingham because of me. They destroyed the place I grew up because they find that stuff amusing. They blew up Birmingham to make fun of me. To show me who they are. And they got paid. Millions. The panic in the streets, the news, the papers. All of that for money."

"This has nothing to do with us," Charlotte says.

"They aren't finished. The public might think that. But it isn't over. They are set up to go again. And the place they'll hit is here. They aren't looking for big important monuments to destroy. They are looking for chaos. Leverage. They want the country at its knees. For money and nothing else. The idiots with the bomb vests are those crazy zealots, but Christoph is a business man and this is easy money. Going after the plebs, the workers, the average man on the street. They are going to blow the crap out of London. Starting here, starting with your street. Because that's what they do."

"Bullshit," I say.

"The truth. And you have decided there's nothing to do beyond running and hiding, until they catch up and kill you."

"When is this happening?" I ask.

"Soon, and no way of reporting it beyond phoning a hotline where all the other nutjobs call in to spout nonsense and elaborate theories. And then Siri gets word and the whole thing moves on. They have a safety net and a contract out on me."

"That's your problem," I say.

Scully nods.

"Yes, it is. But your problem, or ours, is the fact our little part of the world is about to be blown apart, taken down and destroyed by a terrorist group who are going to hunt us down."

Charlotte laughs.

"You want us to take them on?" she says. "Us and whatever muscle you can muster, take down a terrorist group?"

"Running is just going to prolong the agony. And hiding here isn't going to work as it is about to be blown to shit."

CHARLOTTE

The whole deal is a farce. Scully with delusions of grandeur. Raucous buying into hitting out at something and someone so much bigger. Local hoods against global organisations. A joke, but the testosterone flows and the belief in beating odds as low as this builds.

"We were leaving anyway, Raucous," I say. "There's no change. It isn't our fight anymore."

Raucous isn't mine anymore. Stolen away by the death of his friend and the blather of a crook from Birmingham.

"Going where?" he says. "A hot island? Where do we hide exactly? This man, this group killed Michael so they can pull this, destroy our home and kill us?"

"Revenge is fine," I say. "I wanted some myself. But we are three people plus Scully's men. There is nothing we can do."

Scully leans forward.

"I disagree. I don't think it'll end well for any of us. But none of the options do. But I am not running, hiding, bowing down for anyone. I doubt you will either."

RAUCOUS

"What do you know? What is your plan?" I ask.

Charlotte listens, edging to speak. But I asked first.

"They have three places as far as I know," Scully says. "People holed up. People with bombs. Had they chosen somewhere else, we would be running and hiding. I have people here, not any trustworthy. But people all the same. They've chosen to come into my house and cause destruction on my land. They made a mistake."

178

"Where is Christoph?" Charlotte asks.

"Near. I have eyes around, and he is here."

"You'll know where," Charlotte says.

"I do. A hotel off Oxford Road. Posh but not extravagant. I have two people inside. One a worker, another a guest. Neither reliable. Both scared."

"The others?" I ask.

"Three locations. Nothing unusual."

"Call it in."

"They have the connections. They'll just move on."

"Take Christoph at the hotel. An easy hit," I say.

"A lot of people there. Muscle eyes and the like. Not a simple hit. Not something the regular local shooter can do. It isn't a walk up, gun to the head, bang and gone. It is difficult."

"How much time do we have?" Charlotte asks.

"Little. Activity there has increased. They are getting ready to go. People arriving every day. People go in, but don't come out. They think I'm too dumb to know. They think I am simple. They think I am going to show up and be shot."

"Why involve us?" I ask.

"I don't trust anyone. But I share a hatred. We are all dead. And I give you the option of staying here. Not running away. They are weak, arrogant but have muscle. I'll take my shot here rather than hide and wait to be hit. That's no life for me. If you want to run, you go ahead. I'll help you leave. But when you watch your street, your house and your home blow up on high definition TV, remember you ran away and left them to die."

"You let them blow Birmingham."

Scully's mask falls. A face of hate.

"I let them do nothing," he says. "They pulled that, and now they pull this. I'm shooting them down. You can run."

CHARLOTTE

We sat and talked, voices normal. Raucous was in, he was never going to run. I join because what else is there to do? We are dead and revenge is nothing in small doses. Kill them all, take them down. We'll die trying.

Scully has the means. He has weapons, machine and hand guns. Ex-military of Eastern European design. We have brains but not the experience and knowledge. We need soldier's minds but we have street brains. Smash and grab mentality when nasty finesse would be the way.

We know we are talking to delude ourselves. A low level team plotting to defeat the professionals when we know whatever we decide is bound to fail.

But we will not run.

I sit and listen to them talk. They are throwing ideas, looking for something they cannot destroy. A plan of sorts that will wrap enough of a comfort blanket around their future to feel comfortable with inevitable death.

"Take them all down," Scully says.

"Three hits," Raucous says.

"Blow them up?"

"Blowing up bombs is no way to go. Go in, hit, and then run."

"All at the same time?"

"Has to be."

"It won't work."

"We don't have a chance."

"Nothing better to do."

And on they go. No foundations, just outspoken bravado in place of a plan.

"We need logistics," I say. "We need to know what they do. And how we go about beating them. All I hear are two macho men beating chests and shouting out loud so they don't hear the absence of thought. We need a plan."

Scully smiles and Raucous follows. They know. They understand.

"There are three houses," Scully says. "Six bombers in each, plus security. Usually one."

"Babysitters?" I ask.

"Exactly. The suicide zealots are crazy, but some aren't quite crazy enough. They might back out. The muscle sits and keeps them calm. Armed, handgun. No worries and concentrating on looking at what's happening inside rather than out."

"Get in, take them out. And get out?" Raucous asks.

"They change the babysitter regularly. Twenty-four hours. One walks in, the other walks out. That's the way in. The night. Everyone asleep. We walk in as they walk in."

Raucous smiles and leans back like he's been given the solution to life.

"Simultaneous attack," Scully says. "Three houses, three changeovers and one of us at each to take them out. Kill them all and leave."

"One of us fails, it all goes to shit," I say.

"Then onto the hotel," Raucous says.

"Onto the hotel," Scully says. "We walk up to the third floor, shooting as we go, and make our way to the room, blow the door, walk in and have a quiet word."

Nobody says it, but we all think it impossible.

RAUCOUS

"The houses are mine, of sorts," Scully says. "Nothing to trace but mine all the same. The layouts are simple. Three bedrooms on the first floor. A kitchen, front room and hall on the ground. Slightly different in shape, but each similar enough not to need the blue-print."

Scully is talking as we drive. We are in his smooth as silk car of expense. A family car, with darkened windows in the rear to protect babies from harmful light. We sit here as Scully drives.

"The key is to take out the babysitters," Scully says. "If they go first, and quietly, then the rest is simply easy murder of arseholes who believe blowing themselves up and others with them is a way into paradise. Deluded shits."

"The change-over happens at the same time. Midnight. Every night. The bombers asleep, the protection awake. In and out. They have a key. They walk in, the other walks out. Smooth. Never two outside, never two inside. Bang, bang, dead. Walk through the house and shoot – double tap – anyone breathing, sleeping or generally being there. No conscience, no nothing. Kill them all."

"Why don't we just go for Christoph and cut it off there," Charlotte asks.

"Because he'll call it in quick. And they'll be set-off early. A phone call and they go. There is no count-down, they don't know when. They don't have time to think. They get the call and go. If he makes the call, it's a waste. We are shooting at people who are already on their way to destruction."

"You want to hurt these people," Charlotte says.

"I just want them dead."

PART FOUR

CHARLOTTE

Raucous, Scully and I take off at the same time. Three cars, all bland, all clean, all registered to people who didn't even know they owned them.

I drive, following my phone and the commands it belches out. I have seen the place on an online map. I had dragged the little yellow man into the street and had a look. A simple street of simple houses. My number was nineteen.

I think as I drive, killing innocents who are soon to be guilty. A gun, a plan, and no idea of what is inside. It is stupidity dressed up to look like controlled risk.

I only feel the lack of possibility. I'm walking into unknown to kill unknowns and face down people who have never been anything in my life nor that of others. They will die, if I succeed. They will dissolve away into nothing if they come out on top. The noise alone will make the law come. Christoph will move onto the next, lose money and a slice of reputation, but he'll move on the same with his money making off the back of hatred.

I check my gun, unmarked and foreign. I know how it works and I know what it feels like to shoot. I'm beat up but adrenaline beats fast. I park up on the street, my plan is to wait, be ready and move. A simple glide and a few pops. I check my watch. 11.20. I have a wait, but it is not precise. Around midnight, before or after. Within ten minutes, nothing too early and never too late. He'll walk up to the front door and let himself in. The other will let himself out. The start and then the massacre.

I exit my car. I find my spot three houses down. I sit on the garden wall, my hoodie up, my head down. Black jeans, black top. I look like a teenage boy trying to be a midnight man patrolling his street. I'm obvious but nothing. Too short to be a danger, too in-sight to be a threat. I look into the screen on my phone, making sure the light on my face is hidden in the material that drapes my head.

RAUCOUS

We divvied the houses. We have the addresses, we know what we're looking for.

We're each given a gun and two magazines. Plenty of bullets for the people we see. We check and make sure we know what we are doing.

Scully explained, but we know how they work. Safety catches and the ejection of magazines and the clip of a new one. It's easy and practised and we are as expert as we will ever be.

It is ten o'clock and we have two hours before it starts.

"What if there are others?" I asked.

"In the houses?" Scully said.

"Other houses. What if they have other houses?"

"If they do, I am not the man I thought. This is my area. They can't move in, can't operate without me knowing."

It is time to walk to where we need to be.

The three houses are within a three-mile radius. Bigger than the City of London, but not big enough to be a problem. We each have a car. We each have a destination. We each have weapons and the time the babysitters change. The guns have silencers, but they only work to dampen sound. The shots will be heard. Bang, bang, then slaughter. I know this is necessary, I know I hate. Transferring those emotions to people I have never met is a problem I need to overcome. I will kill multiple people tonight, people I want to kill not for them as people but for what they will do. It makes no sense. They have the idea to kill, have been indoctrinated and manipulated. They have seen or heard or experienced moments to which my struggles would never compare. But I will kill them before they have the chance to fulfil their own moral journey. I decide if they live or die. Maybe they'll kill me. Maybe I'm too slow and Scully is very wrong. Maybe they are not the walking zombie of religious righteousness I imagine but hardened men with a goal to exact revenge on any man woman or child who supports the destruction of their own small world. Scully is adamant that they possess nothing but empty souls and a desire to die. I hope he is right. Walking into an unknown house to slaughter unknown men on the word of a man like Scully is a dangerous game of wishful thinking. But running is not an option. A life on alert for the inevitable hit. Take them down and smile. Die where I grew up, die protecting whatever it is that makes me part of this place.

I slow and stop. I park my car. The house I have seen only on an electronic map. I walked the street by clicking a button. I know the area. I know where I am going. I know where I will stand, and I know I will assassinate. I sit and wait. The lights on the car turned off.

CHARLOTTE

I sit and wait, looking at a screen that says nothing. Maybe I have chosen to be out in the open too soon. I wait and do nothing but think. I have come here, a gun and an idea. Nothing else. Two men, one I do not trust, somewhere close, doing the same. Each with their own skills and needs and plans. We are all fools. Each one of us. Raucous wants to kill for his friend. Him and Michael. Michael never visited, not once did he go. He never wrote, they never talked. Raucous taking the fall. He killed two men outside a pub, for nothing. Boys being fools, is what Michael said, and he was one too. Michael made sure Raucous was safe when he came out. Had a job set up. They never met, never spoke. Friends in the past and nothing now. They knew something. Michael knew what had happened, what Raucous did. Friendship but no longer friends. A distance and a check. Michael never involved himself.

Us as teenagers. A group and then we became more than we hoped to be. And now I am here. One of them, I can't question that. I am in and there is no way out.

RAUCOUS

I get out of my car. I'm too big to go unnoticed. I walk the street, number twenty-eight is my destination. I need timing, I need luck. A gun stuck into the back of my dark jeans, hidden under my dark jumper. I am wearing a dark wool hat. I look like a cat burglar gone to seed on junk food and growth hormone. The street is lit but the spaces between the lights make for shadowy going. I slow my pace, waiting. I stop and look at my phone. 11.55. I need luck, or something to happen soon. I see a figure walking, the other side of the street, but the same direction as me. I start to walk slowly, the figure crosses the road. He eyes me, as anyone would. I'm a big guy wearing black on an empty street at midnight, I look back, give my discontent, and look away. The guy touches his chest to the left of centre, he unzips his jacket a few inches. He has told me he is a carrying a gun. A shoulder holster. I walk slowly, leaving him space to accelerate away. He is metres from the doorway. He takes the steps, waits for me to pass, and unlocks the door. He pauses and steps inside. The door closes. And I am ready.

CHARLOTTE

I see him from a distance, a reflected light of a phone lit up. His face non-descript. I would never pick it out in a line-up. Bland and the same as many. No facial hair nor feature. He is paying little attention to the street and none to me. It would be easy to walk up, shoot, get the key and walk in. But a dead body with a head turned inside-out would draw spectators even at this time. I need them all inside or close enough to drag them there. I am alert, watching and timing as he walks, phone in hand, watching or reading something. An arrogant confidence more likely than an attempt at bluffing out a hit. They have been here weeks, according to Scully. A routine has become comfortable. They have never seen trouble and don't expect.

He looks up to see where he is, I check my watch and he is early by a minute. He sees me, and slows but keeps moving. I don't watch him, not directly, but I know. He takes the steps in front of the house. I stand and walk. He sees me, wary but confident. I walk the pavement toward his house. He loses interest, but keeps an eye. He has his key in the lock and I'm as far away as I need to be. I walk past the bottom of the steps. He turns back to the door. I stop as I hear the click of the lock. I turn and pull the gun from the pouch on my hoodie. He hears me, the door is open, I step quickly with the gun raised. He faces me and sees the barrel. His expression tells me he thinks this funny. He reaches for his own gun. I march forward, to the top step, half-a-metre away. I pull the trigger, the gun recoils, his head explodes, the door behind him smeared with biological debris. He falls, more down than backward. I kick his chest as he falls, pushing his body into the door, and into the house. His feet outside, his body in the hallway, a door I will be able to close. Not one that would look clean, but no one is looking. I shoot again at his head. I hit and there is little left, little recognisable. Double tap to be sure, even when you already are. I look up and realise I should have made another plan, I should have thought things through.

RAUCOUS

I have little time to act. I believed the babysitter inside would walk out as the new walked in. I was wrong. But I move into position. I walk the steps up to the front door, my gun drawn, the silencer making the whole barrel too long and off-balance. The door stays closed and I think I have made a mistake. I have ad-libbed a little, believing my intelligence is more than any other. But I'm just dumb, I should know this.

I slide to the side of the front door. My back against the wall, the gun raised up in front of me. I look like Charlie's Angels the hideously ugly drag years. I smile and I know I am nervous. My breathing is calm, my heart racing some but not pounding. That will come, but I'll be gone by then. Lost in the moment. An instinct I hope I haven't lost.

I hear the latch and he steps out. I think, I guess. Does he have the key? Is the other near, saying goodbye? What do I face and how many? I know nothing, gunning in, winging it when the consequence of poor decisions is the end of me. My heart pounds as I convince myself of stupidity.

I turn my left shoulder to the door, he sees because peripheral vision is a genetic must for survival. His focus is the barrel. I pull the trigger and I hear the pop as his head explodes. He drops straight down, outside the house, a double tap is what they said but I have no time and with a head that open a second bullet is a waste. I step into the open door as quick as I can. If someone is there and has watched the scene, they will be drawing a gun, making a call or running to hide. None of these is what I want. I need to act fast, take the risk and move. I look into the narrow corridor, the stairs leading up to the first floor on the left. I see, I know, I should have guessed.

Assumptions are stupid, and I made them all. I can't do this, not everything. But I aim, my finger pressing on the trigger. I'm no Wyatt Earp, no trick-shot specialist nor marksman. But if I don't fire, don't try, I am dead.

I squeeze and fire and the silencer muffles the shots but not the screams.

There was never any plan.

CHARLOTTE

The guy inside sprints toward me. He is chasing down a gun, running toward a bullet with nothing in his hand but crushed air. Clenched fists and a banshee scream coming from a demented face. Maybe I killed his brother or lover because the fire is genuine, the anger complete. I raise my gun and I fire, it hits him, because momentum on his right slows down as his left reels on. He rights himself but does not drop. I fire again, he is there in front of me, but he comes forward like nothing has hit. He grabs me, hands at my throat. He is bleeding, some from his mouth, but adrenaline, fear, survival and revenge keep his systems going.

He lunges, arm out, hands looking to grasp my neck. If he is trained, this is not what they taught. He grabs me, but not the gun. He pushes me back, he is taller than me. His pressure pushes down. I lift my gun, the barrel pressed against something, something low. His stomach maybe, a leg? I don't know. But I fire. The recoil hard, his groans and screams real and close to my ear. I fire again and he gets the message, he looks to my hand, he lets go of my neck, he grabs for the gun. I fire again, this time through his chest, his breathing all wrong and blood spits from his mouth. He flails and claws, he slips down. I point the gun at his head. He closes his eyes. The rage gone, the knowledge in his mind. I don't pull the trigger, I wait rigid as he slides down my body. He hits the floor but doesn't crawl. He breathes, I see his upper body rise. He is still. He is dead. I look at him, waiting for a comeback, a renewed vigour and attack. But he is gone. I watch him, lifeless and still. I wait, not knowing what I am doing. I would stand and look for hours but the voice from the top of the stairs brings me back to the moment.

RAUCOUS

I shoot and I miss. The bullet hits the left wall of the corridor, half-way down, metres short of the man I am trying to kill. He vanishes into the doorway to his left. He steps through, staring at his destination. The room is the kitchen, unless renovations have seen it move. A large room, a back door, an escape to a garden. I don't believe he is running away. I take in everything I can from what I see. The stairs are empty, the landing clear, the corridor smoky but free of people. I step inside and move quickly forward, my gun raised at the kitchen doorway.

I pace, keeping my balance and the gun on a level. I move forward, two, three steps. I hope he has run, but I have heard no noise. He is there, somewhere, waiting or loading a gun. I step again, I keep my back to the opposite wall, giving myself the best angle at the open door. I see nothing, no shadow, no movement. I hear no sound.

I am close, a metre at most. I step across to the opposite wall. I place my back against aged wallpaper, the open doorway next to my right shoulder. I think of a film I once saw while drunk. A man in this position, waiting to enter, ready to shoot. The other man took aim at the wall and shot him through it. I don't remember the title, I don't remember the story. I just know the guy I am was killed because they knew where he stood and they knew the wall was thin. My heart pounds, my imagination on super-charged. I don't want to wait, I don't need a plan. It's easy, I go in and I shoot. This isn't America and this isn't modern. There is no centre island to hide behind. There may be a table and chairs. Formica most likely. I inhale deeply, he probably heard. I just announced my intentions. I'm going to go.

CHARLOTTE

I look up at the landing. A man, tired and dressed for bed. Pyjamas on a grown man never looks good. He stares at the dead man on the floor, he looks at me. His brain works as slowly as mine. He looks to the room to his left. He shouts but I don't understand the words. He races away, through the doorway, I hear shouting in a language I could never understand. I hear movement, and steps. I swear at myself. Stealth and quiet movement are no longer my friend. I walk down the hall, I step into rooms, no one is there, the ground floor occupied by two dead bodies. People are racing upstairs, voices and noise. I walk into the kitchen at the back of the house. Old, used and dirty despite the best efforts of bleach. Too old to be clean. Too used to be shiny. Empty but for me. I look at my gun. I look at my shaking hands. I hear steps, fast paced above me, I know where they are, and I know where they are headed.   I take the breath I don't need. I walk out of the kitchen, turn left, look up and right and aim my gun.

RAUCOUS

He is crouched down, a smaller target, gun raised and ready to fire. He does, but he aims where he thinks I'm going. I walk in, I duck, and fall to the floor. I sprawl out with my gun raised. He has no silencer, the explosion loud and my ears ring. I feel no pain nor impact, but he fires again as if two shots are always going to be better than one. He misses again but I see him making adjustments. His gun lowering to point at me prone on the floor. I'm in no position for fast movement, my gun pointed at him. I fire, his right shoulder, moves a little, I have hit him, maybe full, maybe a clip. He looks at the impact point, and I have bought another moment. I fire again, but too soon, my gun not back in position to aim with clarity. The noise brings him right back to the moment and he brings his gun toward me. I fire again, and he falls back. The impact to his chest. He has lost balance and quite some blood. He sits up, bending at the waist like an old man attempting crunches. He points his gun in the general direction of the door. He fires, again and again and again. He isn't aiming, he is firing, trusting in luck to kill a man who is going to kill him. I wait it out, until I hear the click, click, click of an empty gun. He leans back, the attempted sit-up a bust. I stand and walk over, I stand over him. My gun pointing down at his head. Blood drenches his shoulder, a pool is gathering around his upper torso. He stares at me, defiant and strong. He knows, but he doesn't flinch nor beg. He looks angry that it is me. He doesn't crawl away, he looks me in the eye, waiting for the sign I'll kill.

I watch him, wondering how long he could go in this state. Not more than a few minutes I think. No way he can survive. Two holes in him, the one in his chest the worst. But he ruins it. He speaks, or spits out an insult in a language I don't know. At least the anger in his face shows it to be an insult. Maybe it is a prayer or a call to whatever god he invested in. Maybe a call to a hero of his like the man on death row who shouted for saviour to Joe Louis when the man was seen as unbeatable. Who knows? I don't care. I hear the movement of people upstairs. The patter of feet the shouts and panic. I smile, I nod. I respect the man's strength. I pull the trigger and there is no way that head is still living. I turn to the door and hope the people upstairs are armed only with knives.

CHARLOTTE

Two men race down the stairs. They have shoes but pyjamas. Their hands empty, they race. I imagine for the door. They hit the ground floor, but turn left, turn toward me. They come unarmed, arms outstretched, like sprinting Frankensteins with destruction of their minds. I shoot, low, legs are useful for balance. I hit them both, they fall, and crawl. Scrambling toward me, they scream what I take to be insults. I shoot them repeatedly more than a double tap. Four in each, my own inhibitions gone. They wanted to kill me, tear me apart. They wanted to blow up people they didn't know. They wanted to cause destruction and death to strangers through thoughtless acts of revenge through violence. They rushed a gun and I shot them for their arrogance. They lie there, on an old worn carpet, the last thing in their lives the cheap floor of a non-descript house waiting to complete their life's ambition and falling short. Killed by me, a woman, a woman they will never know. A woman who has killed. I hear no more noise. I step over the bodies and walk the stairs, my gun raised, my heart calm, my back against the wall.

RAUCOUS

Secrecy is gone. I have announced my arrival and thrown out my intentions. I hear movement, fast and with no structure. Movement around and side to side. Voices and screams that I understand as fear and panic. These people, ready to blow themselves to atoms to take others down, now afraid of a man with a gun. I walk the stairs, sideways and slow. I aim at the landing and the door to the right. Three rooms and they cannot escape unless past me. If they are armed, they have the higher ground and higher numbers. But if they had guns they would be on me now. I would be dead.

I step quicker, confident. I reach the top and kick the door to my left. It opens into a box room. A bedroom for the youngest in any house. No room but for a bed and a chest. I look and it is empty. I could be wrong, but I'm not looking under the duvet, and the only person to hide would be a child. I walk the landing with my gun raised like I'm in Miami Vice. The door to my left is ajar. I push it with my left hand. The master bedroom. A double bed, and four single camp beds. No floor is easily seen, strewn clothes and covers. A hiding place for many, but I see no movement, no bumps.

CHARLOTTE

I can hear movement, but nothing much. No panic, like we are playing an adult game of hide and seek. But they all ran and hid in the same room. A grenade inside and the end would come to them all. I wish for a grenade, I wish to be out of here. I walk the landing. There are three doors. One now behind me, a door to the smallest box room. The room I grew up in, small and separate from brothers. No sister to share and no room to grow. My little room that I left and to which I never went back. A door to my left, to the master bedroom, it is open and the camp beds and double bed are clear. I can't see to the far side, anyone could be there. I walk by because I'm not going in. I don't want to be trapped. The door ahead of me is closed. Clicked shut. Maybe they are jumping from a window, escaping away. I sure hope so. I don't want to be doing this.

I hear movement. I can't tell what or who, but the boards creek and the air vibrates. A room with people. I don't know how many, I don't know if they are armed.

I pause, readying myself. A vibration in my pocket. My phone, on silent. I shake my head. My phone, a call now. The only two who know my number, and one of them has time to call. I take the phone from my pocket. The name says Two. It is Scully. One, Two and Three. Me, Scully and Raucous.

I put the phone back in my pocket. It vibrates, he needs to speak but I need to finish.

I walk to the door, my gun pointed ahead. Moving and acting like the detectives I have seen on TV. My plan is clear.

I kick the door, at the handle, there is no lock. It flies open, smacking against the wall. I duck down, gun out, pointing and moving from left to right, a scan of the room. Four men stand at the far side of the room, two either side of a light blue curtain that hides the window. They have their hands raised like I'm robbing their stagecoach. They chatter, in a language I don't understand.

"Shut up," I shout.

The men look at each other, they talk more. A constant stream of high-pitched noise. Back-and-forth.

I point my gun at each of them.

"Be quiet," I say.

They ignore me.

I know what I need to do, what I should do. I should kill them all, now, dead. Walk away and move on to the next stage. I have to shoot. These people would kill, that is the truth, I have to believe that. These four were to be the carriers of bombs and death and destruction. I believe that.

"Down," I say.

The men look at each other as if none of them understand, they chatter, they lower their hands. The two men on either end, start to walk forward. I point at the one on the left, then the one on the right. Back and forth, tick-tock but they don't stop moving. Words come from four mouths. My gun left and right, which man to cover, which decision to make.

The man to my right starts to speak to me. Not in English, but calm and assuring. He reaches out with his right hand, a meter from me, as if offering me a way out. A peace to be made, a way out alive for everyone. He moves slow, hypnotic. I watch his every small edge forward. He smiles, his teeth white but crooked. A man with the ability to connect. He gets closer and I'm frozen.

His outstretched arm, his fingertips getting closer. I watch and I feel the relaxation of muscle. I'm not going to shoot, I'm not going to kill. I feel that, I feel peace. I watch him and he smiles more. He looks me in the eye, I am the only one in the room. He leans forward again, but his eyes flicker, to look over my shoulder. I see the nod, the communication, the order. I feel the second man grab my left shoulder, feel him try to drag me round and down. I turn with the gun in my right hand. I jam the barrel into his gut and I fire twice. Quick succession, and I feel his grip loosen as he drops. He isn't dead, he won't be for a while, but he hurts and there is nothing he can do. I turn and the first man is on me. The gun between us, pointing away from his gut. He wrestles with me, I wrestle with the gun. I pull my arm back and free, as he twists me, kicking my legs away, we fall to the floor. I hold the gun tight as we thud down. I bend my elbow, I ram the barrel up under his armpit. The bullet could ricochet anywhere, but I fire. Three times and the guy stops like all activity to his brain has ceased.

I look up and the two men left alive are coming at me. I point my gun at them. They stop.

The one to my left stares.

"We will kill many of your people," he says.

I pull the trigger and shoot him in the head, the second man runs for the door. I shoot his leg, he drops, he looks at me and I shoot. His face contorts as the bullet enters. My part done, I need to leave.

RAUCOUS

My phone rings. It should be on silent. A button to press in a menu I accessed. Clearly the wrong action. It rings and vibrates in my back pocket. I reach for it slowly with my left hand. My right holds the gun, pointing at the door. I look at the screen, holding it out at arm's length. I'm an old man and my eyes are gone. It is Scully, or number two in the dumb code he insisted on. A phone with no past, and very little future. Three numbers, number three mine.

"I don't have time," I say.

I put the phone in my pocket. I walk on, I raise my foot and kick the door. It flings open, I get a glimpse of the room and the people before the door rebounds back and shut. I push the door with my left hand. I'm not afraid. I'm confused.

I scan across all four of them. They look the same, the same clothes, the same height, the same skin. They could be sisters or clones, or my mind messing with me. Four women, staring dead-eyed at me. Their heads covered in brown, beige and green hijab. They stand, their bodies undefined under billowing material. They could be of any shape or size. A bland blanket of non-descript dress. Women who follow a culture I've seen every day of my life. It is not one I can name, but what's the name of mine? Stupidity? Thuggery? It doesn't matter, they are labels for others. Four women, but not afraid. They stare at me, at my gun. I look around the room, looking for someone hiding, someone playing the fool to jump out and take me down. There is no one. Me and four quiet, strong women. They make no sound and no move.

"Who are you?" I ask.

Scully told me of the people here. Killers, suicide bombers. I had never questioned his word. I had envisaged men. I see four women. Women, this is a problem. If they do not attack, try to kill me then I do not have the cold character to kill them. A stand-off of boredom. They stare at me. No answer. And they do not look to each other to find a leader, a voice, or a community.

"Do you understand?" I ask.

They all four nod.

"Start speaking," I say. "Or we're going to end up dead."

They stare in silence, not a word. Then the woman closest to me, the second from the right, speaks.

"We have nothing to say. Do what you want. We are no longer part of this. We were not selected."

"Selected?"

"We get to live, for a while. We don't give our lives for our cause. Not this time."

I need to think. She would be one, she will be one. At least that is what she says. They are not part of this, not now.

"So if you choose to kill us now, you can. We will give you no fight. But you don't look to be the right type."

"I've just killed two men, in this house."

"You defended yourself. And we are female. That, it is clear, means something to you. You will not shoot."

She knows, and she knows me. My phone rings, I check again. Scully. A message too. I read. GET HERE NOW! Simple, but dumb. I am not late, our meeting is still minutes away. I put the phone back. I have a thought. Someone has Scully's phone. The message from someone trying to lure me in. The plan is not making it through.

The women haven't moved. They stand, waiting, not scared, not showing anything.

"On your knees," I say.

"No, I don't think so," the same woman says.

I walk up to her, she doesn't flinch. But she should. I swipe the gun handle across her forehead, a small bump, not to break, nor damage. A stinger, hopefully knock her down. She yelps, because it hurts, and it is unexpected. She drops to her knee.

"Do I have to do this to each of you?" I say.

The other three drop to their knees. They do it slowly, a defiance, but their voice, their leader is dripping blood from a gash and has no more words.

I scan the room, like I'm going to see rope. I see nothing.

"Where are your phones?" I say

The woman I hit, looks up at me. "We have no phones, no contact. The men you killed, they have the communication. But they are dead now."

I'm lost, no idea what to do. If I leave, they can notify whoever, and the next step is done. I'm not killing them. I know this.

They know this.

"I guess there is no way of getting your word to stay quiet."

"You expect me to scream? We will stay here. And wait. You are doomed, whoever you are and whatever your intentions maybe. You should kill us. That's what you should do. But you don't. Which is why you have no chance. The people you are up against would not be speaking now. They would have gone, and left four women dead."

"I'm not those people."

"And because of that you will die. We can do nothing. We sit and wait. You are free to go and walk into whatever coffin you choose."

I look at the women, the room, at my hands. I'm shaking. She is right, and I am a dead man.

"Why?" I ask. "Why do this?"

"For many reasons. Very few you understand. But there are reasons. You cannot act without any. If you do that, you are to be punished through living."

I place my gun in the back of my jeans. I cover it with my shirt. I smile. Wisdom found in the most obscene places.

CHARLOTTE

I walk out quickly. I close the door. My hood up but I don't run. The noise of shooting heard by all, and we are not in a city that turns deaf to murder. I keep my gun because I will need it again. If I'm stopped and searched so be it. I walk with my head down and turning on streets I have memorised. I hear no sirens and see no cars. A peaceful night. But it can't remain, a country afraid of terror and explosions. Everyone locked up feeling safe when they know they are not.

Far enough away for light, I take my phone from my pocket. Three missed calls, all Scully. All in a row, the last ten minutes ago. There is no reason for him to call. I make the decision and press the button, a reply as I walk.

He answers immediately.

"Where are you?" I ask.

"Outside where I should be," he says.

"Why the call?"

"You need to get here. Not where we said to meet, but here. Now."

I hear something in his voice. It isn't fear, Scully doesn't let people see his fear. He has it, probably why he made it so far. But it is inside. An excitement, a thrill.

"Why?"

"Because he is here. Siri is here. Get here quick."

"You need the help?"

"Siri and two men. Both armed. Others inside. It's a shootout. Or something similar. You in?"

"I'm in. Nothing till I get there. Raucous?"

"I'd love him to be here. But he doesn't answer."

RAUCOUS

I walk out slow. Close the door and keep the gun. I know where I need to be and when I need to be there. I take the route I planned to take. No cars, no sirens no movement. The women I left are free to do what they want. A phone call or confirmation, a story and a warning. I couldn't kill them, and they'll more likely than me kill more. Free to speak and move and tell. They told me things but I have no reason to believe. My phone rings. Scully again. I pull it from my pocket. It is Charlotte.

"What is it?" I ask.

"Change of plan. You need to be where the two is. Soon as."

"What's gone wrong?"

"Nothing yet. But there is someone there who you need to see."

"Who?"

"Siri."

"Alone?"

"With two men and whoever is inside."

"I'm ten minutes away."

"I'm five."

"Wait for me."

"No intention to do otherwise."

I quicken my pace. I need to be there. Siri and a way to redemption. I need to kill that man. I have a reason and a desire. I don't care if slowly or without pain. But it has to be me. Some type of code I couldn't explain. But it is in me, as real as the law in any state. I smile, the women can do nothing. This is where I need to be.

CHARLOTTE

Scully speaks fast and I listen as we wait for Raucous.

Siri turned up in a police van. Two men with him. They have parked and walked in, the two men walking in and out of the house, uniformed and seen. Lights and nothing hidden. Scully watched from the end of the road, in darkness, he called me in as I shuffled along. A wall into an alley, a side street to the back of terraced houses. A scoop from the space of two houses, a smaller room than the rest, and a brick alley with a roof where people slept in damp bedrooms. Scully was smiling and he glowed with the glee of being in the right place.

The two men came out in turns to the Police van, carrying back large bags, twelve of them, locking the van each turn. They stopped coming out after twelve.

"It's the start," Scully said. "They have brought explosives. It's soon, and it starts from here."

"All of it?"

"Who knows, maybe they go to the other houses next. A delivery of sorts. We go when Raucous is here. They won't be ready for a raid."

"They'll know from the other houses something is wrong."

"They won't know anything. This is planned in advance. No communication. No risk. And they're all dead where you came from, right?"

I think and see it all. The deaths. The blood the murder. I nod my head.

"It's OK. They deserved it," Scully says. "Just like these do. Raucous is on his way, so he killed too. We have these and then Christoph has nothing but a hotel room and a gun."

He is right, we are all in, nothing to do but go forward. Twelve bags mean twelve people plus Siri and his two.

"Fifteen inside," I say.

"Minimum, probably more."

"At least five each," I say.

Scully laughs like I've tickled him.

"Easy. Most are zombies. Dead to the world and not trusted with guns. They are tools, been taught and trained to blow themselves up. They are idiots and nothing to be scared of."

200

"I know," I say. "I met some."

We hear movement, a walk. We don't panic. We know.

RAUCOUS

I walk quickly, sweat breaks, I'm sticky but I walk fast. I know where Scully should be, I don't know the end of the street, but I can come in quickly from one end so that's what I choose. I can double back around if I'm wrong, but it makes sense to come at the house from this way. I slow and start to amble when I'm on the road. The house, Scully's house is two thirds down from this end, I stroll. And I see them.

An alleyway, because hiding behind a car is stupid. The two of them, a metre and half in, waiting and smiling like we are playing the most amazing game.

I look down the street. No one is there, street lights and no movement. A dead street at night, with no one coming out and no one looking.

"How many, Raucous?" Scully asks.

"Two dead men, and four women," I say.

They stare at me, the grins going and then Scully's coming back in a different form.

"You killed four women?" he asks.

"No, they are alive. The two men are very dead."

Neither asks what the women are doing. We have reached a point where trust is something you have to do. Too far in to ask questions and point out mistakes and flaws.

Charlotte tells me the scene, the numbers, what they think is going on.

"So we go into a house with at least fifteen people, twelve bags of high explosives, and armed police. Us three. With three hand guns. That's the plan? We've been lucky so far, but that's insanity."

"Any suggestions?" Scully asks.

"How long have they been in there?"

"Thirty minutes."

"They follow a pattern?"

"How the hell should I know? I'm not part of this." We look at him, eyes firmly looking up. "OK, I am part of this, I smuggled the people in to the country, and it would appear the explosives. But the plan I had nothing to do with. No idea how this works."

"We can't go blazing in, we'd lose. Die. Too many of them and too many explosives. If you were running this, how would you work it?"

"It doesn't matter," Charlotte says. "One of them just walked out."

"Siri?" Scully asks.

"A random. Big coat, baggy. Hiding something."

"Shit," I say. "Which way?"

"This way."

We wait, all three.

"This side of the road?"

"Our luck's out. The other side."

I stand and watch the man walk. He has a purpose and he checks his watch. There is nothing in his hands.

"He came out of that house, right?" I ask.

Charlotte looks at me. "Do you think I'd make that mistake"

He is on the other side.

"Where is your car Scully?"

"On the other side of the road."

"Press the key, unlock the doors. Now."

Scully fumbles and presses the key, the lights on his car flash twice as the solenoid clicks and the doors unlock. The man is startled, but calms quickly, a car without owner flashing yards in front of him. I walk out of the alley, toward Scully's car. I'm a man going home, maybe just visited a woman, maybe just going for a drive. Nothing to see here, nothing wrong, I should be walking to my car, it just lit up. I just unlocked it. I walk, trying to ignore the man as he tries to ignore me. He passes the car, walking quicker than he had. I am on the pavement behind him. I look to the house and no movement. I run two steps and grab the man, my right arm wrapping around his neck from behind. I grab his left wrist with my left hand and pull it, twisting it up behind his back. He squeals but not loud enough to be heard. My arm crushes his throat. I feel bumps under his jacket. I'm wrestling with a man covered in bombs.

I lead him across the road, easily enough. He is wiry and tall but not strong. I drag him into the alley way. I throw him down and he starts to scream. Scully quietens him by chopping the man's throat with the barrel of his gun. The man gasps and starts to force his hand into his right pocket. Charlotte acts first, she leaps on him, and forces his elbow into the wrong type of bend.

"What's in his pocket, Raucous?"

I reach down and pull out a cylinder of sorts. It looks like the control on a Scaletrix. The handle of a gun, with no barrel only a plastic trigger.

Charlotte opens the man's jacket. He is strapped with explosives, not that I'm an expert, but it sure looks that way.

"Don't press the button, Raucous. Not yet, eh?" Scully says.

He is smiling like he's in the funniest scene of a classic comedy.

"How many of you are there?" Charlotte asks.

The man spits out some words in his own language.

"How many?" Charlotte asks again.

He spits another insult.

Scully looks at his gun. He looks at us and shrugs.

The man's voice is a rasp. "You all die," he says. "We kill you all."

"How many?" I ask.

"Fuck you!"

I kneel down, I wrap my hands around his throat and I squeeze. His eyes bulge, he scrambles for a hold, he scratches, and I squeeze. The windpipe I feel bend and buckle I feel and see his air going. I watch him and I want him to know it is me that is taking his life. He rasps and scrambles, his heels scraping on the floor until he doesn't. But I squeeze some more all the same.

"He's dead, Raucous," Charlotte says.

"I know. But he's just the first."

"You saying we kill all of them?"

"Eleven to go."

"If they come out one at a time."

"There are three of us."

"The next one is out," Scully says. "And he's going the other way."

"Give me your knife," Charlotte says.

Scully watches, insulted for a second. His smile returns. He bends down, pulls up the hem on his trouser leg. Unclips the knife from its sheath. Flips it so he holds the blade.

"Bring it back, I like it."

CHARLOTTE

I take the knife and run. I don't turn right and run past the house, I turn left, ten metres and then left again, the depth of two terraced houses and their yards and I turn left again. I sprint, my legs pumping, holding good form. Trying too hard will slow me. I breath deep, drawing in as much oxygen as I can. I blow out slow and hard. I hear my feet pounding the pavement, but it is not a roar. A small echo but I'm no elephant rumbling. I know where I'm going, the road curves left then right, but a long way down there is a cross section, a road that cuts the two parallel streets in half. If I'm fast, I'll make it first. I turn left again and see no one. I slow, walking brisk, keeping quiet, breathing, but not loud. I see nothing and hear nothing. I reach the street I came from, hundreds of metres from where Scully and Raucous hide. I look, but I see nothing. I scan the streets, I'm at a crossroads, I look and see nothing, hear nothing. There is no man. I don't know where to go. Four options, two pretty dumb. The other two streets empty. I look and then I see.

The figure cuts across the road. I look left along the street, and the door of the house opens again. Another walks out, I watch alternate, the first and the second. The second turns right at the bottom of the steps, toward Raucous. I fix the first and walk. I pull down my hood, I want to be seen, no danger, hoods cause fear. The man looks behind and he sees me, but he sees me looking at my phone, my face illuminated, my stature clear. A small woman, short hair and engrossed in social media. No threat, I look no threat. He walks on as do I.

I quicken to shorten the distance. They are coming out quick, I need this one dead. I get closer but quiet, but he senses. He turns and I stare at my phone, walking ahead. Making sure the knife I carry in my right hand is hidden along my forearm.

He stops, waiting for me to pass. I look up as if seeing him for the first time, I step closer to the road, an attempt at showing my intentions to avoid. He stands and waits for me to pass. I stare into my phone and see nothing. All on peripheral vision, all ready to see the gap. He turns as he watches me. I step further away, but still on the same pavement. He watches me, turned sideways. I look up from my phone, teenage temperament in my voice.

"What the hell you looking at?" I say.

He watches me, he smiles, he snorts. He closes his eyes. And there is his mistake. The arrogance of man.

The handle of the knife is in my hand, I step to his side quickly and his eyes open. He wants to see me but I have moved from view, behind him now. I jump up, he is taller than me by some distance, and I wrap my left arm around his neck, my phone in my hand like I'm aiming for the most violent of selfies. With my right, my feet off the ground, my weight pulling his head back, I drive the knife up, under his skull, below his right ear, I wiggle it about, slicing through his brain. He stops his struggle, his structure gone. He falls and I land my feet on the tarmac. He slumps down, if not dead then no way coming back. I look at my phone, no message. I grab the man's collar and drag him with all the strength in my legs and back between two cars. As well hidden as he can be right now. Someone is going to find him, and I hope the others.

I look at my phone, no message, no call. I type as fast as I can.

"Dead. Hidden. I have them this way."

I send. They'll understand.

RAUCOUS

My phone vibrates and so does Scully's. He looks and reads, but I have no time. The third one out and he is coming our way.

"Same trick," I say.

Scully nods, smiling away.

The man walks the same way as the one I killed, the same side of the road, away from us. We have the timing, the routine. A beep and I walk, the boot open and the man walks past.

It flows, it works. I am at the boot before the man arrives, my back to him. No danger. I glance his way as I walk across the road as to do nothing is suspicious. I nod, and go back to my business. I look in the back of Scully's boot. Two large rags, and a bottle of screen wash. Everything clean. Spotless. The rags look like they have been cut from the finest cotton.

205

I feel the man walk past, I look right and I don't know why. He sees me, his face drops, he looks behind him, he looks ahead. He starts to run and I know he knows. He pushes off with his right leg, aiming to go back to where he came. I step forward, as quickly as my ambling self allows. I reach out with my right foot and clip his left heel. The impact makes him lose his footing, he falls and scrambles on the floor, crawling, trying to get to his feet. A noise breaks from his throat. I jump on him. My right arm wrapping around his neck. My left hand across his mouth. We are on the floor in some type of playground fight. He reaches for his pocket and I twist and pull. His head popping back and to the side. I pull and push, left and right, fast and uncontrolled. I feel his pain, he bites into my hand. I let go, and he starts a muffled cry. My right arm crushing his larynx acts as a dampener to any sound.

I stand and pull him to his feet with me. He scrambles, his hand going to his pocket again, I swipe his legs from under him with my right shin. He twists but can't go far as my arm crushes his neck. I ram his head against the nearest stone wall. The top of his skull smashes into brick. He struggles still, and I feel the blood trickle. No time. This needs to be quick. I release my grip, I grab around his waist, both arms, a hug, I lock my hands, I hoist him up, and smash him down. He turns his head, like anyone would, but the edge of the garden wall, the concrete covered top, impacts on his whiplashing temple and the thud, the collision, snaps something, cracks open skin and splinters bone. He is limp in my arms. I don't drop him, I haul him up and over my shoulder, my breathing hard and raspy and not quick enough for me to catch my breath. I walk, hoping to run, back to Scully. I throw the man down.

"Charlotte got the other. That's three. Not bad for no plan and no idea what on earth is happening, don't you think?" Scully says.

I stare at him. Scully looks out into the road. He types into his phone.

"Another one," he says. "Going Charlotte's way."

CHARLOTTE

I see the man walk from the house. The same as the last. The same clothes, height, the same gait. Clones of whoever thinks this is the best way to end a life. I scan and make a decision. The last man dead between cars on a road twenty metres from here. I wait at the cross road. Crouched behind a white van, scanning the street. I see him walk. The last went left, I wait for his route to be shown. He heads straight across, which means he can lie dead on another street. How many explosives he has strapped, I do not know. The detonator in his right pocket, unless he is left-handed. He walks, almost bouncing, his steps quiet, and strong. I'm on the other side of the road, and I want him to walk a little more. The further away, the less likely he will be seen dead by the next.

I stand and start my routine. I walk quicker than him, face in my phone, making sure I can be seen as the little kid I look like. He notices me as soon as I start. He turns his head, looks right at me. My face illuminated, my pace quick and heading to him. He doesn't stop and stare, not the perfect clone after all. He quickens his pace and within a moment my plan is gone.

"Hey, you," I shout.

He makes no movement but the ones that propel him forward and faster away from me.

"Hey," I shout.

I start to run. This gets his attention. He turns, his hands raised, clenched to fists, his face angry at my interference.

I keep coming at him and he changes expression from anger to surprise. The tense relaxing as confusion floods. The little girl shouting isn't backing off. He steps toward me and I feel relief. He is a man, he wants the fight, he'll hurt me and send me on my way. He wants the confrontation; he thinks he has me beat.

He walks and I start to alter pace, slow then quick on repeat. Nothing exaggerated, just enough for timing to be a problem. He steps toward me thinking to push. He thrusts out his hands, aiming for my chest, a bounce to stop me in my tracks. I slip my hands between his as he pushes forward, I press out and his hands push against air, either side of my shoulders. His momentum brings him forward, the impact no longer there to stop his flow. I step into his chest, driving my left shoulder up under his ribs. I feel the solid pack of explosives under his jacket, the solid thud of protection. He is off-balance but not hurt nor winded. I drive my knife up, aiming for and hitting the underside of his jaw. The blade slices through and I drag it out and away from me. A weaker muscle movement, but one that has no danger of slicing me. He screams at the impact but the sound dies as quickly as he drops. Blood gushes from his neck, his feet kick, and within seconds he is dead. I kick and roll him into the road. Two parked cars with a ton of bombs and a dead terrorist. I open his coat, just to check, to be sure. A vest of what can only be explosives. I reach into his right pocket and feel the detonator. He was a killer, a bomber. It is ok. It is ok.

"Done," I message.

I move back to the white van. I lean against its side. I smear a darker colour. Red, I know it is red.

RAUCOUS

"This one is mine," Scully says. "Can't have you gasping for air too much, can we?"

I nod, I need air. I try to catch breath by breathing quietly and shallow. It doesn't work. I lean against the wall.

I don't look, but Scully nods and moves. The next one out. I can't be sure which number, but it is early. More to come. I inhale and rest my hands on my knees. I hear the beep of the car and the solenoids click, Scully strolls like he owns the city, and maybe he believes he does. He walks to the car, but earlier than I did. The man is a long way back. Scully leans into the boot, he works on something or at least puts up the greatest impression of searching. The man walks wary, a small angle away from Scully's side of the pavement, closer to the houses, to the brick. Front doors and windows, no light, no movement, just Scully playing games in the boot of his car. The man walks past, Scully plays. The man looks and Scully pays no heed. The man walks, Scully stands straight. He lifts his gun from the boot, takes aim and shoots.

The Man sees and hears nothing. His forehead opens from the inside out. The bullet through the back of his skull. Little noise, a suppressed cough, as Scully has screwed in a silencer to the gun.

The man lies dead on the pavement. Scully looks, kicks the body, drops the gun in his boot, closes the car and jogs back to me.

"If you could be so kind as to hide the body there, Raucous. I think I'll do the killing while you do the lifting."

I stare at him.

"I just forgot I had the silencer. We have it covered. Go drag the body between the cars," he says.

And I do as I'm told.

CHARLOTTE

The next comes and he goes right at the cross-road. He doesn't look, he isn't aware. I walk up and he pays no attention. I'm worried, it isn't normal. When I'm close I hear him muttering. He is lost in thought and deed. It is easy, too easy. I grab his shoulder, drive the knife up and under his skull, he drops like they all have. As he falls, I manoeuvre him as far to the road as I can. He lies, feet visible between cars. I stroll back to the van. Too easy. I send my text, all done, and wait.

Scully tells me they are waiting. I sit and watch and nothing happens. No more people, no more action, no more texts. I wait. My phone in my hand. I look down streets and I can see where the bodies are. I know, they will be found. They are wrapped in explosives with detonators in pockets, there for people to find them, there to be set off by inquisitive kids, or old ladies, or thieves.

I wait and nothing. No news, and nothing to do.

"What's happening?" I ask.

No reply. I watch the street, I see no movement.

RAUCOUS

Scully tells me, "The next is out."

"This way or to Charlotte?" I ask.

"This way."

"Me or you?"

"I'll go he says,"

The routine. The same. The guy walks our way. Scully beeps the car, walks out across the road, gets to the car and pops the boot.

The man stops. Too far from Scully to be killed. He watches Scully, every move, up and down. He looks around the street, he looks at the police van. He looks everywhere. He steps back. He looks at Scully, his face I cannot see. Scully doesn't turn, he continues to rummage in the boot. Too long now. Way too long. Scully puts the gun in his coat. He doesn't look back. He steps onto the pavement, he seems to be going to sit in the car. The man doesn't move. He watches. He takes a step back. He glances across the road. He squints. He sees me. He must. He steps back again, he turns. He runs. He sprints, and he shouts.

Shit. Scully turns, pulls his gun, and fires. Little sound, a loud ping as the bullet hits wall. The man keeps running.

I'm running now, but not fast, not nearly fast enough. The man is heading back to the house. It is a long way if walking, twenty seconds if sprinting. 200 metres at most. Scully grabs his phone, he dials. He isn't running as I sprint past. He speaks, to Charlotte.

"Man running your way, back to the house. We've been seen. Get him."

CHARLOTTE

My phone rings and Scully tells me that. Shit.

I start sprinting along the road, running to the house, form perfect. Stride good, but not too long, and I see him coming, a strange run, not looking forward, but over his shoulder, looking at the massive lumbering figure of Raucous getting further away. He looks forward then back, confident he is escaping, running fast. He looks back, a mistake in most situations. But here it is mocking. He runs, within himself, and the big fat man can't keep up. I sprint, my steps quiet, gliding. I run in the road, the cars between me and the pavement. The house he came from coming up on my right. The curtains are closed, the light on inside. I run, past now, closer to the man. He looks forward again and sees me.

I dart between cars, knife in my right hand, he thinks he'll run by, he has enough time, enough space. He is wrong. I catch him, side on, the impact raises his feet up off the floor. We hit a wall, the front of a house. Centimetres from a window. I drive the knife up as he screams, up under his jaw. The knife bends, but doesn't snap. He gargles, he gasps, he can't make a sound, he scratches at my hand, but he has nothing to give. I wiggle the knife as much as I can, but it is trapped on bone. He loses all strength and drops. I drag him as much as I can, toward the cars, into the road. He is heavy, a dead-weight. I struggle, but in an instant he feels light. Raucous with me, grabbing the man, throwing him between parked cars. Bumper to bumper. A dead man, bleeding out. Raucous grabs me, drags me away from the house. Behind a mini-van, nothing big, but big enough. He forces me down. I fight it, but he is strong.

"Quiet, someone is coming out."

I look and he sees I don't understand.

"The front door just opened. Someone is coming out."

"Shit."

RAUCOUS

We wait, Charlotte and I, crouched in some gym position, our backs against the rear doors of a small van. Our legs at right angles, our backs to the van like we are sitting on invisible chairs. We hear movement and steps, pacing and van doors opening. I dare not look. No movement, no sound. My phone vibrates, but it is my pocket. I don't pull it out. Like a phone in the cinema, light will draw everyone's attention. I look at Charlotte, she grimaces. I nod. We wait. The noise of many people, not just one. The van door, the silence of men breathing and moving without word. I drop down, my legs starting to shake, I can't help myself, I look. I need to know. I see six men, six policemen, perfect uniform, perfect look. Nothing fake, all perfect issue, all new, all with the right gear, equipment and anti-stab vest. Big bulky vests, with radios.

They are sat in the back of the van, at their feet are a number of half empty holdalls. A man slams the van door shut. He walks to the passenger side and gets in. The engine starts and they drive away. No light, no sirens. A smooth, slow acceleration to wherever they plan to go.

"They're gone," I say to Charlotte.

She lets out a deep breath like she has been testing her ability to stay under water.

"How many more?"

"In the van? Six. All police, all dressed as officers of the law."

Scully's car pulls up, silent and smooth. Electric and quiet.

"Get in," he says. "Quick."

"Pop the boot."

"We haven't got time."

"Pop the boot."

He does, and I do what I need to do. It takes more strength than I thought, but dead-weight is heavy weight.

We get in and Scully drives.

"Do you know where they are going?" Charlotte asks.

"Not right now, but there aren't too many ways out of here, and if they are intending on using those police as bombs, then they are staying close, I reckon."

"If you're wrong?"

"Terror on the TV tonight," Scully says.

CHARLOTTE

Scully drives and takes streets and corners, looking for a police van. A novelty, I imagine for someone who has spent his life doing the avoiding.

"How long before they realise their first wave isn't happening," Raucous asks.

"They'll know soon," I say. "The night-life isn't far away, and the people they were going to kill will be packed into pubs and clubs not more than a mile from here. I guess that's where they are hitting."

"That's what I figure too," says Scully.

"Set up explosions, kill people and then send in the police to blow up ambulances, help and everyone else," I say. "Nasty and smart."

Raucous, like we all are, is scanning the street for the police van.

212

"Police walking around as bombers," he says.

"They can mingle in, and when there are enough people. Boom," I say.

Scully speaks but we are all talking to ourselves. We've stopped the first wave. We don't know their plan, we are guessing, hoping we are right. If we aren't, the police with their bombs are going to cause carnage.

"The others? The ones we killed," I say. "You think they were something else? They were the start, the chaos. And then the police step in and it tops it."

"If it isn't that way," Raucous says. "We're going to see a lot of people dead."

Scully drives and we scan, we go slow and we go quietly. Street after street, ever increasing circles. We see nothing, a few cars, a few people, but no van, no police. But we hear no bombs, no screams.

Scully pulls into a large space on a semi-deserted street.

We look at him, Raucous and I. He knows but he waits, words passing through his mind.

"We don't know where he is. Christoph is in a hotel five hundred metres from here. On the road you see ahead. The van we don't know. They are waiting on explosions."

"That's what we think," I say.

"It's a reasonable assumption to make."

"Their plan goes wrong at the start, and they'll adapt. Or they run," I say.

"There is too much money involved to run. They are in. They have made a promise. They can't run. They have bombs, they have police. They are in. It is happening."

"So we wait? For what?" I ask.

"For information," Scully says. "A word. From anywhere."

213

RAUCOUS

We sit in silence for ten minutes, waiting for whatever we hope will happen. We hear no explosions; our phones don't beep. We don't speak and we look, hoping the van reappears. It doesn't.

Scully has his eyes closed, meditating or sleeping. I don't care which. I watch him in his calm. Raucous in the back, I see through the mirror. He is still, waiting, not switched off, but resting.

Scully opens his eyes. He frowns. He leans forward and reaches to his back pocket. He pulls out his phone, looks at the number. He answers.

"Yes?"

He listens.

"What colour and type?"

He listens again.

"How many men?"

He nods.

"Heading which way?"

He listens.

"Any other information?"

He listens again.

"Thank you."

Scully switches off the phone, he places it in a small open shelf on the dashboard.

"We won't be storming the hotel today. Christoph is on the move. Coming this way as it happens. A black Sedan, German in design. Two men with him. Looking a little agitated by my man's account."

"Running away?" I ask.

"I would wager he is a little disorientated as his plan, due to our heroics, has gone to shit."

"I'd wager," Charlotte says, "that if we follow him, we'll meet the van."

"A distinct possibility. They are ad-libbing now."

"We're better than them at that," Charlotte says.

"Debatable," I say. "But it evens things up a little."

"The storm the hotel was a bad idea," Scully says. "I can't deny that, Raucous. I wasn't looking forward to that part at all."

214

Scully starts the car. We wait, lights off, engine running.
We see the lights of a car a long time before we hear an engine.
Scully smoothly rolls the car forward, lights off. A black sedan of
German origin slides by, we pull out and follow. Lights off but the
street illuminated enough for us to see.

CHARLOTTE

Scully drives slowly, silently. We hear nothing of the
electric engine. Who knows how long the battery lasts, how long
before he switches to fuel. The black sedan ahead drives calmly,
indicating, turning slow when it needs to. We stay far back, Scully
letting them vanish into roads he knows.

"They're heading to the industrial estate," I say.

Raucous looks at me.

"It's the only place out here, the only place where that many
men can go unnoticed."

"It'll be my yard they are heading to, or at least my ex-yard."

"Makes sense."

"Does it make it easier?" I ask.

No one answers. I hope it does. The hotel was suicide, in
the hope of a life for a life. Take them out as they take us.

We watch, travelling at five miles an hour, as the sedan
slows, brake lights glaring, and pulls right through an open gate and
into a yard.

"Someone knew they were coming," I say. "The gate all
conveniently open for them."

"Siri inside," Raucous says.

"That's a pretty good assumption. Other ways in or out?" I
ask.

Scully nods.

"On foot, of course," he says. "By vehicle, nothing. In or out
through that gate."

RAUCOUS

I make Scully stop the car. I get out. I see the fire-door, a large metal rectangle in the brick wall. Closed and smooth. No handle on the outside. We need to know. I walk along the wall of the yard. It is a metre taller than me. Concrete set on top with broken glass bottles sticking up. Easy to climb over with a thick blanket.

I walk and hear nothing. No steps, no breathing, no shivers but my own. They should have a sentry; they can't be that dumb. I walk across the road, a large lorry parked up for the night with its rear doors open showing it has nothing to steal. If I'm spotted, it'll look like a hulking driver making his way back to his bed for the night.

I walk and keep an eye on the gate. Nothing, no movement. But then I see. The gate sliding closed. Clanking of metal and a grind of rollers on a rail. It moves slow but steady all the way to the end. Ten seconds in total from open to closed. I look along the top of the wall. No cameras, no external CCTV. No towers with guards like an American penitentiary. They are inside, they are not looking out. They are looking for an answer, or maybe waiting to start. Who knows when the first wave of bombs was set to go.

CHARLOTTE

I watch Raucous jog back. He is no athlete, just bulk and mass and strength. Not built for speed, not built for anything beyond threats.

He opens the door. "Nothing," he says. "All closed up. Nothing to see from outside."

He gets in and the car sags.

"We can wait," I say, "but wait for what? The police? Siri is the police. He'll know and be gone. We can't storm in, they outnumber us. Any ideas, because I'm thinking stealth. But don't ask me how."

"Getting in is easy," Raucous says. "Glass topped wall, stick a coat over it and we're in. Only there to stop kids. Inside, I don't know. Siri and Two plus, Christoph and two. All armed. And six guys wearing explosives. Three of us and handguns."

"What's inside?" I ask.

"Used to be a timber yard," Scully says. "Big open space. Office in the far right corner, in front of the gate. Nothing but space otherwise. If the timber's still there, a lot of that dotted about. It's a carpark. All tarmac and space."

Raucous turns, "First thing we need to do is get this car parked up outside the gate. Not covering it, just making it difficult for a quick escape. All eventualities, right?"

I know his idea, and so does Scully. He smiles. The car starts, the silence of electricity, and we roll toward the gate.

RAUCOUS

We get out of the car. Scully has left space for a truck, but it is tight and there's no speeding without impact. A slow edge around or danger of permanent damage. I feel in my pocket and wonder the distance it works. I wonder if it works at all. They know, Scully and Charlotte. Scully touches his car like it will be the last time they meet. Men and motors, a strange love. I never got it, and I hope I never do.

Scully walks us around the edge of the wall, we turn right and walk. There are bins, the industrial size slide tops on wheels. Blue in colour and worn through use. Their wheels blocked by mechanical breaks. We unclip them and slide one bin to the wall.

"Any guard dogs?" I ask.

"How do I know?" Scully says. "I hate dogs."

I climb up onto the bin. It isn't easy, the slope of plastic not the best of grip. I crouch, keeping my head below the broken bottles. I put my fingers on the concrete, making sure my fingers move between the greens and browns of very old, sharp glass. I straighten, and look over. The yard is dark, one small light on the front of the blue portacabin tries to illuminate the vast space. There are stacks of timber, old blocks of sleepers and scaffold board, tied together tight. There is an order to them, rows upon rows. Some single stack others double. But there is a lot of space. The police van is parked five metres from the far wall. There is another portable office, dark green. Its two windows are yellow squares. I squint but see little. The length of the yard, a hundred metres at least, is too far for detail. The black sedan is parked next to the van as if there are parking spaces and they have followed the rules. I stand, there is no backlight to strike me in silhouette, I look down, the metres drop to the floor below, between the wall and the portacabin. A safe enough place to start.

CHARLOTTE

Raucous describes the yard. It matters little as we will see it ourselves soon enough. We place Scully's expensive coat over the spiked shards of glass. Raucous first, me and last Scully. We drop down, leave space for the next one until we are crouched, backs to the portacabin, guns in hand, breathing hard and smiling. We are a trio of fools, butch Cassidy and the Sundance Kid getting ready to take down an army.

"Best case scenario is they stay in there and we take them out from outside," Raucous says.

"Best case scenario is never happening," I say.

We move as one because there is only one way to go. We walk the gap between the portacabin and wall. We follow it into the corner, turn and follow the path till there is nothing but the expanse of the yard ahead. We can see the office on the other side, the windows bright, the movement inside a blur. There are people standing, I assume all six. The bombers still inside the van. A guess, an estimate, but it can be no other way. There is little light, but we are not concealed. There are stacks of timber we can use as cover. But we have to stay close to the wall. At the end there is a gap, a buffer zone around the office. The van and car provide cover, a metre from the nearest stack.

We move slowly, from stack to stack like we are in some executive paintball game. We have no training, no real idea, but it makes us feel safe. One at a time, from hiding spot to hiding spot, like any teenage kid knows from playing killing games on line. In our heads we are covering each other, in reality we have no idea but are making an effort to look professional. We support each other through faking expertise.

RAUCOUS

I know we have no idea. I feel it, Charlotte going through the motions, quick movement between timber piles, back against the cover, pushed up tight, me looking ahead, covering with a gun. There are six men in the office, all armed, all ready to kill. We have surprise but not enough. Barging through the door, guns blazing, shooting whatever moves is the dumbest plan and not one we'll follow. We are edging closer but to a point where direction is needed and we have none. We can't get them out by deceit, they aren't that dumb and we aren't that smart. Brute force they have the edge, but they are trapped, in a sense. A van with six men and explosives sits there, quiet and still. No rocking from movement and no sound. Someone has the detonator to six human bombs, and if one of them goes, the whole yard becomes a death scene for forensics who deal expertly in the tiniest traces of blood and bone. The van next to a sedan. One way out and the gate is closed.

I am at the last of the stacks of wood. A half stack, if I stand its height is at my chest. Four metres long, wood meant for scaffold boards, but not now. Now they are for show. I crouch down, squatting like a child playing in the sand. Charlotte arrives next to me, Scully three seconds later.

"Any ideas?" I ask.

Scully smiles, Charlotte shrugs. We sit and wait and think. I place my left hand in my pocket. It is there. It makes me feel safe. I don't know why.

"They aren't coming out one by one," Charlotte says. "And if we go in, we get maybe three before they get us."

"I'd prefer to be alive at the end of this," Scully says. "Which is a strange new sensation, because I figured we'd be dead by now."

We sit there, smiling because the worst of humour is the funniest thing. Unhinged and scared, nerves making easy grins.

Charlotte looks around, she looks at the van. She looks at us.

"Make sure no one comes up on my blindside and kills me," she says.

CHARLOTTE

I have no time to explain, and why should I? It is dumb but we can't sit and wait. I saw the van move, a slight small sag in the suspension. They are inside, getting cramp and uncomfortable. They are quiet, subdued, like they are drug calm. I heard stories about soldiers storming beaches because they were calmed. Six men in a van with vests to kill, alone in there, abandoned. The van moves again. Someone inside, at least one, I say six.

I peer out from behind the wood. I look at the office. The door in I see is closed, the two windows illuminate, but I see no shadows of bodies. The light changes inside as if someone moves or paces. Shadows changing slightly, small movements, small changes in shade. Movement but minimal. I crouch and step toward the van, I get there in three small paces. I have the knife and the gun. It is better the knife. Silent is best, a calling card of bullets and fire and smoke is an introduction to a shoot-out. Us in the open and them with cover. Silence is a must. I get to the side of the van that hides me from the office. I see the small movements as someone shifts slightly, a sway in time with weight being lifted then sat back down. I hear nothing, I think but I can't be sure, I hear breathing. The Police sign is across the large side panel. I reach up, the handle of the knife sticking out slightly from beyond my little finger as I create a fist. I look across at Raucous and Scully. They know what I am going to do. I give them time. Scully smiles and nods and moves, he gets to the end of the wood stack, an angle better to cover more area. He has the front door covered as well as the van. Raucous goes the other way, he crouches down, his view, when he looks out, will cover the two windows. They hold their guns ready. I step toward the rear, make sure my feet are close to the rear wheel, nothing sticking out, nothing to be seen. I look again and they nod. I nod too. I inhale, I smile and with force to leave a dent, I smack the side of the van twice. The noise is loud and echoes. The people inside make noise, they scream and shout like they have just been on the end of a Halloween scare.

RAUCOUS

I watch her, understanding more as she moves and looks. Entice them out, at least some. Even out the numbers and the odds. She hides as well as anyone could out in the open. The back to the van is locked, if it isn't they won't come out the same. Sitting there waiting with explosives. If it were open, they would have moved out. If it is open and they didn't then they are zombies on a mission to do the one thing they have learned and that is to give their lives for the deaths of hundreds.

The office door opens, one man walks out. Large, suited, no weapon in his hand. He walks to the Van, three strides and he is there. He walks to the back, not the driver's door. I look to Charlotte, with my right index finger I motion he is going around the back.

Charlotte stays still, her feet hidden by the wheel. It is quiet, I hope she holds her breath. The small changes, small noises give people away. The man disappears behind the van. I hear keys, and the doors open. The man speaks in a language I don't know and has a reply in the same. An exchange of information I cannot understand. A reprimand for making noise and an innocent response of denial. The man closes the Van door. I hear the keys again, and I see Charlotte move fast.

CHARLOTTE

He is there, shutting the van door. I hear the keys and the lock. He is hidden by the van, from me and the office. I don't know his size nor shape. I have a knife but I doubt he'll be as easy as the men who walked from the house. I tense and move.

I step quietly, twice, I turn the corner and he stares directly at me. He is huge. The size of Raucous but better dressed. A tight jacket and suit, a dark colour with a dark shirt and tie. He looks surprised and smiles. I step forward and slash his throat. I hit clean and the blade is sharp. I slice through his skin and cartilage, the blade hardly sticking. He grabs where the blood flows freely. His hands engulfed in warm red blood. He gargles, attempting a shout or scream or noise. I watch him, he has no idea how to react. In shock

221

he grasps his throat tighter as if strangling himself is the only way out. He drops to his knees, looking at me realising he is dead. He falls forward, and right, not moving, but still bleeding. The kosher way to kill meat. I search his trouser pockets and find the keys. A fob with the make of the Van. Heavy metal with a flap of leather. I pocket them. Maybe the only set they have.

Raucous startles me. I turn and he is there. He reaches down and grabs the collar of the dead man. He pulls and bends his back, dragging the man two metres behind a wood-stack.

We sit back and crouch.

"They will come and check," I say.

"One is coming now," Scully tells us.

Raucous points at Scully's silenced gun.

RAUCOUS

I take the gun from Scully. He seems calm with the idea as I swap it with mine. I step across to the van, I stand as Charlotte did with my feet hidden behind the rear wheel. I hear the office door open and a call, a name, the intonation wrong. The name doesn't rise at the end, there is no English lift to mean questioning. The name, the word, is shrill and blunt. There is no reply because the man he wants has no voice-box nor life. He calls again. I imagine he looks back to his boss for instruction on the next step. I hear the paces, I look to Charlotte and Scully, they are sat with guns not looking out from their hiding spot. I hear the sound of leather sole walking on tarmac, small stones occasionally crunching. He is on the other side, walking to the back of the van. His steps stop, something not right. I hear nothing and feel no movement. I stay still, breathing silently.

I hear the small crack of a joint bending. A knee, I think. I hear the small rustle of material stretching and folding, I hear metal tap on tarmac. He is crouching, looking under the van, looking for feet, or a sign or anything. I look down, my feet together like standing to attention. Hidden from view from his side. I hear the small quick scrape of metal and material stretching again. He calls out the name once more. There are noises from inside the van, chatter, murmur, an unease. I hear no movement from the man.

CHARLOTTE

I watch Raucous, stood there still with the long barrel of a silencer held up. I can't see the man. But I know he is there.

Another voice shouts out a different name. The man replies. They exchange words, phrases, but they mean nothing. Nothing at all to be picked out, nothing at all to be gained from listening to the flow of words. The exchange is sharp and short. I imagine question, reply, question, reply. I hear the awful click of a gun being cocked. The second man, I hear step out into the yard.

Another sentence from the same man. I do not know if it is directed into the office or an instruction out. I look to Raucous, he nods like we have made a telepathic plan. The only sense is he takes the nearest and I take the man at the door. Scully nods too, but he smiles and shrugs. He has no idea just like me. I start to move, but Raucous shakes his head. I hold my position. I hear the second man start to step out into the yard. There are three more men inside. Two out in the open. And a van full of bombs. I know nothing about explosives, but I know I don't want a bullet hitting a suicide belt, not when I'm this close.

The first man out starts to step to the back of the van. The company of others gives you the ability to build confidence. I am sure the second man is within two metres of the office door. His gun in hand, his senses high. The first man walks, I hear his steps. I am ready to move, ready to fire. There is no plan and if my gun goes off, the whole yard will reverberate with the sound of an unsilenced gun.

I look at Raucous. He nods. And he moves. Shit.

RAUCOUS

I think the man is two metres from the office door. A bad place to be for him, nothing to hide behind, too far away to get back quick, and not close enough to the van to be safe.

The first man out, if he has any brains or any training, will make a slow loop of the van while the second holds guard. They can see it all in each other's company. If I wait they have the upper hand. They know when they will turn the corner. Slow and methodical and ready and alert. I give Charlotte the nod, she has no idea what I mean. My movement will tell her. I step fast, not as fast as Charlotte but the man, I imagine is a bulk like me and not built for speed. I hold the gun out in front of me. I have it pointing lower than my own chest level. The man might be a bulk but he might be short.

I lead with the gun and hear nothing. I don't want to hear anything. I turn the first corner and he isn't there. But I have made noise, there was no avoiding that. I step again, turn the next corner and I see him just as he sees me. He has his gun raised and I fire. Once, twice, three times. The noise of each bullet louder than the first. The silencer, the suppressor working less efficiently with each shot. The second and third hit him, the first in the gut the second in the chest. He falls, and I shoot him again. I look up and the second man has me in his sight. He doesn't shoot, which saves my life.

"Drop the gun," he says.

I'm pointing down, he is pointing at my head. He has me so I drop my gun. He hasn't asked but I raise my arms anyway. I hold his stare, avoiding the sight of the barrel.

"Down," he says. "The floor."

He speaks perfectly. He is English. London. An accent all of our own.

He shouts out loud, something in another language. He watches me all the time.

From behind him, another man steps out of the office. His gun is raised, he surveys the yard, looking into every aspect as he scans back and forth repeatedly.

The man with the gun on me walks forward.

I don't know why they wait.

CHARLOTTE

We are hidden behind the wood. Scully crouched and ready to go left, me ready to go right.

Raucous took out the man. He should have taken the second but he chose to shoot too much. The man was dead, a double and triple tap meant nothing. The other man needed to be killed.

224

The man speaks perfect English. He sounds like every other man round here. Local to the point of absurdity. Born in this street would be no surprise. But he doesn't shoot. He has Raucous on his knees. But he got another man to come out. Scully smiles and nods, psyching himself and me. He looks to me, he holds up his right hand, his thumb, index and middle finger. He pulls in his middle finger, he pulls in his index finger, he nods and pulls in his thumb. We stand, reveal ourselves, guns out, hoping we have guessed where the two men stand.

The man with the gun on Raucous turns his head to me, I'm stepping and charging, my gun raised and I'm pulling the trigger, explosion after explosion, the first miss, the next do not. His right shoulder explodes, and he twists and his gun hits the floor. I shoot again, steadier as I slow. Four more shots, two more hits and he drops. I turn to see Scully above the other man. He has him dead, lying on the floor. The man looks up, blood coming from his mouth. He says something.

"Whatever," Scully says.

He shoots him in the face.

RAUCOUS

I pick up my gun and the second man's. I prefer mine and push his into the back of my jeans. We three stand, smoke drifting, we start to edge away back to the wood.

"Hey, Siri," Charlotte shouts. "They are all four dead. Just you two now. Coming out?"

We each have our guns trained on the windows. We back away to the woodstack. We move around behind it but rest our arms and guns on top. We are crouching like I imagine three novices at a shooting range. We are watching the windows, looking for movement.

"We could just keep shooting through those thin walls," I say. "How do you feel about that?"

There is no reply, but the sound of the people in the van is difficult to ignore. The van is rocking from side-to-side, the people bouncing and moving, the panels being hit. The back door pushed and smacked. They aren't getting out, not any time soon.

A shouted sentence booms from the office. The movement in the van slows and stops.

"Raucous?" Siri asks.

"It's me. And Charlotte. Scully too, if you need to know the full line-up."

There is no reply.

"The six men you sent out with bombs. They are all dead. We killed them. They walked out of the house and they made it eighty yards before they had their throats slit or brains blown out."

"There are six more in the van," Siri says.

"You going to blow them up now?" I ask. "You two don't strike me as the martyr type."

"It might just leave a hole in the ground, nothing too large. You've been totally incompetent so far. They probably don't even work," Scully says.

"I imagine it would be enough to take out the whole yard," I say. "If not more."

Scully laughs and then smiles.

"Ten pounds says it just leaves a big hole, no larger than a pool."

"I'll take that," I say. "What do you think Christoph?"

We wait, a stand-off. We have them covered, they can't escape. The bombers are locked up. Maybe one of them is crazy enough to set them all off like a chain reaction, but for what? Who they going to kill? Each other and us. No big statement, no dying a hero. Just blowing up timber and a small group of fools.

"I have the detonators," Christoph says. "All six. I die, the whole van goes up and you all too. A single shot toward me, and we are all going to be scraped off the floor."

I look at Scully and Charlotte. They know.

"You aren't them, Christoph. You are a businessman. You won't die for any cause. You want the money."

"We have the money. How much for us to walk out of here?"

"How much have you got?" Scully asks.

"Name a price."

"All of it."

"Never happening."

CHARLOTTE

We wait, we have nothing to do but stand. Tense but calm. A van full of suicide bombs and a trapped man with all the switches.

I hear movement, I watch the door. Christoph steps out, a small ruck-sack in his left hand, a detonator in his right.

Raucous and I cover him with our guns, Scully, the man with another angle moves around trying to locate Siri. But he steps out too, a metre behind Christoph. Siri has his gun raised. But he has three to point at and choses none.

"You can shoot," Christoph says. "But you'd need to kill me. The last thing I'll do is detonate those men in the van."

They understand English, a movement and banging from inside the van. They are all going to blow themselves up only they don't want to do it and be a waste. Fools.

They edge toward their car, a slow large semi-circle of side shuffles, Christoph holding out the bag and the detonator.

"Who has the keys to the van?" Siri asks.

"I do," I say. "But you aren't having them."

"You want to keep six men wrapped in explosives close?"

He smiles, a sneer at my stupidity.

"It is over, Siri. There will be no bombs tonight. Nothing for you tomorrow. It is over. You run away with an old man carrying a bag. But keep on running because your time as who you were is done. The van stays and you go."

His sneer remains but his words stay in his head. Whatever his comeback might be, it wasn't quick enough.

"Let's go," Christoph says. "We have another chance to meet sometime. I have a big family. Many people. They will all know your names."

"We have a problem," I say. "Pretty clear. You drive away with the detonators and we are left standing next to the bomb. You push the button and we all vanish while you get away."

They edge toward the car smiling like their power has returned.

"Trust is an issue here," Christoph says. "I suggest that once we are in the car and driving away that you three use those fire doors to make a quick escape. And get far enough away before an accidental explosion happens."

Siri smiles because he is winning at his game.

I look to Raucous and Scully. Scully is already looking at the double-doors of the fire escape. We can't shoot them, we would all die. A little pressure on that tiny button in Christoph's right hand and the whole world as we know it, in this small little timber yard, ends for all of us. I watch Scully, he is the only one who would make that call. Balance out injustice with a dumb attempt at instant murder of a man who holds the most destructive weapon.

But we know what Siri and Christoph don't. But there is no way of making that pay.

They slide into the car, Siri driving, Christoph in the passenger seat.

"To be on the safe side," Christoph says, "I'd start running that way as soon as we start moving." He looks at us, no smile just stone, "And we will be seeing each other again. I wouldn't stay around here. Give yourself a head start. A game of hide-and-seek that I will win."

He shuts the door. The engine starts. He nods his goodbye. Slowly they reverse and slowly they move forward, second gear and ten-miles-an-hour.

"We letting them go?" I ask

"They aren't getting out of the gate," Raucous says.

"But we are most definitely getting out of the yard. He's going to blow that as soon as he can. Ten quid says it makes the size of a pool, but I don't want to be here to find out. Let's go."

"Raucous?" I say.

"I'm coming. I've got a plan. Catch you up."

"Raucous?" I say.

"I don't like hide-and-seek. Get going. If they make it out they are coming down this road. You catch them."

He doesn't look at me, he won't. He raises his right hand, a dismissal. Scully grabs me by my right shoulder. He pulls me and we are running through the firedoors.

RAUCOUS

Their car is travelling slow and sure. I look at the van, see it move, the people inside know they have been left. I don't care. They can all die, just as long as they take no one else with them.

I watch the car arc and stop in front of the gate. Siri gets out, he glances my way. I can't see the features of his face but I know he smiles. I don't know his plan but I can guess well enough. I place my right hand in my pocket, I feel the shape and weight of it. The same as Christoph. Me and him, the only two alive that know.

I hear the gate screech and squeal on the metal rail as its mass slides slowly opening up space. They will see now, the expensive electric car, a minor inconvenience, there is space either side, not enough to get by without scratching bodywork, but enough to race through in a noise of scratching metal.

Siri sees because he snaps his head to see me again. I look behind me, Scully and Charlotte are long gone. I hope they have run fast and long. Six men with explosives will leave more than a small crater. That's a lot of bang in a small space. I look at where Siri is, where he stands. He is close enough, the car no protection. I saw the news, I saw the devastation. I saw the destruction. The car won't protect, and even if it did, how much? To survive would be worse. Mangled beyond recognition. The explosion will set off his, I'm sure of that. Why wouldn't it. I'm never lucky and I won't be now.

Siri looks at me and I hear a noise, a voice, Christoph's. Siri turns to get into the car.

I nod my head, inhale, look down at my hand and the detonator and press the button.

Nothing. Nothing at all. The dead man in the boot of Scully's car, wrapped in explosives, heavy to lift. Nothing, no bang. Nothing.

I press the button again and again. Nothing. I look up. Siri knows, senses something. They are still too close to blow the van, they have to be. They can't, they won't. Too close.

I run. Toward them. I raise my gun, I fire. Shot after shot, nothing close, but everything loud. I run and fire, one impact on the car, just one from eight. One hole in the back of the car. Siri pulls his gun and aims at me, his stance trained and still. I pull the trigger, and no more bullets to fire. Siri stands tall and chooses not to shoot.

229

He aims at me, getting closer, he wants the shot close. I run pulling the trigger, firing nothing but the noise of a click. I can see his features now. He smiles like I knew he would. He wants me to see. I stop. As quickly as I can, a halt. Twenty metres away, maybe less, maybe more. Twenty feels right. Siri looks at me and raises his gun. He aims, at my chest I think. Not my head, he wants to see my face.

I bring my left hand up. I give the thumbs up while holding the detonator. A little luck, a little good fortune to go with the bad that is to come. That is all I need.

Siri looks at my hand, he doesn't understand. He knows what I hold, but he is slow to make a connection. But he does, faster than most, slower than some. He looks to Scully's car, just a glance with his eyes, not moving his head. I nod. I press the button. My luck, if it is that, holds. I don't hear the explosion, but I see it. Light travels faster than sound. Yellow and white, a flash, as I am smashed off my feet, lifted up and back. I don't see them, I don't see the car. I fly up and back and down. And I see nothing at all.

CHARLOTTE

The explosion is loud, the energy wave fierce. We are too far away to be blown off our feet, but that energy, the vibration shatters our run. We stop and look back. Smoke rising from the far side of the yard. A flame, I think, a bright light for sure.

"He did it," Scully says.

I stare at Scully, his little giggle, developing into a roar. I turn and run, sprinting back the way I came. I run, the pain in my legs not close to the pain in my lungs. Sprinting, arms pumping, the noise of my feet slapping against the floor on every stride telling me I have lost all form. I draw deep breaths and exhale fast. I see the doors of the fire-escape closed. Not by hand. I don't run for them, I take the road, along the wall, the side of the yard. I see the burning mass of Scully's car, the explosion the one we heard. Raucous blew it. I hope he timed it perfect. I hope he killed them. I run, but I think. I hope they are alive, I hope they are in pain, I hope they are breathing fire and going slow. Michael held on, and they hurt him all the way to the end. They dragged his death out for pleasure because they could. I run and I pray they are alive.

I get close and slow. I walk and slow further. The fire burns hot, but the car has flipped and moved from the gate. A spinning top two car-lengths from where it sat. I edge to the gate, the wall in pieces like the background in a film set in World War Two. I peer round the corner, I see their car, further from the gate than I thought. Pushed back by an explosion I do not know. The front a mangled mess, fire covers the body, small eternal flames, the glass gone, the metal wrecked. I see a body, or what I think is a body, against the far wall. A crumpled bag of flesh turned inside out. Fallen to the ground like a crash-test dummy bathed in blood. From the remnants of the clothes I assume it is Siri. Skin blown off and the underneath burned. Patches remain, but they are small. It is not Raucous. Even in that state Raucous would be too big. In the car there is movement. The passenger side. A red mask of raw flesh moves. It is Christoph. I don't know if he fell or if he lives. But I am looking for someone else. I look into the yard and I see him. Sprawled like a knocked-out drunk. I run, slower this time. Less urgency and I don't know why. As I get close I see his chest rising. I kneel down at his side. I whisper his name. He opens his eyes.

"They dead?" he asks.

"They're dead," I say.

He lies there, breathing hard, blinking, squinting, hurting. A minute maybe, a minute of nothing but waiting for pain to dull.

He sits up and accompanies the move with groans. I help him to his feet. He is too big and heavy for me to support. We hobble toward the gate.

"He is alive," Scully says.

Scully is stood, a metre from the car peering into the passenger side.

"What's that, Christoph?" he asks. "You aren't making much sense."

Raucous pushes me away.

"Do it," he says.

He sits down where I leave him, cross-legged and limp.

I walk over and lean into the passenger side. He has his eyes open, only one works. The left one is a ball of red. Not exploded but not in use.

"Can you see me, Christoph?" I ask.

He says something I take to be an insult.

"You didn't make it," I say. "We did. But you, your superior air. You died. Siri is back there against the wall like a ball of mince, and you are here, in your car, blown and crushed and soon dead. Where is your god now?"

"Money," he says.

"Money?" I ask.

"Money."

He smiles, and spits, but he has no force and dribbles blood down his red chin.

He looks to his right. Scully holds up a rucksack.

"These?" he asks.

Everything leaves Christoph's body. He goes limp.

I take out my gun.

"What are you doing?" Scully asks. "He's going to die. Nice and slow and nice and painful. Just how we like, isn't that right, Christoph?"

Scully leans past me and smacks Christoph's face.

I watch and Christoph shows nothing. No pain, no indignity. Nothing.

"Christoph," I say. "You know who is taking your life?"

He doesn't answer.

"No words anymore. Nothing?" I ask.

I look at Raucous, I call his name. "He doesn't speak anymore," I shout.

Raucous looks up and nods.

I understand.

"Christoph, I am taking your life. No bomb, no collapsed lungs. Me, Charlotte. You understand that? You got beat by me, a woman. The shame, eh?"

He turns to face me, he starts to speak.

I'm not interested in anything he has to say.

I fire my gun through his head. He drops dead. Brains and skull mixed in with carnage. And it is me who killed him.

RAUCOUS

We walk for a half-a-mile. Scully stays, he asked for the keys to the van. Charlotte gave them without complaint. Me and Charlotte walking. We hear the van start, and we hear the van drive. A police van of bombers with Scully at the wheel.

"I'll be in touch," Scully said. "You'll need the work."

I nod because speaking hurts, and I know I'll take the money.

"I'm a millionaire," Charlotte says.

"That is true, but you have a low threshold for boredom. We'll be seeing each other."

We walk away and don't look back.

Me and Charlotte walk and stumble for another mile. We find a bench and sit. We don't speak but we huddle close. A small park for kids in the day and homeless at night. We sit and breathe and say nothing. She slides her left hand over my right and we squeeze hands tight, fingers locked. We sit like that for an age, looking at the sky, thinking about the past, and people we knew and loved. Thinking about what has happened and not what would be. A silence, but for sirens of fire engines and police. We sit and drift away into sleep. The first time with ease. A homeless couple snuggled up for warmth, waiting for another day.

It is an hour before we wake. And we wake with everyone. The light breaking through for the morning. We wake quickly to the noise, we wake startled, we look to the source, a huge grey cloud twirling in the air, noise of alarms going off, the sound of tremors.

My phone vibrates. As does Charlotte's.

I take it out and look at the screen. Scully.

"No one hurt. Other than six. Took the van for a drive. I owe you ten pounds. A lot bigger than a pool. Lose the phones. Speak soon."

We stand, break the cards in the phones, hold hands and walk toward my home.

Printed in Great Britain
by Amazon

25456404R00138